PREMIERE

a love story

TRACY EWENS

PREMIERE

a love story

Ebook ISBN: 978-0-9908571-0-5
Print ISBN: 978-0-9908571-1-2

Book design by Maureen Cutajar
www.gopublished.com

For My Mom,
Who taught me books are
very precious things.

Chapter One

Samantha Cathner liked understated. She appreciated it. Certainly she believed it was better to be a quiet surprise than a loud letdown. For this reason, and many others, the Norton Simon Museum spoke to her. She arrived early to double-check everything for the fundraiser. The Norton Simon was a special venue, part of the neighborhood. The famous umber-tiled exterior walls and the beautiful grounds blended well with the rest of Pasadena. It was simple and yet able to hold its own among the most sophisticated houses of art, even stacking up to The Getty.

Streamlined but welcoming, that's what she had pitched to the board, and as Sam approached the main exhibit hall, she was confident they had achieved just that. The charcoal table linens worked to bring weight and warmth to the room. *Deception*, a magnificent bronze statue of an actor holding a mask, sat center stage in the cocktail area. Servers were filling simple hand-blown champagne flutes and placing them on muted pewter serving trays.

The museum did not normally host private functions, but they tried to accommodate at least one fundraiser a year for the Pasadena Playhouse. Pasadena had a very tight-knit arts community.

Everyone worked to hold each other up during lean years. It was almost seven o'clock. A large crowd was expected.

Sam spotted her parents near the bar as the guests arrived and began mingling. Jack Cathner cut a large, engaging figure with his salt-and-pepper hair, a nose that sort of bulbed up more on one side than the other, and booming voice. He had recently put on some weight. Sam thought it looked good on him—and so did her mother—but his incessant tugging at the front of his jacket was obviously driving Susan Cathner crazy because she swatted at him again.

"Stop pulling at it."

"I feel like I'm going to bust out of this damn thing. Maybe if I unbutton the top one." His wife's look was enough to stop Jack. Her kiss on his cheek brought a smile to his face.

"You look wonderful. Stop and enjoy the evening."

"What do you make of that statue we passed on the way in? Male? Female? Unless I'm slipping, those are breasts, right?"

"It's bronze, I think it's the material that makes the chest look larger. That's a male," Susan said, looking again at the sculpture.

Sam stood quietly next to her father, enjoying their conversation.

"Sam, do I look like I'm busting out of this tux?"

"No, you look great, and the statue is neither male nor female. It's abstract, asexual. It represents humans, male and female."

Her parents looked at her and then back at the statue. Jack rolled his eyes. He understood creativity, but he would never understand eccentricity.

"Beautiful dress, honey. This whole event is stunning. Margaret and the rest of the bridge club are setting up the silent auction. Do you need help explaining the auction as people arrive?"

Sam looked toward the front of the museum. "No, the volunteers are here, and they'll cover that. Mom, you're here to enjoy."

"So what does that make the statue, I mean if someone asks, what do I say?" her father asked.

"I doubt anyone's going to ask you, Dad, but stick with abstract, okay?" Sam patted her father on the shoulder and turned to order a drink.

Her skin knew he was there before her mind had a chance to catch up. Even after all this time, all these years, he could still change the air she lived in.

"Well, look who's here. Peter, my boy, how are you?" her father boomed, extending his hand.

"I'm good, Mr. C. It's good to see you both." Peter shook hands and kissed Susan Cathner on the cheek. "Mrs. C, you look fantastic."

"Thank you, Peter. Are they taking care of you in the big city? We can't thank you enough for bringing your new play here. Your mother is so proud." Peter's mind tripped for a moment at the thought of his mother and her pride, but he moved on.

"Oh, no thanks are needed. It's the perfect venue for this particular play. New York is great, but it's nice to be home, at least for a little while."

"Well, we hear you're quite the success," Jack said, patting him on the back.

"I'm making my way, thank you, sir."

Sam's back was still to all of them while she pretended to be incredibly interested in the bartender revealing what made his Manhattan so special. She tried to steady her breath, but it was no use. She likened the moment to that time in Phys Ed when she saw the softball coming toward her, but froze and was unable to stop the impact. Sam took another large sip of wine, and a shallow breath, before turning slowly with her father's drink in hand. Her hair tousled over one bare shoulder, Sam looked right at her father's face.

"Dad, your drink." She smiled, hoping she appeared casual. She was grasping for casual.

"Thank you, Button. Look who . . ."

Their eyes met, and Sam's knees softened. She gently took her father's arm for balance and willed herself to stop being obvious.

They stared at each other for seconds that seemed longer. Neither of them heard Jack and Susan discussing the last time Peter was in town.

Sam let out a slow breath and allowed herself to look at him.

His hair had grown out; it curled slightly around his ears. And facial hair, more than a shadow, but not quite a full beard. Eyes that were still that indescribable green hooded by dark lashes. She remembered them, those eyes. One minute bright and sparkling; the next, a dark forest of hidden secrets. Sam had never met another pair of eyes like Peter's. After he left, she spent a good year looking for eyes to replace his, before she learned to settle for men with different eyes.

Sam was taken aback, she would admit it: looking at him was much more than she imagined it would be. She tried to see Peter as her friend, tried to conjure it up. The little girl buried inside her desperately wanted go to back to being best friends. Her pulse was pounding now with the realization that nothing could be done; with one look she knew Peter would never be *only* her best friend again. She had to get out of the room.

"Peter, welcome home. Good of you to, well, it's great. Thank you so much for what you're doing to help the theater. Speaking of which, I really should check on the auction." Peter's mouth opened as Sam nodded to her mother, turned with her very best professional purpose, and walked away. The casual observer would see it as an employee diligently attending to an important event detail.

Peter smiled at Mr. and Mrs. Cathner, took a sip of his drink, and saw it for what it was. While he hadn't expected her to turn and bolt, he had known for months this wasn't going to be easy. Her rejection tonight felt like a punch. He was sorry their first new meeting made her uncomfortable, but after what he'd done to her, Peter was relieved to see a reaction at all.

She was more beautiful than he remembered—and his memory was perfect when it came to Samantha Cathner. She was older now, more fluid and polished. Sam had always had that scrubbed, girl-next-door look, but she had never been ordinary. Her lips had a perfect bow, like in a painting, and her eyes were so open and vulnerable. She had always hated that Peter could tell what she was really thinking. It was the eyes. They often betrayed her, even when her tongue was wicked.

Her hair was shorter, but still that ink-dark brown. He wondered if summer still kissed her hair with gold and brought freckles to her nose and shoulders. Back in New York, when he allowed himself to remember Sam, he had always pictured her in jeans. This Sam was in all that black silk. He let out a deep breath he hadn't realized he was holding. She was different.

She had never been more grateful for something to do in her entire life. The caterers were two people short; six invited guests had shown up with an extra person, throwing off the food count; and they were dangerously low on champagne. Candice, the creative director of the Playhouse and Sam's boss, had arrived thirty minutes ago and asked for help. Sam was secretly thrilled. Details, she loved the details, the problems to solve. Right now, calling the local liquor stores to see how many bottles of Krug Clos d'Ambonnay she could scrounge up was a welcome distraction. There were answers to these problems, solutions. By the time Sam sent someone to pick up two more cases of champagne she was halfway to normal. Walking out of the kitchen, she told herself she was Samantha Cathner, assistant creative director for the Pasadena Playhouse. She did not cower or hide, and apart from her quick exit from Peter, she never ran. That was Peter's game, but Sam was a sticker. Always had been, always would be, and his was her home.

She was no longer the overly confident woman whose first step into the "real world"—as her brother put it—had been full of bluster. Sam knew it. She had recognized long ago that she had moved on from the disappointment and become a new, more humble person. It had taken her a while, but she had discovered what she was good at and what mattered. She could not let anyone, especially not Peter Everoad, drag her into a past she had worked so hard to forget.

Sam went to let the bartender know he would not have to explain any champagne shortage. He was grateful and offered her another glass of wine. She turned to rest her elbows on the rich, polished wood bar. Grady's father, Senator Malendar, had made his entrance and was working the room. Grady, her other best friend growing up, was now officially late. Sam watched as the senator glad-handed through the crowd. He exuded confidence. She wondered if he'd felt that self-assured all his life or if a solid sense of self was something to look forward to with age. The jazz band glided in to play behind a soulful singer Candice had chosen for the evening, and with that, the mood was complete.

"Would you like to dance, gorgeous?" Her heart skipped a beat. But it was only her older brother, Henry.

"Where did you come from?" Sam attempted a smile.

"Were you expecting someone else?" Henry asked, brushing his naturally curly hair off his face. He was dashing in his tux.

"No, you'll do just fine." She kissed him and smoothed the shoulders of his jacket. "Very nice tux, black on black, I approve. I'd love to dance."

Henry put his hand out as Sam joined him on the dance floor. He stood a full head above her, even when she was in heels. Sam could feel the other women in the room looking at him as she rested her head on his shoulder. She was used to the looks, her brother was a handsome man. Henry had recently broken up with his long-term girlfriend. Sam could only assume there were women at the fundraiser hoping to take her place.

As his sister, Sam didn't care what Henry looked like, all she knew was that he was her rock. He protected her, always had. No strings attached. He had been her fortress when she was younger and life was not so kind. Sam had slept on Henry's couch in Los Angeles when she couldn't yet bear to return home a failure, and he met her in Paris for a week when she went off to "find herself." She was her own woman now, but spinning in Henry's arms was a nice break. She felt safe.

Across the room, with his hands in his pockets, Peter had just finished listening to Mr. Callaway, his former high school principal, talk about "the fly fishing trip of a lifetime." Mr. Callaway swiped another canapé off a passing tray and asked Peter what he thought about the future of Broadway.

"I mean with the commercialism and the melding of theater and movies, especially Disney. What do you think the future holds?" Mr. Callaway inquired.

Peter found it strange that people he had known all his life now regarded him as an adult with knowledge and valuable insight. *The power of a little recognition,* he thought to himself as he answered in the most authoritative tone he could muster. They had no idea he was still the same messed-up kid they'd watched leave for New York, all of them secretly anticipating his failure. Now older and more removed from all he had grown up with in Pasadena, Peter wondered if these people had actually expected his failure or if he had imagined it all because disdain was easier to deal with than pity. Above all, he hated pity and the holier-than-thou bullshit that came with it.

Peter pulled at his collar, amazed at how quickly the past could seep into his consciousness. Clamping down on his thoughts, he tried to—as his father used say—"Remember who you are, son." Right as he was preparing to suck up to another set of deep pockets in the hopes they would help the Playhouse, he turned and his eyes fell onto swirling melting movements of his past. *Christ, she still undoes me every time*, Peter admitted to himself, watching Sam dance with her brother. The money men would have to wait. Peter took a deep breath and made his way to the dance floor. It was time to talk. If that meant getting past Henry, then so be it.

"Hey, may I?" Peter asked, tapping Henry on the shoulder.

"Well, Mr. Big Shot. Long time no see." Henry pulled Sam around to get a better look at Peter.

"Hair's longer," he observed.

Peter ran his fingers through his hair and looked away. Henry was confident, always had been. He was older than Peter by two years and enjoyed giving him a protective brother's once-over.

"You want to dance with my baby sister? I don't know. She was pretty messed up when . . ."

"Henry!" Sam interrupted. "I'll be fine. Go find your rebound girlfriend."

"All right, but you keep your hands where I can see them." Henry passed Sam's hand to Peter while she rolled her eyes.

Chapter Two

Her stomach twisted at Peter's touch. When he pulled her close, her heart remembered. He was bigger, more solid. He smelled like something so familiar yet oddly mysterious at the same time. Sam looked over Peter's shoulder, then closed her eyes, followed his lead, and said nothing. She knew that, dancing this close, he could probably feel her heart pounding, and she wondered if his heart was mixed somewhere in that thunder. If he felt anything as they began to sway, he wasn't giving it up, which was fine with her, easier actually. She simply wanted to get this over with. Move on.

Peter's body responded immediately. It was as if he'd never left. He had danced with her dozens of times, but it had been years ago. His body should have forgotten how she felt in his arms, but it remembered instantly. The feel of her hair, a hint of Coco Chanel, the long sweep of her neck: it was all right there. While his mind was racing for the right words, his heart ached and begged to stay right where it was.

"Sam, it's good . . ." Peter said quietly at her ear.

"This is a great event, isn't it?"

"Yeah, it's nice, but I . . ."

"It's great that you've agreed to come home and save the theater."

She was trying to keep things professional while willing herself to release her death grip on his dinner jacket.

"Sam."

"What?"

"Now that you've established that everything is 'great,' will you look at me?"

"Peter, we're dancing. It's not exactly conducive to looking." She blew the bangs out of her face. Why had she let her stylist talk her into bangs? *Had something happened to the air conditioning? Or was she the only one starting to sweat?*

"Sure it is."

Peter eased her back slightly, and Sam was once again lost in that face. Creases between the eyebrows, maybe a little deeper now. Peter, grown-up Peter, was really lovely. She knew it sounded absurd, but gorgeous wasn't enough for the Peter dancing with her. It was too shallow. He was like a tailored suit paired with comfortable running shoes. His hair was deep brown, almost black now. Dressed up, it was off his face, as it was now, but Sam preferred Peter a bit mussed. He was warm, lived in. Cultured with a trace of a dirty joke.

Despite her best efforts, Peter continued to steal her breath. She reasoned that it might be the confidence, his new sense of self, that caught her off guard. Whatever it was, she willed herself to stop. Peter was going to be in town for the next few months, and she needed to put this away. They could no longer be friends, but she could work with him. She was a professional. One dance would not undo her. Besides, Sam was no longer about living in the past—at least that's what she told herself. She looked right back at him and tried to relax. Peter held her firmly and without hesitation. Sam was more comfortable with the shy, uncertain Peter who had left her years ago. This version made her unsteady.

"There, happy? I'm looking at you. Now what did you need to say?" *Good girl, Sam,* she thought. *Oh, for Christ's sake I'm praising myself like a dog now.*

"I didn't *need* to say anything, I *wanted* to say that it's good to see you." Peter's hand moved along her back. It was a small movement, only an adjustment, but his fingertips brushed her skin, and she forgot where she was. She was drowning in his eyes and unable to call anyone for help. There were so many questions, but the most urgent, the one aching to get out, was . . . why? She would never give him the satisfaction of asking and she was positive his answer would never be enough.

"Good to see you too, Peter."

"Really? Because it seems like you're dancing with your old uncle Joe. You know the creepy one that always used to kiss you on the lips?" He smirked.

The announcement that the auctions would be closing in fifteen minutes brought Sam back to reality, and she glanced over toward the tables. Her mother was watching them. She smiled. Her mother gestured that everything was under control. Sam didn't have time for dancing, but she couldn't let go, not yet.

"Uncle Joe died last year," she deadpanned. Peter's face fell.

"Oh, Sam. I'm so sorry."

His cool playwright exterior was gone, and he looked like fourteen-year-old Peter standing against the wall at his first etiquette class. Sam buried her face in his shoulder and laughed. It felt good to laugh. Peter spun her around and she felt his breath on her neck. *Some kind of wood? Cedar, maybe? Is that his new smell? God, whatever it is, I've missed him so much.*

"I can't believe you. Did he really die?" Peter whispered. They were now dancing chest to chest, his arms around her waist, hers intertwined over his shoulders.

"No, he's living in Florida. He still kisses all of us on the lips." They both pulsed with laughter, and the tension spilled onto the dance floor. That was all it took, one laugh, one gesture, always. During the most intense times in their lives Sam and Peter could still manage to make each other laugh. In that moment, it felt so natural, as if Peter had never left.

Sam was certain those biceps were new as she allowed herself to be held just a little longer. Then the song changed, and it all became too much.

Peter's smiling gaze shot through her chest, and she knew with all her being that she could not do this again. She would not survive it. Things had changed. Peter had changed them when he chose to ignore what happened between them. He left, and as much as she wanted to, she couldn't forgive him for making her feel so, so lost. The music continued, but they were no longer dancing. Sam unwrapped herself from his arms and smiled politely.

Peter knew the instant she was gone. He could feel it. She came back to him for a flash, and as his heart warmed, he felt the cruel pain of someone being torn away. He deserved it, all of it, but his mind scrambled for something to hang on to. Maybe she wouldn't forgive him, but he had to try.

"Peter, it was nice to see you. Please excuse me."

"Sam," he followed her off the dance floor and grabbed her arm, stopping her. Sam glanced around to assess how much of a scene they were making. No one seemed to care.

"Peter, please let me go. I have a million things to do."

"We need to talk."

Sam turned quickly.

"We do?" Sam released a pained laugh. "What exactly do we need to talk about, Peter?"

"About the . . . play, we need to talk about that, yeah." He settled for a bit of distance, because the look on her face was killing him. "Candice tells me you're handling my production. We should meet. There are a few things that need ironing out."

"I'll be there tomorrow, the first day of rehearsals. We can get everything taken care of then. Peter, I need to go."

Sam turned to leave without giving him a chance to respond. He gave up and realized he could still smell her on his jacket. She had worn Coco Chanel since her father had first given it to her on her sixteenth birthday. Peter loved it. Was he actually sniffing his jacket? *Get a grip, man.*

Walking among the patrons and swirling waiters, Sam stopped to clap for Mr. Weaver who had won the trip to Vail in the silent auction. She chatted her way through the crowd and noticed the petits fours and coffee service. Sam accepted gracious praise from Candice who was wearing a tight red dress and long gold earrings. She looked more like a statuesque model than the creative director for The Pasadena Playhouse. Candice was thrilled with the turn out and in a great mood. Grateful that things were going well, Sam turned to make her exit, and ran straight into Grady. *Fantastic! The third musketeer has arrived, late as usual.* Growing up in Pasadena, it had always been the three of them. Peter, Sam, and Grady had been best friends until *that day*. Peter had moved on and while Sam knew that he and Grady had kept in touch, she hadn't heard one word from Peter Everoad in four years. Not until today.

"Whoa, where's the fire? Wow, is this silk? You know how I love silk, Sam. Did you wear this for me?"

Sam swatted at Grady's hands, and right as she wanted to swat his face, he leaned in and kissed her cheek.

"You're late and not even fashionably."

"I know. But I'm here now, so you can't leave me here alone."

"I can, and I will. I've been on my feet all day and it's time for me to go."

"You love this stuff, and the night is young. I, at least, deserve a dance if I'm going in there to play Happy Senator's Son. Why are you so quick . . ." Grady saw Peter and looked back at Sam. He ran his hand over the stubble on his obnoxiously beautiful face, and even though Sam's eyes pleaded for him to let her go, he called, "Peter!"

He smiled, wiggled his eyebrows, and pulled her back into the fire.

"Sam, look, Peter's here."

"I can see that, Grady."

Her eyes were daggers.

"It's been a long time since we've been to one of these swanky events," Grady said, gently pulling Sam across the crowd and extending his hand to Peter. Peter shook it, and Grady pulled him in for the one-armed hug and pat on the back. Grady looked perfect, as always, decked out in black Armani and with that dazzling smile. Expertly cut honey brown hair and a day's worth of stubble that said, *I'm rich and successful, but I don't care about any of this.*

Sam and Peter both knew him better, but Grady, who had spent his life in the public eye, was a master at the game. Sam noticed the light in Peter's eyes changed, softened. Grady could tap into a side of Peter no one else had access to, and he was one of the few people Peter could truly be himself around. They had their quirks, as all friends do, but they were bound by a deep brotherhood.

"It has been a long time. You're late, missed the shrimp and cream cheese thingies," Peter said, handing Grady some champagne.

"Wrapped in the little wontons? Damn, those are my favorite."

"Um, excuse me, we did not have cream cheese anything here tonight."

Peter and Grady both laughed. It was still fun getting a rise out of Sam.

"Did you guys have a chance to catch up?"

Sam was pretty sure she was going to kill both of them.

"She tell you she recently broke up with Brian? Remember that weekend we all went to Vegas, and you and I were going to get married, Sam?"

Grady had a way of making the most inappropriate comments sound like standard fare. It was clear to her now; Grady, at least, would have to die.

"Oh yeah, you dropped to your knee right there at the black-jack table," Peter added, laughing.

"Who is Brian?"

"He was not on his knee! I would have never. Christ! Do you guys ever grow up?"

Peter and Grady both looked at each other and shook their heads. Sam rolled her eyes, grateful the Brian question had been dropped. Her face felt warm. Grady leaned over to touch her cheek, she squirmed, and his hand dropped.

"See," Grady smiled, "the passion. Someday you'll wake up and I'll be gone."

"Oh, and that would be a shame," she said with more than a hint of sarcasm.

Grady feigned a broken heart by holding his hand to his chest: "Ouch!"

Sam knew it was time to get even.

"Grady, you are an incredibly attractive," he lifted his eyebrows as Peter shook his head, "self-absorbed man, and though during a drunken trip to Vegas several years ago, I did agree to marry you, I believe I've recovered. I'm sure there have been, and are currently, dozens of women waiting to be Mrs. Malendar, but I'm not one of them. I love you, always have, like . . ."

Peter slapped Grady on the back as an early condolence.

"Oh God, don't do it. Don't say it again," Grady begged, and Sam once again dropped the bomb.

"I love you like a dear, sweet, immature, brother."

"Ahhhh," he fell back into Peter's arms and the two of them laughed.

"The pain. Well, sis, I'm off to get a beer to numb the ache of rejection. Do they have a decent beer in this place? You two kids stay out of trouble, or hell, get into trouble for a change. Pete, we still on for tennis tomorrow?"

"We are. Ten o'clock. You promise to go easy on me? It's been a while."

"Oh please, I make no such promise. You're all grown up now. I've seen that fancy gym of yours in the city. Don't pull that 'I don't work out at all' shit with me."

Grady kissed Sam's hand: "Samantha, you look ravishing as always."

"Thank you. You know some day I may flirt back when I'm sober and then where would you be?"

"I would love to see that, sweetheart," Grady said over his shoulder as he walked away.

Peter laughed. "Some things never change. You know, I'm pretty sure he was actually on one knee."

"Not talking about it," she said cutting him off. It was now past time to leave. "I'm checking on the swag bags and going home."

"Do you need any . . ."

"No. No, Peter I don't need anything." She turned to him and saw her message was received. Things had changed. She'd changed, and Sam needed to close this memory lane in honor of self-preservation. There was nothing left to say. She put her empty glass on the nearest linen-draped table and walked away.

Chapter Three

With her ridiculously high heels now put away in the closet and her face free of makeup, Sam sat in pajama bottoms and a UCLA tank top, a mug of tea beside her, looking over images of the Peter and Grady years, before it all went to hell. She had not meant to pull the box out from under her bed. She hadn't looked through it in ages, but she had been in Peter's arms a couple of hours ago, and something in her wanted to remember.

Since she had returned two years ago with a pretty tattered self-image as just another out-of-work actress who hadn't made it in Hollywood, Sam had been living in the guesthouse. Built in the same style as the Cathners' sprawling mansion, this space was more accessible. Dark hardwood floors and pale yellow walls topped with white molding. Sam was aware that this little guesthouse was larger than many people's homes, but not the homes she grew up around. Compared to those, this was a tawdry little shack, but she loved it.

Sam had taken a photography class in high school and from then on and all through college she snapped tons of photographs. Grady used to call her "the preserver of all deeds good and evil." As she took a small sip of her tea, Sam realized that she hadn't taken pictures in years. Sure, there was the occasional shot, but she used to want to hold on to everything, and now, well, she didn't know.

Cool air of a late spring evening trickled through the open windows. The smell of lavender danced around her space. Looking over at the floor-to-ceiling bookshelves across from the couch, Sam reflected on the images she'd framed. There used to be many pictures of Peter, but they had been put away and replaced with landscapes or family and friends. She had kept the bamboo photograph and the jar of rainwater. They both sat among her books on the fourth shelf, up by the window. A subtle reminder of Peter that her heart could handle.

She looked back at the images on the floor, the ones she had taken from the box, and Peter was everywhere. The tea warmed Sam's cheeks, and she allowed him in, knowing it would hurt later. A lot of the photos were black and white, and most of them made her laugh. All through high school and college Sam had considered herself a lucky girl. Grady went off to Stanford—father's orders— but he came home often. She had loved them both and then she found herself loving Peter differently. After Peter left, she had wondered if there were any signs. Sam had always felt something with him: a kindred spirit maybe. Looking back on it, he was her type. Brooding artist, tormented soul, and clearly that was her weakness when she was young, but she knew better now. He was a self-centered ass.

There were times in their past, late-night study sessions, when they had spent midnights talking about their families or issues they were dealing with, but it was always in the context of the three of them. Sam went to high school dances with Grady and Peter; they all dated other people through college. They talked boyfriends and girlfriends, but nothing was ever serious. Grady dated more than Peter and Sam put together, but that was part of his DNA.

Sam sipped her tea and thumbed through shots of her and Peter's first year at UCLA, the weekend they met Grady in San Francisco, and one Spring Break in Mexico. They had a tradition of posing seriously for any event and then making the most ridiculous faces for the second shot. A wave of warmth washed over her now looking at the photos. These were great years and she had always imagined they would be together forever. Live on the same block, talk crap about each other's spouses, laugh together, vacation together, and grow old together. Sam realized a while ago how naive she had been. Unlike a photograph, people don't freeze. People grow up and they leave.

Peter had always had a roaming spirit. He talked about wanting more, or wanting something different. After high school he backpacked alone through England and France. He was gone for two months and called it his "deep breath trip." His father had died two years earlier, and he "wanted out," as he put it. Sam should have seen it then, yet he always came home. They had both gone to college close to home. She had known he didn't want to start his career in Hollywood. He talked a lot about New York, but she never thought he'd leave. Maybe she knew, but after what happened between them, she thought he would have at least asked her to go with him.

Well into her second cup of tea and feeling quite relaxed, Sam picked up the stack of shots from their last day at the Huntington. That day, the day everything changed. Mostly pictures of plants in the gardens at first and then one of Peter standing next to *Diana of the Chase* with her bow outstretched. It was a famous statue near the entrance to the rose gardens.

He looked younger, but those green eyes were the same ones she had been lost in only hours earlier. If in fact eyes were the windows to the soul, Peter's soul was glorious. The picture took her into the memory. He loved that statue and on that day Sam had asked, "What's with her? With everything else here, why do you always come back to her?"

Peter had put his hand on his chin like a philosopher, then looked up at the statue, and said plainly: "I think it's because she's naked. Yup, that's it, the lack of clothing. I like that, and that bow, my God, what guy's gonna resist?" For all his culture and prose, Peter was still just a guy.

They had both laughed like children, and she had snapped Peter's picture with his arrow-wielding ladylove. Looking at his big grin now, tears pooled in her eyes. She was at home and alone, so she let the hollow empty pain in and then quickly wiped it way. Sam was fine. In fact she was good, great on some days. Hearts broke all the time, she knew that, friendships ended, but this was bone deep. While she had learned to stand on her own in the past four years, at this moment she just wanted to jump into the photograph and go back to that time when she and Peter simply *were*, when it had been effortless.

She set the photos down, closed her eyes, and leaned back on her hands. She would need to deal with the way things were in the present, but not tonight. She'd had enough for one day. Sam finished her tea, wiped her eyes again, and crawled to the couch.

Peter arrived at his mother's house, at what used to be his family home, shortly after midnight. He'd played the part of successful playwright most of the night. He'd sucked up and danced with his mother's friends. Grady's mom was a personal favorite. He genuinely loved Bindi Malendar. She had been his mother's best friend all his life, and no one knew better than Peter that his mother was often hard to love.

She was asleep on the couch when he got in, having opted out of the fundraiser because she "had absolutely nothing to wear." Truth was she preferred to stay home and drink. Peter carefully carried her to her room and ignored the fact that once again she was too drunk to wake up and notice.

Now sitting at the dimly lit dining room table, Peter opened his laptop to check his email and the call schedule for the next morning. He kept thinking about Sam. She had left early; Peter had pretended not to feel hollow for the rest of the evening. She hated him, and he didn't blame her. What man, even a young, insecure, and stupid one, would leave a woman like Sam? She was essential even back then. It had been a long time, but Peter still remembered feeling small. Needing to be more if he was ever going be enough for her.

Peter answered a few emails from his agent and agreed to two telephone interviews the following week. He started to do a little research for the play he was currently writing. It was a comedy, a full comedy. Thank God his new play had nothing to do with his actual life.

His eyes became heavy, and he picked up his phone. Maybe he could hide behind a text, maybe she would listen, let him explain. That all sounded great to his exhausted brain, but he hadn't yet figured out how to explain. Sitting back, he could still feel her in his arms. His heart, the heart he thought still dead in his chest, pulsed at the memory of the brief moment in which she had let him back in. Peter swore at his foolishness, plugged his phone into its charger and decided to call it a night.

Walking toward the staircase, he stopped at the study door. It was always closed now. He hadn't been inside since his mother had redecorated long before he left for New York. The last time Peter was in his father's study it still smelled of leather and cigars enjoyed late at night with three fingers of scotch. He put his hand on the door. It wasn't as frequent anymore, but sometimes he could still feel his father, still hear his voice. His hand slid down the oiled wood, and Peter closed his eyes.

"Goodnight, Dad."

Chapter Four

The next morning, Sam arrived early and sank into the rich gold upholstery of seat BB4 in the dark theater. She tucked her legs to the side. She had not slept well, or at all for that matter, and the paper cup of strong black tea warming her hands provided little comfort. She had climbed to the balcony, to the power position of the theater, hoping for some clarity. She wasn't sure what to do, if she could even move.

The smell of fresh paint and sawdust ushered in the start of a new production. *Beginnings are always so wonderful*, she thought.

She leaned toward the front edge of the wrought iron balcony and saw two young actors, center stage, in animated conversation. A wash of warm light bathed them, blurring their features and making them almost dreamlike.

Her mind drifted from the list of props and supplies she was supposed to discuss with Peter to the magnet on her refrigerator affirming: "Everything happens for a reason." Peter was back, she had seen him, danced with him, and survived. He had not come home for her, but to save the theater he loved. That was the reason, nothing more.

"Could we get some of the main scenery pieces out here for the first act?" called a voice from below.

It had been four years since Peter had thrown away a lifetime of friendship and everything she had ever imagined love was supposed to feel like. He could have called, should have called, but never did. After about a year, Sam stopped crying and decided never to be a fool again. She had rebuilt her life, a life that was working now, and she desperately needed it to stay that way.

She could see the designers moving boxes around the stage to simulate what would evolve into scenery. Sam normally loved the early days of a production. Correction, she still loved the early days of a production. Any minute now her shit would fall together, and she'd be down there. She was just waking up, reviewing her notes, whatever she could come up with, that was why she wasn't moving. *Good girl, you keep telling yourself that, honey.*

"Good morning, Peter," Spencer, the director, called from the stage.

Spencer's dirty blonde hair was long, but pulled off his face by a cheap rubber band. He wore glasses that spent more time in his hand than on his face. Spencer spoke in a calm, coffee-shop voice, most of the time.

"Julie left you a copy of the notes from yesterday's read-through," he continued while moving a box upstage.

"Morning," Peter said, walking toward the stage.

Sam's eyes found Peter at the sound of his voice. God, that voice crawled into her. Even when he was younger, it had been deep, raspy, and sexy—before she ever knew what that meant. She watched him pull the beat-up leather bag off his shoulder and put it into a seat. Peter continued toward the stage, rolling the sleeves of his shirt right above the elbows. He wore jeans. She found herself noticing his dark hair again. The memory of what it felt like to run her fingers through his wet hair and the citrus smell of his shampoo filled her mind. It was so unexpected, she physically jolted.

"I'm thinking we need to start by running the dream scene again and figure out what's missing?" Spencer queried, hopping off the stage.

"Sure, we can start with the dream," Peter said while flipping through a few pages of notes, adding, "Did you meet with Gordy last night about the light cues for that scene?"

As both men looked toward the lighting booth, Sam inched further down in her seat to be sure she wasn't seen. *What am I hiding from now? Absurd*, she thought.

"We did meet and I think they're done. I'll ask him to at least hit the major cues while we're working the scene. Give me twenty minutes, I'll get him away from the doughnuts, and we'll get started."

With one more labored push, Spencer paused to wipe his forehead, exclaiming, "Aw, Christ, where's the guy that's supposed to help me move these damn boxes?"

"Getting old, buddy?" Peter laughed and turned back toward his seat.

"Sam?" Spencer moved to the end of the stage, holding his hand up to block the light.

"Sam, are you out there?"

The jig was up, as her grandfather used to say. Sam stood up, threw her tea out, and leaned over the balcony.

"I'm here, Spencer. Be right down."

As she walked toward the lobby, Sam dialed Chris, their set design intern, to see if he was going to be on time.

Sam knew Spencer Asher and liked him. He had started as an actor in a few of the early one-acts Peter had put on while they were all at UCLA. He assisted on Peter's first full-length play before graduation, but she didn't know he had followed Peter to New York. Spencer had married recently; when he had arrived in Pasadena, she had taken him to lunch and learned that Peter had spent last Christmas with him and his wife at a cabin in Colorado. They were friends. Every time Sam thought of the pieces of Peter she no longer knew, it hurt.

Sam walked down toward the stage and saw Peter standing in the aisle, rubbing the back of his neck. Telltale sign he was stressed or nervous, or both. Sam hoped she was the cause of at least some of that stress. It took her mind off her own scratchy, sleep deprived eyes. She could do this. She was an adult and the assistant creative director of the Playhouse. The silliness of long-ago love was over, she had a job to do. Sam fixed her eyes on the stage, breezed past Peter, and walked right to Spencer.

"Here, Spencer, I'm here. I called Chris. He's your guy for moving the set pieces. He's just pulling into the parking lot, so leave those, and we'll get them moved for you. What else can I help you with?"

"Great, thanks Sam." Spencer looked at his notes. "Hey, Peter. Peter?"

"Uh, yeah sorry. What's the problem?"

Peter was distracted by something on his phone, but he was now standing in the aisle, and looked up. Spencer jumped down from the stage and walked toward him. Sam followed, trying desperately to look at anything and everything except her past—her older, more stubbled, more rumpled, and sexier past—now standing casually in front of her with a pencil in his mouth.

"Do we know where we want the swing set yet? Sam says we've got it backstage, but I'm not sure we ever decided if it was going to be in front of the scrim for Act I or behind. I can just tape it off for now, but if it's ready we should probably get it out here."

"I thought we decided it would be behind the scrim for Act I, and then we'd bring it forward at the last scene change before Act II?"

Peter put the pencil back in his mouth, and his eyes flicked to Sam making breathing difficult yet again. Thank God she didn't need to say anything.

"Right, right. We did say that. Okay."

Spencer turned to Sam, asking, "Sam, can we get it moved onstage? Wait, you know what? Is it too late to get it put on wheels?"

So much for silence. It was time for Sam to find her words. She took a breath.

"Actually, it's already on casters. We can leave them on, even see if we can have set design put on a false front."

Spencer smiled and put his arm around her.

"I love this girl," he said, kissing her forehead.

Sam knew her face flushed, but there was nothing she could do.

"Hell, have you guys even seen each other yet?"

Spencer looked back and forth between Sam and Peter.

Peter smiled and replied, "We did. Saw each other at the fundraiser last night. Sam, it's good to see you again."

Sam did not smile.

She nodded, however, acknowledging, "Peter," before looking back at Spencer, continuing, "Okay, so I'll have them pull the swing set out and," looking over her shoulder, and finishing with "it looks like Chris is getting everything else in place."

"Okay." Spencer looked confused at Sam's sudden chill.

But she just kept moving. She had to. If she stopped for too long, if she lingered, everyone in the whole theater would see her hands shaking.

"Let me know if you need anything else," Sam said as she hopped up onstage to take care of the swing set and get as far from Peter as possible.

Sam pushed through the curtain and stood up against the cool concrete wall backstage. *Damn him!* Wait, she had no right to damn him. This production would bring in enough publicity and money to keep the theater in the black for a few seasons. She should be thanking him, but the pain was sharper than she had anticipated. In the dark, she closed her eyes.

The Playhouse's creative team had accepted Peter's gracious offer without so much as a full read-through. That was unheard of, especially in a town like Pasadena, where keeping up appearances was as important as breathing.

"You'll be taking most of this one, Sam. I'll always be here, but you know Peter and the director. So no biggie, right?" Candice had proclaimed months before while smashing her lipstick-rimmed cigarette into the owl ashtray on her desk.

"I'll need you to take notes at the production meetings, monitor rehearsals, and report back any resource needs, that sort of thing. Peter is footing the bill for the entire thing, but we need to make sure we're on top of everything so money is not wasted. We may even need to pitch in if need be."

No biggie? I'm pretty sure this is the biggest biggie, Sam thought at the time, but of course she was the logical choice. It was a great opportunity. Sam had accepted the assignment with a smile.

So why, she mused, was she so stupid, heart fluttering, stuck? More importantly, at the age of twenty-eight, in her hometown, in her theater, why the hell was she shaking and avoiding him? She would have to talk to him eventually. They would be working together for the next few months. He was saving their ass, right? Sam let out a slow breath. She would be professional, cordial even. *It's been four years, Sam. You were kids, get a grip!*

Peter flipped through the notes from the read-through, one hand still rubbing the back of his neck. He tried to put her out of his mind. Those jeans, the slight shake in her voice, the smoldering hatred she tried to mask behind a professional facade. It was all there, even the lips. He needed to focus.

Writing, going to New York, had made Peter his own man. It freed him from the shadow of his parents, his tragic little story. Peter was always good with words. Sam used to tell him that he single-handedly saved her grades during freshman and sophomore English. It surprised no one when Peter became a playwright. He was sure this town would always see him as that awkward high school kid who put on the neighborhood talent show. The kid whose life seemed pleasant enough until the day his father blew his brains out.

Mrs. Fillmore, their plump music teacher whose hairline receded unusually far for a woman, had once cornered him at Junior Assembly and whispered, "Peter dear, you'll really need to develop some confidence if you ever hope to marry or make any money."

Peter was able to laugh, thinking about it now, sort of. This town had always underestimated him, so when his mother called to tell him the Playhouse was in trouble and might close its doors, he made excuses and then hung up the phone. He was successful in

New York. In Pasadena, he was some poor rich kid with a dead dad and a mother who lived in a bottle.

Being that kid—coming back to be him—was the very last thing Peter wanted to do. Yet he loved the Playhouse. It had been his shelter when the storm hit. It was a beating heart when his simply stopped. That's why he had called his mother back that same night and told her he would do whatever they needed. He couldn't lose the theater as well. It would break Sam's heart and he had already done that once.

Sam was everywhere while he was writing this play. He knew on some level that his therapist had yet to tackle that he would one day share it with her. Sure, it would generate revenue for the theater, but the play was for her. It was all the things he couldn't say. At least what he had finished so far. He still had to write the ending. For the first time in his career, he was stuck. There was still plenty of time. He wasn't worried yet. Maybe being home would jog . . . something.

When he had spoken to the board and offered up his play to help them fend off bankruptcy, he had been so resolute. He knew it was the right thing to do, but that didn't make it easy. Maybe, as his friends in New York had said, he was returning home a wild success so he could swoop in, save the day, and prove he was now "the man." He honestly had no idea, but looking at the stage now, Peter definitely didn't feel like "the man."

The play, *Looking In,* was a coming-of-age story about three friends growing up in a small, affluent community. Peter smirked thinking about it now. Not exactly original, but in public he would only own up to it being semi-autobiographical. He had written a couple of endings, but none had worked. He knew he could make something up, he had tried, but most of the play was so honest and organic that any ending he attempted to create fell flat.

Peter moved to his seat and added too much sugar to his coffee. Candice, the tall, leggy blonde, head of the theater, had told him Sam would be managing the production. Peter had nearly fallen off his chair during that video conference. He had heard from Grady that Sam was now the assistant creative director, but given their history, he was surprised she wanted anything to do with this particular project. Maybe she didn't have a choice.

He knew she was somewhere backstage now, he could feel her. He wondered if she'd stay back there for the entire rehearsal. Peter looked up from his notes again. She was going to try and avoid him—understandably so, but she wouldn't be able to hide forever. Like it or not, they had a job to do.

Three actors were now onstage. Two young men, one with very dark hair and the other with light brown, and a young woman with long dark hair tied into a tail low on her neck. She was several inches shorter than the boys, and they were all laughing as she stood on one of the boxes to achieve eye contact.

Spencer called the rehearsal to order.

"Okay, let's take it again from the top of Phillip's dream sequence. This is the first time the audience gets to be inside Phillip's head. It's only a dream, but in Phillip's mind it's real, so we need to bring it to the audience."

"Jacob," he said to the actor with the almost black hair, the one that looked like a young Peter, "remember that Phillip has known Sally his entire life, so there's history that we need to see, but there's also something new. Do you get what I'm saying?"

Jacob nodded and shoved his hands into his pockets, testing out the physicality he would need to play young Phillip.

"Great. Let's give it a try from the top."

Sam stood in the wings and wondered if Peter had had a hand in the casting. The young woman playing Sally looked so much like her. She pulled the three actors' headshots out of a folder Candice had given her.

Minka Randolph, from Los Angeles, had been cast as Sally. Sam looked at her photograph. She had big brown eyes, even Sam's freckles. Christ, Minka could be Sam's younger sister. *Unreal.*

Minka was now in the middle of a scene with the young actor. *What was his name again?* Sam sifted through the file once more. Jacob Pratt was obviously playing Phillip. He too was a dead ringer for Peter back in the day. Wow, was this a damn autobiography because the actor standing next to Phillip, eating an apple, could he be Grady's long lost son?

The three of them, well their actor counterparts, stood onstage, and Sam couldn't look away. Grady's character, Greg in the play, turned and exited stage left, right past Sam. The other two stood lost in each other's eyes. Both still holding scripts but managing to look nervous and awkward, hearts racing and full of something Sam recognized, but hadn't felt in a very long time. They were terrific actors. When Sally touched Phillip's face, Sam's heart jumped. It was as if she was right there.

Sally said, "I never realized your eyes had that little dark brown part. I guess this is the first time I've been this close, I thought they were just green."

Phillip nodded and let out a deep breath. Sally closed her eyes and grinned.

"Mmm . . . your breath always smells like Life Savers."

Sally opened her eyes and Phillip moved closer. Sam's hand came instinctively to her chest, she could not breathe. Her heart was clinging to the actors, and she felt a pull toward a time when what she and Peter felt was possible.

"Okay, hold it," Spencer said jumping back on the stage.

"Let's go back three, no four lines. I need you both to make your way further downstage during those lines, so you end up," he took three large steps downstage and looked back at them, "here by the Lifesaver part. Let's try that again."

Sam sat in a folding chair in the darkness, put her hands to her warm cheeks, and told herself she was being ridiculous.

What the hell was this scene? A dream? She knew Peter was only giving out the play in pieces, but maybe she needed to read the whole damn thing. Exactly what story was Peter going to tell all of their friends and family? Sally, Phillip, and Greg? Those weren't exactly names meant to disguise, were they? *The Life Savers, he put the Life Savers candy in there?* Was any of this fiction? There was no way their story was a feel-good play—more like a cautionary tale. Sam wasn't sure how their story would even make good theater. No one likes a sad ending, especially not in Pasadena.

Her phone vibrated with a text from her brother asking if she wanted to go on a blind date with an actor from one of his films. Sam sighed, slid her phone back in to her back pocket, and decided she needed to leave. She had solved some problems, taken a few pages of notes. She'd seen enough to tell Candice things were under control. There were suppliers to contact, union reports to file. She didn't have time to spare exploring Peter's childhood dreams, if that's what this was. She had dreams of her own now, and Peter was not part of them anymore. With one last look onstage, Sam wrote her mobile number on the Dry Erase board, checked in with Chris (who was still moving scenery), and went through the green room to make her exit.

Chapter Five

The production was off and running. The actors and the crew were all adjusting well, with the exception of Julie. Along with Spencer, Peter had brought Julie, his neurotic, psychic, Queen of Fixing-All-Things-With-Superglue, stage manager. Julie was a handful, she was actually a pain in the ass, but she never missed a thing, and, according to Spencer, she had no life outside of the theater. That was maybe a little sad for her, but a huge benefit for him. Sam considered herself detail oriented and maybe a bit of a worrier, but Julie started stressing about things long before anyone else had even begun to think about them. Peter and Spencer fed her chamomile tea and chose to focus on her sheer brilliance at putting up any show, because otherwise she was just plain crazy.

Peter was very protective of his play. Act I had been given out at the first rehearsal. Subsequent scenes would be distributed one week before they were to be rehearsed. Spencer was the only one with the entire script. The cast and crew were given a pretty detailed overview, but Sam imagined it was tough for the actors to put together a character without all the lines. It was unorthodox, but no one seemed to mind. The cast and crew appeared thrilled at the opportunity to work with Peter. Sam had majored in acting, she'd worked in professional theaters for years, and she was well versed in the artistic temperament. Peter wrote a one-act at UCLA that had literally five lines of dialogue. It had received rave reviews, but it was a huge risk. Apparently Peter liked risk as long as he could hide behind a script.

Relegated to watching the scenes as they played out, Sam observed intently every chance she had, just to find out the story, Peter's version of their childhood. So far, she was intrigued. His dialogue was real and he conveyed so well what it was like growing up in their little world. Peter showed the joy and the pain of his own childhood with such eloquence.

They were starting to block scenes with the three friends: Sally, Phillip, and Greg. Sam was a little confused because the Sally character seemed to be a bit of a priss. If she was Sally, Peter had definitely taken artistic license, or maybe he saw her as the type of girl who would send poor Phillip back into the house to change into a more appropriate jacket. *I never did that,* she thought and then reminded herself this wasn't her life.

Spencer began walking through what looked like a high school scene. Rolled up script pages in his back pocket, his hands were flailing around showing the three principals how he wanted the hall scene entrances to go. Sam was backstage, sitting near Julie, who was at her podium barking orders into her headset before calling for a ten-minute hold while they fixed the lighting cues. She ripped off her headset in a huff, releasing her blonde, frizzy hair. Sam feigned sympathy as Julie plopped herself down into her chair as if the weight of the world was sitting right on top of her.

"You okay, Julie? Maybe it's time for some tea?" Sam laughed a little to herself.

"No, I'm fine." She rubbed the bridge of her nose.

"I would give up my right arm if Gordon could get his lighting together. I mean, you'd think this was the first damn time he's done this? When we worked on that revival of *All the Way Home*— did you see that one? Oh, of course not, you live here. Sometimes I forget where I am. Anyway, he pulled the same shit with that one.

He's so unorganized. Lighting guys are usually meticulous, yeah not Gordon. He's trying to drive me crazy."

"I'm sure that's not it. You're doing such a wonderful job and everything is ahead of schedule. It'll work out."

Sam tried to appease her. A calm and collected stage manager meant a happy cast and crew. Sam would stroke Julie's ego all day long if that's what it took.

"Sure, right now we're ahead, but you know how these things can turn, Sam. I need this to go perfectly for Peter. He's so . . . so damn brilliant and this needs to be right. I think he's nervous about this one. Hometown, saving the theater, you know."

She pumped tea from the little Thermos tied to her podium with a yellow bungee cord and yelled across the stage to some poor stagehand: "Stop! Just stop. You cannot run those cords through there. Back it up!"

He did as she instructed and looked like a bunny caught trying to cross a four-lane freeway.

"So, you grew up with our Peter," she said, sipping her tea.

"I did. We like to think of him as our . . ."

Appease, Sam reminded herself.

"Yes, yes, I grew up with *your* Peter."

"This is a cool little town. It's so relaxing. Your food is pretty bad, but Peter always tells me I'm a New York food snob."

She let out an odd pseudo-laugh that told Sam Julie didn't laugh much.

"Do you see yourself in any of this? In the play? I mean what you've seen so far?"

Sam was caught off guard and looked at Julie's crinkled little nose as she tilted her head and waited for Sam to respond. Was she serious? It was obvious Julie had no idea what "her Peter" was to Sam, and there was no need to share.

"Oh well, not especially. Peter and I were good friends, but the play seems mostly about him. You know, at least semi-autobiographical, his experiences, so . . ."

"Good friends? Christ, are you Sally? We've all, all of us from

New York that is, been trying to figure out who he based her on. She's so vivid and clear. She must be someone in this town. You're the only one of his female friends so far . . ."

"Is that your headset going off?" Sam asked quickly, trying to change the subject.

"Shoot," Julie put her headset back on, and Sam was saved. Julie waved her off and began barking at Gordy. Sam slipped away to the side stairs and walked down to sit in the front row corner. Worst seat in the house, but it was quiet and Sam needed to finish the day's notes for Candice.

A few minutes later, Julie and Gordy were toe-to-toe onstage, still arguing while Spencer and Peter looked on in exhaustion. Rounding out the New York crew, quite literally because he was a big boy, was Gordon. Peter had met him through Julie. Gordon and Julie had actually dated at one point, which, according to Spencer, was a huge disaster. Since their breakup about a year ago, Julie had not stopped yelling at him, and Gordon seemed to be eating his feelings. Peter apparently didn't care because Gordy—as everyone but Julie called him—was "an artist with light." That's the title Peter had given him in an article Sam read a week before they arrived.

"He took forever and always had powdered sugar in his beard, but no one lit a show like Gordy," Peter had added. The New York Times went on to say that the three of them, Spencer, Julie, and Gordy, were Peter's team, his backbone. They had started together when Peter was still in theaters with leaky ceilings and broken house seats, and he had insisted on them when he went to Broadway. Now they had agreed to return home with him.

Gordy was pointing to his lights and trying to explain the difficult angle to Julie, when Spencer called it quits: "Thanks everyone, that'll do it for tonight. We'll pick up right here tomorrow. Julie, please make note of the area that's still giving us trouble."

Julie nodded and hurried off while Spencer collected his things and talked to Peter, who was on his third or fourth coffee at this point. Black, three sugars. *Funny the things you remember*, Sam thought. She closed her notes, grabbed her purse, and walked back toward the lobby. Peter made his way through a row of seats; she saw him out of the corner of her eye. He was wearing a shirt she had given him for his birthday when they were in college. She would recognize it anywhere. It was orange, his favorite color. Plaid flannel with patches on the elbows. *That shirt is five years old, why wear that shirt? Is he doing this crap on purpose?*

"Sam, I want to talk to you for a minute."

"Right now? I should get going."

They'd been doing well, and it was late. Late and Peter's rumpled, birthday-present shirt were not a good combination for her right now.

"If this is about the paint, I already talked to Spencer and I'll have the samples for him in the morning, but . . ."

"It's not about the paint. I need to, we need to talk."

His eyes changed, and Sam knew in an instant what he wanted to talk about. It was easier if she kept moving. She wasn't sure why they needed to talk now, things were fine. Almost two weeks had gone by, and they were making things work as colleagues. In fact, despite her past being played out every day on that stage and the realization that her nagging question—"why"—would never be answered, Sam was proud of how professional she'd been.

"Here?" she asked, making one more effort to dismiss this.

"Let's go sit for a minute. I won't take up a lot of your time, but, I . . . I only need a minute, please."

Peter walked to the back of the house. He couldn't ignore it anymore. Things were tense, and she was being so professional it was making him sick. Being near her every day and looking into the void in her eyes was painful.

"I think pretty much everything is moving along. It would be helpful if I could see a bit more of the script."

"Sam . . ."

"I know there are issues with needing to add lights to the opening scene. I told Candice yesterday, and that supplier is in town, so it shouldn't be too difficult."

Sam's hands were now moving on their own, flipping through papers in her binder as she babbled. Peter put his hand on hers, and she froze.

"Stop, please. I don't want to talk about the play. I want, I need, to talk about this."

He moved his hands indicating something between them.

"This weird, awkward situation. It has to be strange for you. I know it is for me, and I really want to find a way."

"Find a way to what?"

Sam felt her face warm and she turned to look at him. This was what she was trying to avoid. There wasn't a discussion that would explain, so Sam saw no reason to discuss anything. The play: that was the focus. Not the actual content, because that was proving difficult, but the details of the production. Sam was choosing to stay focused on paint, lights, timecards, union breaks. She was comfortable as long as they stuck to the details.

"I want you to. . . I want to be able to . . ." *Jesus, you're a writer, man. Spit it out!* Peter took in a deep breath. "I guess I want us to be able to work together and not . . ."

Spencer and Gordy walked up the aisle and Peter was grateful for the reprieve. They looked at Peter and Sam, noticed the tension, and wisely kept moving.

"Goodnight, guys. You're the last ones here," Spencer said. Peter nodded.

"Hey Sam, thanks again for getting me those gels," Gordy added as they reached the back door.

"Oh sure, you're very welcome. Have a great night." Sam grinned as both men left through the lobby and then her smile dropped as she turned back to Peter.

"We are working together. Done. Is there something you're not getting that we need to address?"

"No, it's fine. The show's getting a great start. I don't want you to feel uncomfortable. If you need to hand this off to someone else, I'll understand."

"What? Hand it off? This is my job. I'm going to hand this off because, because you and I have, whatever you want to call it, history? I don't think so."

"I didn't mean to upset you, I thought, I don't want you to feel . . ."

"Peter, you gave up needing to worry about my feelings years ago. As far as I'm concerned you're a playwright, just like any other playwright, putting on a production in this theater. We grew up together and you moved away. Period. If there's any awkwardness, it must be yours, because I'm fine."

"I thought, since we haven't talked about it."

"Please! You want to talk now? No, the time for talking is over. We have a job to do, our, my theater is counting on this. All I want from you is a good show."

"That's all?"

"Yup, that's it. So, unless there's something the play needs or your staff needs, I have to get going."

Peter looked at Sam as she stood to leave. She took a breath, looked down at her papers, and then over at the stage. *Hand it off, was he out of his overly inflated mind?* She tried to keep a handle on all of her feelings nagging for release. She wasn't strong enough, and the words slid off her lips before she could pull them back.

"One question before I leave."

"Sure," he said, standing.

"What's the ending? How does the play end? I mean, is everyone happy when the curtain finally drops?"

"I, Sam . . ."

"You know what, forget it."

She turned to leave.

"No, wait. It did all work out. Didn't it? Grady is happy and you, you're happy, aren't you? I'm sure after I left everything eventually . . ."

"Worked out? Yeah, sure Peter, eventually."

Sam stared back out to the stage and Peter said nothing. So, he asked if she wanted to hand it off, he had wanted her to step aside to make things more comfortable. He had pranced back into her life without an explanation other than that he was there to save the theater, and now, now after four years, he wanted to talk? *You want to talk? Let's talk*. Sam let the anger course through her, it was good to feel something other than pain.

"Are you happy, Peter?"

He didn't know what to say. There was no right answer. He went with a gentle dodge.

"I, I'm happy that I'm able to help out the theater. Yes, I'm happy."

Sam, recognizing a classic Peter maneuver, shook her head.

"Is that easier? Walking away, skirting around things?"

"Sam."

He went to touch her arm, turn her to face him.

"No, don't," she held up her hand, still looking at the stage. "You know, you write plays, 'words to paper' as Mr. Keeley used to say."

Peter noticed the reference, Keeley had been his favorite English teacher in junior high school, but the memory faded as Sam continued.

"Do you ever get onstage and read your words? Step out into the light and live in the world you create, or are you always on the sidelines? Observing, sitting in the dark theater? Critiquing. Like when we were kids, always watching me onstage, watching Grady get the dates. Ever get out there?"

Sam could feel her breath quicken, but there was no turning back.

"Oh wait, you did make a move, on me, right? Confused the hell out of me and then ran back to the sidelines. That's right. Is that what you want to talk about, Peter?"

Peter instantly felt like he did as a child when his father took him out too far in the ocean. *Shit*, he thought.

"Are you ever on the stage for the whole damn thing, Peter? The good parts and the ugly parts?"

Sam turned to face him fully now. Peter decided it was best to treat this like a bear attack, so he locked onto her eyes and spoke softly.

"Sam, I was there with you, but I needed . . ."

"You, you needed. Oh wow, yes let's talk about what you needed." Her anger became too much and she actually let out an odd laugh.

"Peter, it's always been about you, hasn't it? You're a character of your own design. How can a person be so there with me one minute and then coldly walk away? That person . . . Christ! Do you have anything to say?"

Sam laughed again, it was all she could muster.

The cleaning crew rolled in with their equipment, Peter said nothing, and Sam decided she had had enough.

"Have a good night, Peter. Good talk."

Sam turned and left through the double lobby doors. Her heart was beating out of her chest. He wanted to talk, and then he stood there, and she did all the work.

"Typical bullshit," she hissed as she stormed to the parking lot. By the time she closed herself into her car, she had pushed the pain back where it belonged.

Chapter Six

Sunday morning breakfast at the Cathner house was a tradition. Henry, the oldest, lived in Los Angeles but drove over on most Sundays. He worked as film producer for a large production company. He handled mostly art films and documentaries, carrying himself with an air of casual cool that covered his ridiculous mind for business. Henry had been recently dumped by his girlfriend Britney. This thrilled Sam because last year for Christmas she gave Sam a gift certificate to the spa for what Brit called, "seriously needed maintenance." At Christmas, in front of her whole family. *Bitch!*

Sam's parents were, simply put, great people. Like everyone else, they had their flaws and just enough dysfunction to foster a dry sense of humor and material for great stories. Sam not only loved her parents, she liked being around them. Jack, her dad, came from money, but he worked at being so much more. When someone asked him what he did for a living, he said, "I run the family business." When asked what the family business was, he said, "Oh, we're in tile." There's a sign on his desk that says CUT THE CRAP. That little piece of wood described her dad to a tee.

Sam's grandfather, Michael Cathner, had been a tile artisan on Catalina Island. When he married her grandmother, Gwendolyn

Ross, and moved to Pasadena, they became very well known within the arts community. Michael designed tile and artistic treatments for high-end homes and public buildings during Pasadena's growth in the thirties. He worked with some of the most well-known architects and contractors, and it was hard to go anywhere in neighborhood or downtown Pasadena and not see his work.

Jack earned an MBA from UCLA and then worked closely with his father. They grew the company, Cathner Interiors, into an international corporation. Jack was a warm, humble man, with an addiction to hazelnuts and an obsession with baseball. He had even considered buying the Dodgers once or twice over the years. Jack married Susan, who was funny, independent, had a filthy mouth when anyone got her alone, and was a horrible tennis player, though she continued to try.

They were Sam's foundation. They did have dark sides. They tended to hold grudges, they rarely forgot, and the women in the family had tempers that seemed to simmer for eternity and then explode.

Walking through the front door of the imposing two-story home built by her grandparents, Sam was filled with the familiar. She was desperate for Sunday breakfast. She needed these people.

"Samantha, is that you?"

Her mother called from somewhere in the house.

"It is. Where are you?"

"Kitchen."

"There are flowers sitting by the door. Do you want them?"

"Oh, yes, your brother brought those. Could you bring them in here and also grab the vase on the piano?"

Sam stepped into the living room, which was filled with morning light falling on the lush red Oriental rug her parents had shipped home from their trip to China. She had always marveled at how such an intricate design could sit in such a traditional home. It didn't look busy, but rather joined in somehow with the rest of the furnishings. Her mother had not even flinched when it was delivered. She didn't care if it went or not, she loved the rug, and it would simply have to work. Susan Cathner was daring that way.

Sam grabbed the vase and the bundle of paper-wrapped flowers on her way into the kitchen. Her mother was whisking eggs at the counter. No makeup and her hair pulled back. She was lovely, Sam thought. No one dressed up like her mother, but she didn't need all of that for Sunday breakfast. She had no one to impress and Sam liked her best this way. She put the vase on the counter and opened the flowers over the sink. Susan, still whisking, leaned over and kissed her on the cheek.

"Good morning, dear. You look tired."

"You always say that."

"Well, maybe you always look tired," she laughed.

"Susan, I can't find those damn little knives for the . . . Button! When'd you get here?"

Jack barged into the kitchen holding what looked like toasted muffins.

"Hey, Dad. Got here a few minutes ago."

He tossed the muffins on the table, gave her a big, two-armed hug and a kiss on the cheek. He held Sam by both shoulders.

"Let me take a look at you. Yup, still gorgeous. A little tired maybe."

Her mother raised her eyebrows as if to say: "See?"

"What's with you guys and the sleep thing? I'm getting plenty of sleep. Maybe I just look this way."

"Jack, tell me you didn't already toast those muffins. I haven't even finished the eggs. They'll be cold. Oh, this whole breakfast is hitting the fan, damn it!"

He wrapped his arms around her and whispered into her ear, "They'll be fine."

"Your charms won't work on me, Mr. Cathner. I hate cold muffins. At least wrap them in tin foil until we eat. The little knives are right there on the table. Put them by the butter and jam. Oh, and put that spoon in the fruit salad, please."

He wrapped the muffins, grabbed the other stuff, winked at Sam, and walked off before he got into any more trouble.

"Where's Henry?" Sam asked, finishing the flowers.

"Out back, two mimosas into breakfast." She rolled her eyes.

"Flowers arranged. Where would you like them?"

"Oh, they look beautiful, let's put them on the table outside."

Sam walked toward the back doors and looked out on the large redwood patio. Both men were reclined around the table, and she could hear their laughter before the doors even opened. Sam loved that sound.

"The thing is, he was way too old . . ."

They both turned as Sam walked onto the patio. Henry stood, took the vase from her, and set it on the table.

"Hey, sis, could you tell our father that we saw my very ex-girlfriend in Los Angeles last week having dinner with a guy that was old enough to be her dad?"

"We did," Sam said, kissing Henry.

"Dodged a bullet breaking up with that one, no question."

She joined them at the table.

"Henry, come get these plates and set the table."

Susan peeked her head out and handed him a stack of plates and silverware. Henry obeyed, while their father was ranting about what a mistake it would have been to marry his old girlfriend and that he was better off.

"Speaking of better off," Henry added, setting the plates down, "or maybe not . . . Sam should tell us how things are going at work?"

Both her father and Henry grinned right up into their eyes. Sam shook her head and got up to pour some orange juice. They were both waiting for her response.

"Really?" Sam asked. Henry wiggled his eyebrows up and down. She laughed and pushed his shoulder.

"Are you sure you two have only had a couple of mimosas?"

They were still waiting.

"Wow, okay. Well, the play is off to a great start. You both saw Peter at the fundraiser. He's fine, the same I guess. He works. I work. That's all there is to it."

Jack and Henry both saw something in her eyes and without a word between them, they stopped joking. The table got quiet as Sam added some champagne to her orange juice.

"What?"

She looked at both of them.

"Are you all right with this? I mean, how are you, Sam?" Henry asked.

"I'm fine with it. I'm assuming that you're asking me if I've returned to the heartbroken mess that lived on your couch for two weeks? No, I have not. That was a long time ago. We're both different."

Jack and Henry looked at each other again. Sam was saved when her mother finally joined them.

"Well, this conversation looks like it's turned awfully serious," Susan said, putting the eggs on the table and pouring herself a drink.

"What's so dire?"

"Peter, Peter Everoad."

"Oh, well. Let's start eating before everything gets cold."

She handed Sam the muffins.

They all sat around the large glass top table, and Sam was thankful the passing of plates took center stage, but of course they swung back around once everyone had settled in and begun eating.

"So," her mother asked gently, "have you read the play? Bridge club gossip is that it's about the three of you?"

"Really?" Henry asked while putting jam on his muffin.

"It is based loosely on his growing up in Pasadena, and there are three friends. I have not read the whole play. It's being given out in sections. That's how Peter wants it."

"Hmm, well it should be interesting," Susan added.

Seeing Sam's obvious discomfort, she attempted a change in conversation.

"Is he excited about his sister's wedding? I spoke to April last week, and Cynthia went for her final fitting. Can't believe it's only a couple of months away now."

"Oh yeah, I'd be excited if my sister was marrying a tool like Alan Christian Ferrimore. Please, he's . . ."

"Henry, do you need to go sit in the corner?" Susan asked, pointing her fork at him. The whole table laughed.

"Very funny, I'm just saying. Have you met the guy?"

"I don't know if Peter's excited. We don't discuss his personal life. It's professional, so if it doesn't have to do with the play we're not talking about it," Sam blurted out and the table became awkward again.

Her parents and Henry sensed Sam had feelings, things she wanted to discuss, but they weren't sure she was ready.

"It really didn't look like you were talking about the play at the fundraiser a few weeks ago."

Henry kept picking away, hoping for a reaction.

"I swear to God, I'm going to hit you. Shut up."

"Hey, let's settle down. Wow, you two revert back to kids in a flash. I half expect you to start throwing food at each other," Jack said.

"If you say everything is fine, Button, then we believe you. You just seem a little tense, edgy. Are you sure you don't want to talk about anything? Everything's all right?"

"Everything's fine, Dad. Sure, it has taken some getting used to. I haven't seen Peter in years, but it's professional, there's a distance, and that helps. He brought Spencer with him, who I knew in college, and Grady has kept in touch with Peter. They're playing table tennis this afternoon. We are simply working together, it's good. I promise, it's fine."

The table was silent. Sam was in pain and her mother wondered if she even knew it herself.

"Be sure you're . . . yeah, just take care of you, Sam," Henry said and looked at her with a smile that reminded her why she'd cried on his shoulder after Peter left. Henry went through it with her and he wanted her to be careful. Sam nodded and he knew she appreciated his concern.

"Right, well, you've got this under control, and we're here if you need us," her mom added.

Sam couldn't take the tension.

"Now, can we please get back to Henry's narrow escape from the wicked witch of Prada?"

Henry threw a strawberry at her. They all laughed and the topic was dropped. Jack leaned over and kissed Sam's forehead. Breakfast was delicious, in spite of Susan Cathner's worries, and the company filled Sam up. On the drive home she thought about the conversation. She had this under control. She was in the power position this time, not him.

Chapter Seven

Sam had not seen Brian Frackis in what seemed like forever. They had dated while she was trying to make it in Hollywood, but their relationship fizzled out, not unlike many of Sam's relationships. Brian was a solid guy, a Los Angeles firefighter with a geology degree: an interesting combination. They'd seen each other on and off for a little over a year, but this trip was unexpected. He called and wanted to have lunch. Sam felt a tug mainly because Brian was beautiful, distractingly so. He was well over six feet tall, muscular, lean, with deep, chocolate brown eyes—and kind. That was the right word, Brian was a kind man. When they were dating Sam always felt cherished; he was a great lover. Other than his need to watch and rewatch *Dirty Harry* movies, there was nothing wrong with him. It was a bit annoying that every woman on the planet ogled him, but Sam got used to it. He barely noticed the fuss, which made him even more appealing. Having given up on making it as an actress in Hollywood, Sam decided to lick her wounds for six months in Europe. It never even occurred to her to ask Brian, not only sure he couldn't go because he had to work, but also—she didn't *want* him to go with her. The night before she left, Brian took her to dinner, made love to her, and at the airport he told her he loved her. Sam smiled, kissed him, and knew her heart wasn't there. It was the last time she had seen him. Their break up followed shortly after in a series of polite, awkward, phone calls.

Maybe he's coming to tell me he's getting married? She thought, getting out of her car. *Like in the movies, tying up loose ends with women too blocked or stupid to take advantage of a great thing.* Sam walked into La Grande Orange Café. She was greeted by the smell of cookies baking and jovial, lunchtime chatter. Sam spotted Brian on the patio, she only needed to follow the line of blushing waitresses. *Okay, maybe it was annoying.* Brian stood, smiling as she approached the table.

"Sam, so good to see you."

The waitresses scattered. *That's right, ladies!* She was being silly, but it felt good. Brian was light and fun. Not a lot of that in Sam's life these days. He kissed and hugged her gently. He smelled like . . . well, clean, beautiful man, and Sam held on for a second longer.

"You, too. Are you taller?" she joked, breaking the ice.

They both laughed and Brian pulled out a chair for her. He sat, folded his towering body into the seat next to her, and pushed his brown hair off his face. Sam noticed his hands, she always did, big working hands. His right thumb was smashed from when he had slammed it in a car door as a kid. Sam smiled, remembering when he told her that story one night in bed. They had been in that wonderful beginning period of every relationship, discovering everything about each other. The waitress took their order.

They lunched and laughed as Brian brought Sam up to date on how things were going with him and some of their mutual friends. She told him about her adventures at the Playhouse, and it was a perfectly lovely afternoon. Beautiful weather, great salad with a very attractive man who, unless he was going to start showing pictures of his new fiancée, she might consider dating again, maybe. Brian reached over and touched her hand. *Nope, no fiancée in the picture.* She took a sip of her wine. All was right with the world, and then she saw Grady. Brian did too and stood to shake his hand. They knew each other from the community service Grady did in

Los Angeles, and while Brian and Sam had been dating they went out with Grady and a couple of his lovelies from time to time. Sam stood as well and laughed as Grady jokingly compared biceps with Brian. *What was he doing here?* she thought, *wasn't he playing tennis with . . . oh, dear God . . .*

Peter walked out onto the patio, and Sam went rigid. *Damn it, am I not allowed a minute to . . . what was I doing? Relaxing, right, am I not allowed to relax?*

"So, Brian, you may not know this about me, but I'm a table tennis champ."

"No kidding?"

Brian laughed as Grady mimicked his paddle moves. They liked each other. Brian had tremendous respect for the time and effort Grady gave to many communities.

"What are you doing here? I thought you were playing . . ."

Sam's breath was shallow and she tried to maintain some semblance of calm, but all she could see was Peter as he walked toward them. Shorts, tan legs, damp T-shirt, those eyes, and that damn look in them that said he knew her better than any man on the patio.

"We did play, but I can't stand their food so we came here for booze and burgers."

Grady looked at Brian and then at Sam, who was now looking at Peter.

Peter and Grady had played table tennis since their sophomore year in high school. Not quite a mainstream sport like regular tennis, Sam even joked it was simply ping pong, but they both enjoyed the oddity of the sport. They joined a club because Grady was trying to go out with Esther Lu, who happened to be a state-ranked table tennis champion. Peter went along for the experience. He wrote an article for the school newspaper cleverly comparing table tennis to dating and Grady went out with Esther for a few weeks. The romance died, but the table tennis continued. Grady and Peter actually went to the state championships as a pair. They didn't win, but Sam was there cheering them all the way. Watching table tennis can be stressful stuff. Looking at Grady's sweaty wristband, she couldn't help but smile at Grady's mixture of sophisticate and complete nerd.

"Peter," Sam finally said awkwardly.

"Sam. Nice to see you."

He looked at Brian.

"Oh, sorry," Grady said, trying to cut the tension.

"Brian Frackis . . . Peter Everoad."

They shook hands.

"Peter is a . . . family friend," Sam interjected as her nerves got the best of her.

Peter winced a little at the distant introduction.

"Peter's our resident hot shot," Grady added as they all took a seat because it seemed odd to continue standing.

"He's a famous playwright. Premiering a new play at . . ."

"The Playhouse, right! We saw your first play in New York. Remember, Sam?"

Her pulse went from calm and crisp like a glass of wine to full throttle in under five seconds. *Spots, are those spots in front of my eyes?*

"It was excellent. Heavy stuff, man. Remember, Sam, you couldn't stop crying?"

Sam managed a nod. She didn't dare look at Peter, which was just as well because he was struck dumb.

How was she supposed to know Brian would remember the damn playwright? Christ, she had forgotten she even went with him. The whole thing was excruciatingly awkward. Grady kept grabbing breadsticks off the table, like he was watching a boxing match. Sam needed to say something.

"I eventually stopped crying. Please."

She attempted to sound playful, pushing at Brian's large perfect shoulder.

"You were in New York?" Peter managed.

Brian nodded as if the question was directed at him and Grady mouthed "Uh-oh," like a toddler. Sam looked up and tried to meet Peter's face without fear. He was stunned.

"You saw it?"

She forgot how to breathe. The simple in and out of it all had escaped her. She was sure she started to sweat. This wasn't a secret, she told herself. Maybe she didn't want Peter to know that she had flown all the way to New York, seen his play, and not seen him, but it certainly wasn't some embarrassing secret.

"Yes," she said, feeling her mouth dry up.

She had never wanted him to know. His last words to her before he left for New York were, "Look, this was a mistake. I need to go. Take care."

What kind of pathetic person still flies to New York after that kind of heartbreak? Sam could hear Brian and Grady talking about football—and Peter was still looking at her.

"Why? Why didn't you . . ."

Grady tuned back in at Peter's tone and decided to give Sam a break. He patted Peter on the back: "Well, let's let these two finish their lunch. You owe me food."

Peter pulled his eyes off Sam, which broke the tension and saved her from having to explain to him why she had convinced her boyfriend at the time that the only thing she wanted for her birthday was to go to New York and see this new off-Broadway play.

Brian had, of course, obliged, and they had spent three days in New York City. She had done more than read Peter's first play, she had seen it, and Brian was right, she could not stop crying. She had to go to the bathroom after the final curtain because she was sobbing. It was emotional for the average audience member. She had lived it with Peter; it was heartbreaking for her.

An intimate story of a father and son, the father's suicide, and the conversations they have after his death. The play touched on so many things she was sure Peter wished he had told his father or vice versa. It was a young man coming to grips with his father's death and learning to let go. Sad, intelligent, and funny at the same time. Sam saw it as true confirmation Peter was an exceptional writer. She and Brian didn't go backstage. Brian didn't even know she knew the playwright at the time. Sam never saw Peter while she was in New York. Looking back on it after she got home, Sam realized she simply wanted to be near him. Stupid, since he clearly didn't want her, but the need to connect on any level drew her to the theater.

"Right. Wait, how is it I owe you food? I kicked your ass," Peter said as he stood and pushed his chair in.

He was over the shock and now wondering if Brian worked out all day. *Were they dating? Grady would have said something, right? Oh, wait, was this the guy Grady said she broke up with?*

"Brian, is it?" Peter asked and shook his hand again.

"Great meeting you. Enjoy the rest of your lunch. And, hey, thanks for coming to see my play. If I'd known you were there, we may have met sooner."

There was an awkward pause as Brian tried to figure out if Peter was talking to him or Sam. Peter then looked at her.

"Sam, enjoy . . . Brian."

With that, he turned and walked away with Grady. Sam stood, now alone with Brian, feeling . . . she couldn't figure out what she felt. Was he mad or jealous? He didn't have a right to be either. Why would she have seen him in New York? Did he really want to get into that mess? She all but had the argument in her head and then sat back down with Brian who was somehow much less appealing.

Peter let Grady choose two seats at the bar. Peter's heart was still too quick. He was angry, but he wasn't sure at whom or for what. While he could hear Grady rambling something as he looked at the menu, Peter's brain didn't process one word. She'd been in New York, and she'd seen his play. She'd been in the theater and it was as if they were strangers. That thought seemed the source of his anger, but at the same time, what did he expect? He had taken responsibility for leaving her a long time ago. He knew the pain she must have gone through: he went through it too. Somewhere in the mess of his thoughts, the anger eased, and his mouth curved. She'd been there, two years after he had torn her heart, she'd been in New York, albeit with that Adonis, but it didn't matter unless they were now dating again. He'd get it out of Grady later.

She could have stayed away, ignored his work, but she didn't. Grady was now staring at him.

"What the hell, man? Are you going to order or sit there with that stupid grin on your face?"

Peter ordered, but the smile stayed, he couldn't help it. It felt like hope and hope was so much more than he had expected.

Chapter Eight

Two days later, Sam was cataloging some final props while Carmen, the props mistress, looked like she was about to lose her mind. Even beyond how any normal woman who was seven months pregnant with her first child and simultaneously bringing up a major production with an out-of-town creative team might look. She waddled over to her main prop table with what appeared to be a bunch of dried flowers. Throwing them down on the table, she wiped her forehead with the back of her hand and then rested an arm on her belly. Sam was standing off stage and caught Carmen's eye.

"Tough morning already?" Sam asked with a hesitant smile.

"You have no idea. Do you honestly want to know?"

"Um, yes? Is that the right answer?"

"Well, you know the scene in the second act with the oleanders?"

Sam pursed her lips because she had been given Act II last night and tried to think back to where there were oleanders.

"The one . . . oh, I need to sit down."

Carmen eased into the chair, took a sip of water, and began again.

"The outdoor party scene that we blocked a couple of weeks ago. It's after the father's passing."

"Oh, right. His birthday?"

"Yes, Sally is on the other side of the oleanders, the bushes. It's the part with his mom. Such a sad scene, remember?"

Carmen continued to explain her dilemma once Sam nodded. Sam did remember. How could she forget? Phillip, *Oh please we might as well use the real names,* she thought. Peter hadn't wanted a party. His father had killed himself six months earlier, so, understandably, Peter had not been in the party mood. His mother, on the other hand, had finished having the house repainted and wanted to throw him a surprise party. Sam gathered the courage and pleaded with April Everoad, arguing that it was a bad idea. Sam's mom and Grady's mom, who was April's best friend, had both chimed in and suggested something quiet, but April had been drunk since her husband died, and she wanted a party. She invited half of Pasadena to wish Peter a happy birthday. Sam had tried to help as much as she could. She told Peter about it before he was surprised and he asked her and Grady not to attend. That's how Peter wanted it, so they stayed home.

Grady lived right next door to Peter, so he covertly checked over the fence to see how things were going. He called Sam once the party got started and told her she needed to "get over here right away. He looks like a fucking zombie."

Sam was there in twenty minutes, looked over the wall of oleanders, and Grady was right. Peter looked lost and numb. Her heart broke again for him as he sat on the periphery watching his mother smile and serve drinks to the guests and to herself, of course. Looking at him, so lost, Sam felt the need to do something, so she threw pecan shells over the fence until she got his attention. The other guests were so busy kissing each other's asses they never even noticed. Peter moved a chair over right in front of his side of the oleanders, and they talked. Well, Sam talked and he listened.

It took her a while to break him out of the survival trance he had put himself in. She and Grady spent the rest of the party reading from a dirty joke book the senator kept in the bathroom. It was juvenile, but they were willing to do anything to keep Peter away from his pain. Sam or Grady would read a joke and Peter would pretend to cough as he laughed. Aside from a brief absence when he had to go cut the cake, they sat there for hours. Grady eventually had to leave for a date, but Sam stayed and talked Peter through what was, as Carmen said, a very sad scene. At the end of the party, as the caterers were cleaning up, Peter reached through the oleanders and took her hand.

"Sam, thanks."

"Anytime. Great party ... fabulous, just fabulous, darling." They both laughed and he squeezed her hand.

Thinking about it now, she remembered noticing warmth. If his touch stirred something more than friendship back then, she didn't recognize it at the time.

"Sam ... seriously, thank you."

"You're welcome. I'm so ..."

He let go of her hand and was gone.

"Sam? Hello!"

Carmen was now standing again.

"Oh, Carmen. Sorry, I was listening. I was thinking ..."

"That's all right, it's insane, right? I mean why can't Spencer have Gordy shine little pink lights on the bushes so they look like oleanders? And, and why is it props job to fix a set design screw up? I need to glue every flower on that plain green bush, wall ... whatever the hell it is. How am I supposed to even reach? And who cares if they're actual oleanders? If they screwed up, can't it just be a plain bush wall?"

While Sam had not been paying attention to Carmen's tirade, because she was lost in memory once again, she gathered from her last comment that she would need to glue flowers on a plain bush wall to make it look like a wall of oleanders for the audience.

"Carmen, it's fine. Deep breaths. I'll help you with this. I'll even do it myself. You're right, you'll never be able to reach or stand for that long in your condition. You concentrate on the place settings for Act II, and I'll glue the flowers tomorrow. Okay?"

Carmen started to cry.

"Oh, no don't. It's fine. Everything is going great. . ."

"I'm so sorry to drop all of this on you, Sam. I'm really so . . ."

Carmen rubbed her belly.

"Pregnant. Carmen, you're beyond pregnant."

Sam walked over and put her hand on Carmen's shoulder.

"Give yourself a break."

She handed her a paper towel from the prop table for her tears. Carmen rested her head on Sam and sighed.

Julie came blowing in from the green room like a dust storm. Hands filled with stacks of paper and her tea dispenser thing dangling from one finger. She plopped everything down. Always the sympathetic one, she said, "Oh Christ, hormones again?"

"Good morning to you too. And my hormones are . . ."

Carmen broke off and continued in Spanish. She did this a lot when she was angry, and Julie usually made her angry. They were different women to begin with and the fact that Julie was from New York made her that much more abrasive in Carmen's eyes.

"Julie," Sam said, patting Carmen on the shoulder, "Carmen and I were talking, and I'm going to work on turning the large green wall into oleanders tomorrow. She has so many other things to work on, and her crew's busy with the outside flower boxes, so I thought I'd help."

Julie looked at Carmen just as she said something under her breath.

"Did she insult me in Spanish?"

She then began doing a million things at once around her podium while Sam assured her that Carmen was really tired and would be fine after a little rest.

"Okay, yeah, that's fine if you're sure you don't mind helping with the oleanders. I don't see why Gordon can't project damn flowers on the bush wall with his lighting scheme, but since I can barely get him to light the stage correctly, I decided not to argue in this morning's design meeting."

She huffed and looked at Sam. Sam was definitely starting to realize that everything, in Julie's eyes, was poor Gordy's fault. Must have been some breakup. Sam nodded and with that Julie turned, put on her headset, and was gone: lost in her world of shouted orders and professed disappointment.

Chapter Nine

The next day Sam walked into the theater prepared for oleander blossoms. She was ready to pick up a glue gun. It still struck her as ironic that she was adding finishing touches to a set of Peter's back-yard for a replay of her childhood. It was surreal actually. She opened the doors, letting the morning sunlight spill into the darkened thea-ter. As the doors quietly closed behind her, it took a couple of minutes for her eyes to adjust. When they did, she stared at the stage stunned. Her stomach, empty of the breakfast she skipped, began to turn. The stage was lit cool blue and there were plants everywhere: a weeping willow, bamboo, and birds of paradise. Billowing green silk covered the stage. *My God, he's going to show everyone,* Sam thought. She had hoped, based on what she'd read so far, that the play would stop just short of this scene from Peter's life, her life.

Overhead the sound guys were testing different levels of pounding thunder. Stagehands repositioned plants and fussed with the set, adjusting the details on one of the best days of her life. Sam's heart raced into what felt like an anxiety attack. She had never had one, but she'd heard about them, and this seemed pretty close. She slid into a seat in the last row of the theater.

The stage was set up as the Huntington and it was clearly going to rain; it couldn't be any other scene. Peter was going to show all of Pasadena—and then most likely the entire country—something so private, intimate. Sam closed her eyes and tried to will the memory away, but it was too strong.

Peter and Sam had been celebrating a victory over their medieval history professor. He was truly crazy, and his final exam had 300 questions. They had been studying for it since the first day of class and they had survived. Peter took Sam to lunch and then to their favorite place, the Huntington Library and Gardens, alone. Grady still wasn't home from Stanford, and Peter had said he didn't want to wait. It was the two of them, and it was a perfect day. They felt like a weight had been lifted. They were finally going to graduate. By the time they got through the exhibits in the galleries, the afternoon light descended diffusely through huge clouds. It didn't yet look like rain, so they decided to go through the gardens quickly and see as much as they could. Sam remembered feeling exhilarated, running through each region like school kids on a field trip. She had slipped on the grass.

My God, please make it stop, she begged, closing her eyes and clutching the seat, but the images kept flooding her mind.

Peter took her hand. They were running toward the bamboo forest, when it began to pour. Sheets of rain soaked them instantly as they entered the forest. There was nowhere to go, they looked at each other and began to laugh. They stood drenched, on the bridge, wiping water from their faces, looking up at the massive bamboo that seemed to disappear into the clouds. Sam shivered, Peter ran his hands up her arms, met her eyes, and that was all it took. Everything crashed like the thunder above. Peter never hesitated. He took her face in his hands and kissed her. Her fingers found his hair, their bodies connected, and they lost control. Peter's lips were cold, and his mouth was so warm as one kiss melted into the other. He pulled back for an instant to look around and then lifted Sam up on the bridge railing. She wrapped her body around him as if her life depended on it. It was—continues to be— the most passionate, desperate moment of her life. Suddenly Sam knew she had been waiting a very long time for his touch.

They could not get close enough. It was crazy and wonderful at the same time. Eyes still closed, Sam now touched her hand to her aching chest. She remembered every second as if it had just happened. It all felt so natural with Peter. There wasn't a beat of awkwardness. It was as if they anticipated each other's moves, and there was a flow she'd never experienced with another man. Their clothes clung, tongues twisting, the steam huffed from their mouths as the cold rain tried in vain to extinguish what had been building their entire lives. Time slowed, and Sam noticed everything about Peter's face, his hands, his body. His eyes were the most exquisite bursts of green as he slipped his body into hers and began to move. They were suspended, inside of each other and grasping to stay right where they were forever. Peter's face was buried in her neck and Sam kissed his shoulder, as the rain began to slow. They held on, exhausted, having given everything to one another. Running back to Peter's car that night, she was soaked and happy. Genuinely, down to the bone, happy and lucky. She had always loved him, and now it would be much more.

Sam's heart hurt, sitting in the theater and going back to that day. She could still feel his lips touch hers for the first time. Still feel the instant they . . . the look in his eyes as he slipped over the edge with her. *Isn't that insane?* she thought. *Four years later and countless talks with myself and I'm right back there in his arms. . . .*

"It's not the whole thing," Peter whispered as he took the seat next to her.

Startled out of her memory, Sam's eyes flew open.

"What?"

It barely came out of her mouth. She recoiled from him as if anticipating the pain all over again.

"Easy. It's not what you think. It's not the whole scene."

"Not, not what I think . . . what was I thinking? What is this? I didn't see this in Act II."

"It's toward the middle of Act III. We're working it out of sequence because of the sound. They need extra runs."

Sam tried to collect herself, but her heart would not stop.

"Sam. Listen, you weren't supposed to be here today and I thought we could work on . . ."

"I wasn't supposed to be here today? What the hell, you're sneaking rehearsals now? Peter, it's clearly your play. If you want to include things from our, from your past, that's your business. I'm just a little . . ."

"Sam, you know what this scene is, and I can't tell the story without it. It was huge and important to . . ."

"Was it?"

Peter saw the anger take over her face.

"Huge and important?"

"Of course it was. I never said that it wasn't."

"No, you said it was a mistake, that you, what was it again? Oh yes, that 'you should have left well enough alone.' Do you remember? Is that in your play?"

Peter remembered, he'd replayed his choice of words over and over for the past four years. He was young and stupid, and he'd long run out of excuses. He tried to touch her hand, even though he knew she would pull away. She did.

"You left. You were my best friend, you made love to me, we were . . ."

Sam felt lost all over again.

"And then you were gone. How? Why does someone do that? If it was so important?"

"Sam, I was young, we were young and I wanted more. It was a special day."

"Special?"

She was embarrassed and could feel her face flush. Peter was looking at her with . . . *was that pity?*

"Oh God, please don't, special? Wow! Peter, do whatever you want with your play," Sam said, getting out of the seat.

"Show the whole thing."

She shook her head.

"Tell everyone how Peter Everoad screwed Samantha Cathner in the rain on his way to his successful life in the big city. How he looked into her eyes, shaking, and told her he'd wanted to touch her like that for as long as he could remember."

Peter stood and instinctively reached for her. She pulled away.

"Do whatever you need to do, but please don't sit here and tell me it was 'special' because I don't want to hear it. I obviously meant nothing to you. I was disposable. Or maybe somewhere in your screwed-up mind, you decided it was all too much for you. You, Peter, because after all it's always about you, right? You must've needed some steam for your pitiful little self-satisfying story. And damn it."

She was losing control.

"This is a good one, Peter. Be sure to include all the details, so you look like a real man. Just make sure you leave out the part where you told me you loved me. That makes it look like you . . ."

She stopped, backed away from him and begged her heart for sanity. The pain was unbearable. The original, awful pain. Peter looked away because he couldn't physically take it one more minute.

He wanted to tell her that he did love her, still needed her. Wanted to hold her and say that he'd been a scared, insecure idiot who thought he needed to make something of himself to even be worthy. He wanted to give her those words to help ease her pain, but he stood there and let her wallow in the ache of her heartbreak.

"Please, Peter. Please, leave me alone."

Sam pushed through the heavy wooden doors and into the lobby of the theater. The oleanders would have to wait. She was not working today. For the past two years nothing had been more important to her than this theater, her job. One stupid scene in his play, this stupid scene, had reduced her to a puddle. Sam was angry. Angry with him for coming back and furious with herself for letting him see how desperately she had loved him.

It had almost killed him putting it down on paper. It was completely insane that he left it in the play, but it was perfect. Some of his best writing. The scene was all from Phillip's perspective, Sally was depicted as only a light, she wasn't even on the stage in the scene. Peter didn't want to share Sam's stunning kisses or the curves of her body under his hands with anyone else. While it was a love scene, it was abstract and mostly an inner monologue about Philip's feelings, physical and emotional.

Peter stood up, watching her walk away again. He felt like one of those stupid cats that proudly drops a dead bird at its master's feet and is shocked when the human doesn't see the brilliance in the deed. How had he managed to hide it from her all those years ago, how was it not all over his face? That day changed his life, brought him back to life. She became everything wrapped in his arms. His air, his touch, it all changed.

Sure, making love to a beautiful woman in the pouring rain was great, there isn't a man alive who wouldn't cherish that memory, but with the first touch it was instantly more, and it had scared him shitless. He had always loved her mind and wanted her body. Her rain-soaked skin was so soft it almost hadn't seemed real. He could recall it like he was right back there, but he wasn't prepared for her to completely crawl inside of him. Her warmth took over and he knew he would need her, the fire she gave him, for the rest of his life.

He couldn't need, not then, he could barely allow need now after years of therapy, but back then his twenty-three-year-old, screwed-up self definitely didn't allow need of any kind. He was so focused on making something of himself during those years. He knew the pull of what he felt for her would keep him in Pasadena. Hell, he could spend a whole day just sitting in a coffee shop talking to her in those days. He couldn't stay. Even though he loved her to desperation, he needed to find himself outside of his family, or one day she would wake up and realize he was nothing more than a shadow of a man she thought she knew. So, he memorized her, her magic, and with a little push he left her behind.

He did say cruel things; he had to. She knew him too well and would have never let him go. He had hurt her and now she thought he was simply back to pick the wound. Peter turned back toward the theater and accepted that. Messed up childhood or not, he had been a real bastard.

Chapter Ten

*P*eter's sister, Cynthia, was getting married in less than two months on Catalina. April Everoad had agreed to let Bindi Malendar host a wedding shower overflowing with champagne and desserts. Sam was invited and was relieved it would be at Grady's family home and not Peter's. Mostly because champagne and Peter's mother did not mix well, and also because Sam had always found it so difficult to be in Peter's home after his father died.

She really had not wanted to attend the shower at all, but her mother would be there, and it would be rude to not make an appearance. Sam, always appropriate, found herself making small talk in the large formal living room with a few women she knew from school as well as a larger group of debutantes and new brides in the community. There was a small buffet of real food, but the highlight was a huge table with thirty-five different desserts. Cynthia Everoad was a self-proclaimed sugar junkie so the shower was themed "Bubbles and Confection."

Belinda Malendar, or Bindi to everyone who knew her, was a tall and beautifully put together woman. She was one of those women one doesn't want to run into on a bad hair day. A collection of thoroughbred features, she was perfect: perfectly beautiful all of the time. Sam was sure being a senator's wife did that to a woman. Bindi had been married to Senator Patrick Malendar since they graduated from college. Despite his wandering eye and a penchant for hard liquor, Senator Malendar was a sweet man. He and his wife, while a little artificial for Sam's taste, always seemed to complement one another.

Bindi had been friends with April Everoad, Peter's mom, and Susan Cathner, Sam's mom, since they were Bindi Parker, April Whitmore, and Susan Braxton back in boarding school. All three women were dear friends and anyone who thought otherwise did not witness the round-the-clock care given to Mrs. Everoad when her husband died. Bindi basically took over her friend's life for the first month after the suicide, and Susan was the one who threw open the curtains when April had spent one too many nights drinking. Both women tried to help her in the beginning, but now they simply accepted it, and ran interference for April's "problem."

Senator Malendar, who was out for the evening, was gearing up to run for re-election again at the end of the year. Grady had already started complaining that he hated election years. The guests were all sure to give Bindi and the Senator their best wishes, but Sam did notice the Malendars were a little on edge. Perhaps because keeping up appearances could be tough when your son was Grady Malendar. Grady liked to party, and he was very good at it.

Sam excused herself from the giggling festivities in search of some air. While standing on the balcony, she heard a car pull up the circular drive. Black Lincoln Town Car, one of the fleet maintained by the Malendars. The car stopped, and the driver walked around to open the door. Grady stepped out steadily, but then put his arm around the driver, who grinned politely and then bent to help the other passenger. Sam hoped Grady had the good sense not to bring a woman around during the shower.

Peter emerged from the car, a little less gracefully. Grady moved his affection from the driver to Peter. While Sam was relieved Grady had not brought one of his many lady friends home to his parents' house, her pulse quickened at the sight of Peter. It had been a few days since she had seen him at rehearsals—the day he decided to parade their private life in front of everyone—but she was still clouded by a mess of feelings she couldn't shake.

Grady and Peter held each other up, waved to the driver, and turned toward the door, the front door. They couldn't see her standing on the balcony, so Sam watched as they both wobbled together. Grady held his liquor well, but Sam wasn't sure about Peter. It occurred to her that she no longer knew how Peter held his liquor. Either way, intoxicated or not, Grady and Peter heading into Cynthia's wedding shower was not good. She had to give it to them for sheer courage, thinking they were going to walk through the front door in their current state.

Leaning over the balcony railing now, Sam watched as they both laughed, turned from the front door, and began walking around the house right under her. *Side door, good choice guys,* she thought, watching as they walked below her joking like they were in high school.

"Did you already finish that, that Slurpee? Such a stupid word . . . Slurpee," Peter said trying, and failing miserably, to whisper.

He was in tan pants and a navy jacket barely hanging on to his broad shoulders. Grady was in a full suit with his tie shoved into the pocket of his jacket. They were both quite disheveled, curling over laughing as they stumbled around the corner. In spite of herself, Sam relished seeing both of them relaxed and silly. Peter's mother had fallen into a serious drinking problem after his father died, so that even when they were in college Peter rarely drank. Which was fine, but it was refreshing to see Peter let loose. Grady must have dragged him to the club with his famous line: "Let's go blow off some steam."

Sam moved back into the study, still not ready to rejoin the shower. They'd been starting to play "How Well Does the Bride Know Her Groom?" when Sam had stepped away. She honestly couldn't take it; backing away, she'd gone up the stairs and into the study unnoticed. Sam figured that the game and the two or three that would follow should allow her a few moments of peace, unless Grady and Peter actually decided to crash the shower. If they were smart they would just stay in the kitchen or get back in the car and go to Grady's house. Why were they here? Bindi didn't give Grady much slack when they were growing up, so she certainly wouldn't take kindly to his behavior now.

Sam sat in one of the high-backed, dark green chairs facing a massive, heavy, wood and glass cabinet of bookshelves. This library was part of the original house built back in 1929. Sam had always liked this room. The three of them prepared for their SATs in this study. Sam's memories reached back even further as she picked up the book on the table in front of her, *The History of the Ottoman Empire*. No doubt a little light reading for Grady. Sam remembered coming to Grady's house after grade school and playing store in this very room. Everywhere Sam went there were pieces of her past. The rich chocolate cake and crème brûlée she had eaten earlier were now both ganging up on her and turning into a headache. Sam closed her eyes.

"She sleeps. . . ." Peter whispered a few minutes later.

Shit! Sam thought and cracked open her eyes expecting to see the two of them looking like kids sneaking home after a night of revelry, but it was only Peter. He was leaning in the doorway with his jacket over his arm like someone propped him there.

"What are you doing? Where's Grady? Tell me he's not . . ."

"Bathroom," Peter answered while leaning to point down the hall. He almost lost his balance and swayed back, grabbing the door molding to steady himself.

"Whoa, that was a close one," he said, now brave enough to walk toward Sam.

She was still unsettled and upset about the scene in the play, but damn if he wasn't sexy and smoldering as he threw himself into the chair next to her. His eyes were heavy and his navy jacket, probably linen, dropped on the floor. Peter rubbed his hands over his face, stretched his long legs, and crossed them at the ankles. His hair looked like he may have taken a nap in the car ride over.

Peter closed his eyes, and Sam allowed herself to notice, once again, that Peter had grown up very nicely. How could she hate him and want to drag him to the floor at the same time?

"Tough night?"

Peter opened one eye and turned toward her. She couldn't help it, she smiled.

"We, there was this thing. Grady came by the theater and said we should go, he invited me, said we could blow off . . ."

"Some steam? Oh, Peter, you fell for that? Hmm . . . you have been gone too long."

"I know. I know, but he's so damn persuasive, and I felt wound up. It seemed like a good idea at the time, but how do people do this all the time? I only had four, maybe five, beers. I should be embarrassed. I love the fact that my face is completely numb along with my brain, but the spinning . . . what kind of a man admits to spinning after only four beers?"

Peter closed his eyes again and rested his head. He looked wrinkled and tired, but a little reckless. It was different. Sam found herself forgetting that she hated him.

"I should get back," she said.

"Yeah, I was going to ask you why you were hiding in here," he said, eyes still closed.

"I'm not hiding. I needed to take a break, but I should get back."

Sam stood, and Peter opened his eyes.

"The shower sounds great. We heard a lot of happy giggling while we were sneaking up the stairs. You're not having a good time?"

"No. I mean, yes, I'm having a good time. Your sister's fun and clearly very much in love. Mrs. Malendar is in charge of the whole thing, so of course it's scary perfect."

Sam let out a laugh.

"Right, that's the well-rehearsed token answer, Miss Cathner, so why are you sitting in the study?"

"You've definitely had five beers."

"True, but that's not why you're in the study."

"Christ, Peter, I needed some air, a breather. Aren't you worried about Grady? Where . . ."

"I make it a habit never to worry about Grady. He's probably taking a little nap or he's downstairs. Now that would be worth the price of admission. I'm pretty sure he's dated half the women at the shower."

He laughed and then put his hands to his head. Laughter erupted from downstairs, and they could hear Cynthia shouting answers to the next game.

"Oh boy it's starting to get rowdy," Peter mocked.

"I'm heading back down. Will you be all right?"

"Probably not for some time, but I'm going to sit here until someone finds me or the room settles down."

Sam walked toward the door.

"Sam, you don't need to leave yet, they're still playing stupid games. You're not into that."

"Oh really, how do you know what I'm into? It's been four years."

"I know."

His eyes were closed again, and he sounded a little sinister. When she walked back toward him, the corner of his mouth turned up.

"Still know how to piss you off, don't I?"

"You are quite good at it."

"I like games. I only needed a . . ."

"Break. Yeah, so you said. Cynthia does seem happy. I used to think Alan wasn't really the guy for her, but they're good for each other. She deserves happy."

Peter grabbed his jacket off the floor, reached into the pocket, and pulled out an open bag of peanut M&M'S.

"Want one?"

"Peanut, my favorite."

"See, I told you . . . I know you."

Sam took it, poured a few into her hand, and sat back down.

"When? Where did you get these?"

"Right around the time Grady declared he needed a red Slurpee, and we had the driver pull over. For some reason I wanted peanut M&M'S."

Their eyes met and again it was effortless.

"Hmm . . . well, they're the very best candy."

Peter laid his head back and closed his eyes again. Sam did the same. Other than the crunch of peanuts, it was quiet. They sat there for a while and said nothing. Peter began to laugh.

"What?"

"Remember when you went to that dance with . . . oh, what was his name?"

"Harrison," Sam moaned immediately and he laughed harder.

"Right, right, Harrison of Pasadena Prep. God, remember him?"

"I do. He was . . . he had very nice hair."

She tried to keep a straight face.

"Oh please, he was a complete lunatic. His teeth were capped before he was fifteen."

Now they both laughed.

"He was . . . high maintenance."

"That's an understatement. Remember when you called me from their big ball, cotillion thing and told me to come get you?"

Sam remembered.

"I do. It was so bad. I should have known when the corsage he gave me took up half my arm, but when he ever started doing the running man . . ."

Now they were belly laughing.

"What did you say to him? I remember pulling up and you came running out to the car in that, that dress."

"Cramps, I used the steadfast excuse for all things awful or un-comfortable. I pulled him aside and said I had to leave because it was my time. The look on his face, it was priceless. Guys never ask any questions when you bring up cramps. It was perfect."

Peter shook his head and reached for more M&M'S.

"What was wrong with my dress?"

"Oh, nothing. It was, wasn't it black?"

"Yes, it was. I loved that dress. It was my first dress that wasn't pink with some kind of bow or ruffle. It was my slinky dress."

"I remember it very well. It was short. My seventeen-year-old mind remembers it being short, and you were wearing very high heels. Yeah, I remembered those heels for quite some time."

She looked over at Peter, whose eyes were still closed. She'd never realized the dress or the heels left such an impression. She wanted to stay in the memory with him.

"Well, if I forgot to say it then, thank you for rescuing me."

"It was my pleasure."

Quiet filled their space again.

"What made you think of Harrison?"

"I remember that we drove to Memorial Park after I picked you up. We sat in my car and talked for hours."

He looked over at her, and the warmth was back. Sam nodded.

"There was a concert at the Levitt Pavilion. For some reason that memory is so vivid. It was a gorgeous night, and you, you were in those heels."

"I'm pretty sure I'd taken the damn things off by the time we got to the park and you brought me M&M'S."

They both looked at each other. Even though they were older, and Sam tried to remember to be angry, it felt so wonderful, like being home, so unstudied sitting there together.

"Well, I thought you might need them after your Harrison trauma. If I'd known about the running man moves, I would have brought two bags."

"Who was playing that night? I can't remember."

"I think it was some jazz band. They did that song 'I'm All Right,' and the woman singing had such a great voice. I bought that song when I moved . . ."

Peter's voice trailed off, but not before Sam saw for a minute how important the memory was.

"So, I wonder where old Harrison is now," he added.

"I think he married one of the teaching assistants from his school."

"No!"

"Yes, yes, I'm pretty sure that's what I heard. My question is were they dating while he was still in high school? Now that'd be a scandal. Such a shame it didn't work out with us."

More laughing. Her chest squeezed. Sam needed to bring the conversation back to the present, remind herself how all of this ended. Why did she continue to allow him in?

"Cynthia's wedding is in less two months away. Are you, excited, nervous?"

"Umm, I'm excited for her, maybe a little nervous. The whole man-of-the-family thing can get to be too much, but I want to be there for her, so it's fine. Looking forward to going to Catalina."

He smiled.

"Me too. When was the last time you were there?"

"Jeez, it's been years. Sophomore year in college maybe? When were . . . you were there too. The summer Grady broke his arm playing rugby? That was sophomore year, right?"

"Yeah. Wow, it has been a long time for you."

"And you? When were you there last? Did you and Brian go to Catalina too?" Peter jabbed, his eyes still closed, but the corners of his mouth curled.

"Nice. Very mature."

"What? I'm just asking. So?"

"Catalina, I went to Catalina with my family last year, and Brian stayed home. The town dedicated a memorial to my grandparents in the botanical gardens. It was touching. Every time I hear about them, I learn something new. They were wonderful people. We spent a week there, had a blast. Watching Henry perfect his pick-up lines was worth the trip."

Peter was listening, watching her, as if seeing her for the first time.

"You have a great family, Sam."

"I do," she said, feeling a little sad for Peter, but there was no question, her family was the real deal. Generations of great people, in fact, and huge, huge shoes to fill.

"Definitely some pressure there too, you know. I'm sure my father was hoping one of his children would at least get a law degree or something."

"I know, but they're so solid. Besides I remember you handling the pressure perfectly fine. You've always been, you still are. Jesus, why is it I can't seem to speak? You're a fantastic woman, Sam. I'm sure your family is very proud."

It was silent again, and the M&M'S were gone. Sam's heart started yearning to stay, to be in the present with Peter, and it hurt. Peter took a deep breath and she said nothing. Her mind returned to the wedding shower and the thought that someone might be looking for her. Crazy as he made her, painful past and all, Sam realized she would still rather sit and talk with Peter than with anyone else in the world. Some things truly never changed.

Peter opened his eyes to look at her.

"Sam, you ever think about marriage, getting married?"

"Well, if Harrison . . ."

"I'm serious. Marriage, spending your life with one person. Ever think about it?"

She said nothing.

"Well, do you?" he asked again.

"I guess, sure, I've thought about it."

"Settling down in some big house here, Bunko on Saturday night, kids at the park on Sunday?"

"Umm, not a fan of Bunko, and the house can't be too big. People can get lost in a big house. I want to be close."

Peter wanted to tell her he did too, but this was the first civil conversation they'd had since he returned, and he did not want to blow it.

"As for the kids, you asked me about marriage. I can't say I ever think much about kids, but I'd like to have them someday. Right now, I'm enjoying my work."

"Here? You'd live here?"

"I don't know. I wouldn't live in Hollywood, but it depends on who I'm marrying."

"Brian? Grady said you two dated for quite a while, right?"

"We did. Brian's a wonderful guy. Solid."

Sam decided to have some fun. He brought it up.

"But, he's a firefighter. Really tough job and when I moved back here . . . I don't know. We'll see."

Peter suddenly felt anxious. *Of course he was a damn firefighter!*

"He did seem nice, but . . . not really your type."

"What? Peter, you don't know anything about my type. I'm going downstairs now before you make a complete ass out of yourself. Sleep it off."

Peter stood up just as she did, and they were face to face.

"I know more than you think I do. I know you, Sam. Even after all of these years, I still, I know."

He brushed the hair out of her face and trailed his fingers along the side of her neck.

"It feels the same. Your skin."

Heart drumming, all Sam could do was stare at him. She wanted to touch his face, but didn't move. For the first time since he had arrived home, Sam wasn't angry.

"I used to think I could never live in Pasadena again. I couldn't wait to get out of here, especially once Dad was gone."

The words coming out of his mouth and the messages in his eyes, his touch, were once again all full of Peter's conflict.

"Is that so?" Sam wondered where he was going with this.

"If you couldn't wait, why are you back?"

"I, my play's here. I didn't mean to hurt . . ."

"You brought it here to help the Playhouse. You could have just written a check. Why this play? Why now, Peter?"

"It needs to be here. I need to be, I want . . . why didn't you tell me you came to New York, that you saw my play?"

He leaned closer and she could feel his breath as he hovered. Everything told Sam to pull away, do something, but she physically could not move. She was searching for some air where there was none. Peter brought both hands to her face, leaned into her neck and whispered, "Samantha. I came home because I need . . ."

Peter searched his fuzzy brain for the perfect words and failed miserably. She was so close, and he fought the urge to simply grab her, to show her why he'd come home.

"Well, am I interrupting something?"

Sam jumped and the back of her hand smacked Peter on the chin. He fell into his chair putting his hand to his head again.

"Hello, Grady. Perfect timing as always. Pretty long piss you took there," Peter said.

Grady walked toward them laughing.

"Peter, please, where are your manners, young man? Good hit, Sam. Nice work. Was he getting fresh with you?"

Sam continued to stare at Peter. *What the hell was that?* kept ringing in her head. He was drunk, and he was playing with her. For a blink, right before Grady came in, it looked as if he was going to kiss her.

Sam was angry. Peter was gracing his little hometown with his presence, and he had decided to mess with the hometown girl. Peter looked at her once more for a split second and then, rubbing his jaw, closed his eyes again. Sam walked right past Grady and toward the door. Grady dropped into the empty chair.

"No, Sam. Don't leave, I think they're opening gifts down there. Sounds dreadfully boring."

Grady was clearly enjoying the awkwardness of his intrusion. Sam was not sure what game Peter was playing, but suddenly the games at the shower seemed a lot safer. She told herself it was the five beers, cursed herself for being foolish enough to play along, put on her fake smile, and walked down the stairs.

Chapter Eleven

Susan Cathner was the only woman Sam knew who could pull off wearing capris with red, white, and blue pinstripes. Most women would look silly, even on the Fourth of July, but she looked festive and classic. Her mother wore them every year, sometimes with a white shirt, but mostly with a navy blue polo and cute little flip-flops sprinkled with glitter. She was a patriotic vision greeting guests at the front door for the Cathners' annual Independence Day celebration.

Sam wore her solid red shorts and a dark blue denim shirt, tied at the waist. Her flip-flops were white and that was about as exciting as her patriotic outfit got. Still, she was genuinely excited for the party, a long-standing family tradition. Since before Sam was born they'd been breaking out steel buckets filled with cold beer and firing up her dad's Lynx grill. Headquarters, as Jack Cathner called it, had grown over the years into a station of four grills, a sink, a full-size refrigerator, burners, and some hickory smoker thing Sam never understood. Jack was clearly an obsessed grill master and Fourth of July was his day to shine.

Sam looked out back and savored the gift of home, the simplicity of seeing her father, apron on, with a huge smile. She remembered being a little girl and pushing past her brother and his friends to help at the grill. The smell of smoke and her father's big hands as he hoisted her up into his arms.

"You can be my co-captain, little nut. Co-grill-captain, that's what you are," and he'd kiss her on the cheek with his Saturday stubble.

She looked at him now, surrounded by his family, a family he'd worked hard to support, to love, and most importantly to keep laughing. He had his arm around Henry; Sam was sure they were telling some tasteless jokes before too many guests arrived or her mother overheard. Sam was still restless, but she felt a little less off-center when she was with her family.

The yard began to fill with guests dressed in patriotic colors. The only requirement on the invitation was that all guests must dress in red, white, and blue. It became a competition for many of their neighbors, friends, and relatives. Mrs. Gressling always wore a sundress that looked like Betsy Ross herself made it. Grady's mother would arrive with a patriotic silk scarf tied around her neck, and April Everoad always wore the same stars-and-stripes skirt that she bought once at a boutique in Santa Barbara. People wore crazy hats, Bermuda shorts, and even carried purses with glittering American flags. Sam's uncle always brought his big English bulldog wearing a coat saying "No More Taxation" over a Union Jack background.

It was a blast to see the turnout every year. It was a tradition. Without fail, no matter what was going on that year, her parents had their Independence Day barbecue. Sam loved that about them, their consistency. On days like this she saw the very best of her neighborhood. They were a community—not all the same, not cookie-cutter as many would have it—but a community rooted in traditions and relationships. There were plenty of ugly stories and scars to go around, but Sam chose, especially on days like this, to see everything that worked, everything that was right.

Sam was putting buns in baskets when Grady arrived with his family. The Senator and Mrs. Malendar came in first, carrying a covered dessert, and raving about the new painting in the entry-way. They were followed closely by Grady and Kara, beautiful, eternally stuck-up Kara, his younger sister. Sam smiled over her shoulder at Grady. He was a sight—for any woman, as she was well aware. Dark navy linen pants and a loose white linen shirt rolled to his elbows, tucked in barely, the whole thing pulled together with a red belt. Crystal blue eyes peeked out of his just-showered hair as he removed his sunglasses and shot Sam his killer, little boy-with-a-secret grin. Grady Malendar was pretty devastating by anyone's standards—and for the most part a wonderful guy.

Underneath all the posturing that came from the crap he grew up with and his own need to fill at least a portion of his father's shoes, Grady was a loyal and funny friend. Sam had asked herself many times why she couldn't simply fall head over heels in love with him and live happily ever after, but she had never felt that way for him. When they were in junior high school, he had been her very first kiss: at Sheila Fernell's birthday party. But as they grew up, Sam and Grady were just good friends, and the rest took a backseat. Grady could never and would never want to handle a woman like Sam. She was too strong-willed with too many thoughts and not enough curves for Grady. So, they settled into being there for each other, and that was enough.

"Happy Independence Day, beautiful," Grady said, sliding his arm around Sam's waist.

"No fair copping a feel, I'm busy with the buns."

"That sounds very interesting."

Sam blushed, and his mission was accomplished. They both laughed as Grady kissed Sam's mother on the cheek.

"I've never understood why men stay out of the kitchen," he said, stealing a chip from the table, "the kitchen is where all the women are. This is where it's at."

"The kitchen is usually where the help is at, Grady. I suppose it all depends on whom you want to hang out with," Kara said, setting her platter down.

"Sam, good to see you. Mrs. Cathner, interesting pants."

They both nodded politely and, as she did every year, Kara floated by them and out to the patio. Kara was in a red, white, and blue wraparound dress, her long blonde hair tied back in a red ribbon. Her lips were tinted red, and her dark sunglasses hid what Sam knew were a stunning copy of Grady's eyes. It was a shame all that perfection was wasted on someone so incredibly unlikable.

Grady chomped on another chip and rolled his eyes.

"Has she always been such a, well, bitch?"

"Grady Malendar, watch your tongue, you're talking about you sister."

He froze and looked at Sam's mother.

"But, to answer your question, yes, we'll always love her dearly, but yes, she has."

They all laughed, and Grady hugged Mrs. Cathner.

"I should go mingle. Thank you, ladies, for brightening my day once again."

Sam watched him through the kitchen window, as he joined their fathers at the grill. He extended a beer to each and seemed to fall right into the conversation.

"Well, the buns are done," Sam said, wiping her hands on the kitchen towel.

"Do you want me to bring them out?"

"No, just leave them there on the table. The caterers will bring the rest in a few minutes. I love their barbecue, but I've never been a fan of the . . ."

"Buns, I know. Did Henry bring these from Los Angeles this morning?"

She smiled.

"He did. I asked him to order the kaiser rolls early because they always run out. He brought extra hamburger buns too. I'm picky about my buns."

She giggled like a schoolgirl, and Sam shook her head. Her mother was really the definition of young at heart.

"Go outside and relax. Everything's under control in here," her mother urged.

"I'd rather stay busy."

"Something wrong?"

Susan knew Sam was having a hard time with Peter in town. But she hadn't said anything. It was usually best to let Sam sort those feelings out on her own.

"No, fine. I just like to stay busy. When does the farmer's market start today?"

"Eleven o'clock. They moved it up an hour because it gets so packed. You could go before lunch this year."

"That's the plan. I'll go see if Dad wants anything and then head over. Tomatoes and avocados for you, anything else?"

"If that sprout guy is there, pick up some radish sprouts. I love those and Dr. Weil says . . ."

"Oh, boy. Radish sprouts it is," Sam said, opening the door and escaping another wellness-after-sixty excerpt. Strawberries were added to the list, at her father's request.

Sam walked around to the side gate and took one of the bikes from the rack by the garage. It was her mother's: wide handlebars and a big basket on the front. Every year she snuck away to the farmer's market in town, usually after lunch, but Sam was antsy this year. She felt nervous and knew Peter's family would arrive any minute. Sam wasn't sure if Peter would be with them, but she hated that she couldn't stop thinking about it. She needed to step away.

Peter had been at rehearsals all week, but they had not spoken since his little night out with Grady. He'd had five beers, she kept telling herself, but then she would picture his face and his hands, the need. Sam paused for a minute to catch her breath. The thought of Peter made her aware of her breathing, and that was annoying. She was clearly an idiot. What more did a person need to put her through before she stopped feeling? How could she even be in the same room with him after the mess he left? Sam let out a deep breath. She'd always had a weakness for Peter, maybe she always would. Just something else to accept about herself. Sam pushed up the kickstand and backed the bike out toward the driveway.

"Want some company?"

Sam jumped and the bike fell to the ground. She whipped around to face Peter, who was standing right beyond the house, and her sunglasses flew off her face.

"Christ! Jesus, where did you . . . ?"

Peter kneeled to pick up her glasses while she struggled with the bike.

"Sorry, you were in your own little world there. I didn't mean to scare you."

Sam snatched her sunglasses from his hand. Peter's eyes were hidden behind his wired-rimmed shades which was a good thing because Sam was in shorts and she still had the most fantastic legs he'd ever seen. They were barely tan with the most adorable freckles at the knees. Peter felt his pulse quicken. *Really? You're turned on by knee freckles? Pull it together, man.*

Sam quickly put her glasses back on.

"You didn't scare me. Well, maybe you did a little. Why the hell are you lurking in the bushes?"

She glanced at her legs in a flutter of insecurity, wondering if she was still too pasty white for red shorts.

"I'm not lurking. Your mom said you were going to the farmer's market and I thought. . ."

"You thought you'd scare the crap out of me?"

"I'm not much into parties, and I thought I'd see if you wanted me to . . . Forget it."

He turned toward the house. She should let him go. She told herself to get on the bike and let it go, but . . .

"Make sure you get one with a basket," she said pointing to the bike rack, "we have a lot of requests," Sam said as she hiked up onto the seat and started down the driveway.

Peter ran toward the bikes and was close behind her by the time she got to the street. They rode side by side on the wide neighborhood street in silence. Peter looked over at her every now and then. They both looked up at the sun twinkling through the huge trees that canopied above. Peter was rumpled and perfect, not Grady perfect, but perfect in Sam's eyes. Khakis loose around his narrow hips, a navy blue T-shirt fitted over a much larger chest than she remembered, and leather flip-flops. His dark brown hair blew in the breeze. They pulled into the open-air market set around Victory Park and parked their bikes.

"Where's your red?" Sam asked, collecting the empty bags out of her basket.

"What?"

"Red," Sam stopped in front of him and forgot herself, the bike ride having made her silly.

Sheer stupidity set in when she touched his blue T-shirt and daringly the white rope belt that hung around his waist.

"Blue shirt, white belt . . . no red."

Peter looked at her suspiciously for a beat and then took her hand gently and laid it right at the neck of his T-shirt. Sam could feel his chest moving in and out. She lost her words and her courage.

"Red," he said, showing Sam a string necklace around his neck.

It was in fact red, white, and blue. She tried a casual smile as he let her hand drop. Peter's mouth curled into a grin as he tried to steady himself.

"Do you enjoy doing that?" she asked.

"What? You touched me first."

"Seriously? Okay, actually, I believe you touched me first. About four years ago. I should probably keep my distance. We all know how that turned out."

It came out with a soft, sarcastic chuckle.

For some reason it felt good for Sam to make light of it. Maybe it was the warmth of the day, but she suddenly felt stronger and so tired of the weight and drama. Peter's heart had jumped when she touched his chest and that made her feel in control and a lot less like the girl left behind.

"Oh, aren't you quick with the clever quips this morning."

Peter nudged her, and they both laughed.

They walked past a barbecue pork stand manned by big and bald Al from Al's Chicks and Ribs. Sam nodded a hello, took a deep breath of his honey barbecue sauce, and felt ten years old again.

Peter walked next to her and took the empty bags as Sam started to pick out tomatoes.

"I haven't been here in years. Remember when we used to come back three or four times in one day just to get another churro?"

"Correction, you and Grady would drag me back here so you two could get another churro."

They laughed and were again swimming in nostalgia.

"But, yes . . . I remember."

"It's pretty much the same, maybe a few more kids, but it hasn't changed."

"Probably never will. Ari's son, do you remember Namir?"

Peter nodded.

"Well, he finally took over their hummus and pita stand, so that's new. Namir and Melanie are having their first baby this Christmas, also new."

They walked and Peter looked around. He tasted the cinnamon roll samples and helped Sam pick out avocados. The hum of a farmer's market, any farmer's market, reminded Peter of home, but this one with Sam was special. He gave himself this time with her and focused on what was right with his hometown. Locals, people they had known their whole lives selling goods they had sampled and brought home for their parents since they could remember. He was right, it was all the same, and yet it felt different to be back. Sam felt different. She had grown up, the sun lit the highlights in her dark hair, and he was so grateful she seemed to be letting him get closer. He had loved her his whole life. He would find a way back to her.

"Peter!"

A woman called from behind. They both turned toward her voice.

"Brandy. Look, Peter, it's Brandy."

Sam's smile was deep as she held off a laugh. Brandy went to Junior High with them, and even though Grady had warned Peter she was a barracuda, Peter had asked her to the eighth grade dance with disastrous consequences. By the time they were all in high school Brandy had herself a reputation for being very, well, friendly, with the entire football team.

"It is . . . Brandy."

Peter was gracious as always.

"Oh my God, it's you. Wow! Welcome home! I've heard so much about your success. You look so . . . oh, hi Sam. Peter, you look great. Wow!"

Sam rolled her eyes as Brandy continued to salivate over Peter.

"Thanks, you look great too. How've you been?"

Peter looked at Sam, bewildered.

"Oh, you know, good. I'm better now. You've gotten taller and your hair . . . very New York. How's it in the Big Apple?"

Peter tried not to laugh and managed what came off as a warm smile.

"It's . . . big. Listen, great to see you, Brandy."

"Oh, you too."

She touched his arm.

"Hey, while you're in town, you should come by and see me. Mother and Daddy bought me a new house, and it's so lonely."

She made a little pouty face, and Sam had to turn away, pretending to look at the radish sprouts.

"Ah, well, I'm swamped with the play, but if there's time. Nice to see you."

"You too, you too, Peter."

Brandy walked off in her wedges and stupidly tight pants. Peter turned toward Sam, his lips pursed. He squinted his eyes in thought.

"Did she wink at me?"

"Oh, well . . . she sure did, Peter. Wow!"

Mocking Brandy, she held his bicep.

"You've gotten so big!"

Sam burst with laughter and tried not to notice that Peter's biceps were in fact quite nice.

"Cut it out," Peter said, pulling his arm away and gently pushing at her.

Sam bought the sprouts her mother wanted, and they continued through the market.

"Brandy never gave me the time of day. Remember she wouldn't go to the formal with me unless I picked her up with a car and driver? Christ, we were in the eighth grade and now, now she's lonely? What the hell?"

Sam's sides were hurting now from laughing.

"You're all grown up now."

He shot her a warning glance.

"Seriously. You're more, maybe she's drawn to your . . ."

Sam gestured toward Peter's body.

"Yeah, yeah I'm glad you're having fun with this. Give me some of those bags."

She handed him two of the bags and they walked toward the bikes.

"I am having fun. Thanks for . . ."

Peter stopped by the bikes and looked at Sam.

"Thanks for coming," she said.

Sam knew she should check herself, be angry or bitter, pull back, but she couldn't help it. It was like walking in the sun. He warmed her. She was never more herself than when she was with Peter. Even now, she wanted to pretend nothing had happened and just throw herself into telling him her secrets, asking him about his life. Sam had so many memories, but the pull of what Peter was now, the man she was discovering, was intoxicating. He was more comfortable with himself, as if New York had given him the strength to be his full self. Maybe it was time to admit to herself that she still wanted him. She couldn't allow him back into her heart, but there was no sense in lying to herself. She couldn't start over or stop feeling. He had been her friend and her lover, she was at least ready to stop hiding.

Peter could look at her all day, be with her all day. It was clear, hiding behind his glasses, that was why he came back. In spite of everything he abhorred about who he had been in this town, she was here, and he couldn't stay away.

"Thanks for bringing me back, back here. It was great, seriously."

Peter loaded the bags in the baskets. They had to pay attention to the increased traffic on Sierra Madre Boulevard, so they rode again in silence, with nothing but the cars buzzing by and the smell of fresh cut grass. A bit later, they turned onto Oak Knoll and then into their neighborhood. They were now able to ride side by side, under speckles of sunlight falling through the canopied trees.

When Peter had arrived in Pasadena, he thought his feelings for Sam might have diminished over time. Maybe they had both moved on, changed even, and he would be released of the heart aching need. He glanced over at her now, smiling, cheeks flushed with sunlight dancing on her face and he knew he would need her forever. Now if he only knew how to find her heart again.

Chapter Twelve

*M*onday was insane. As Susan Cathner would say, "it all hit the fan," on about every level at the Playhouse. They lost an air conditioning unit at the bungalow where they housed their community outreach program, Child's Play. Today was the first day of summer camp, and July without air conditioning was not a good thing. The Playhouse used the revenue from this camp to fund their student matinees, which allowed under-privileged, or at-risk children, to attend their productions, at no cost, throughout the year. Campers and parents were complaining and threatening to pull.

Sam arranged for fans and rented an emergency air conditioning unit that would arrive Tuesday morning. She spent Monday morning on the phone trying to convince the credit card company to extend their credit limit an additional five thousand dollars to pay for a new unit they could have in by Friday. Candice even canceled her meeting with the board and got on the phone to patrons to see if anyone was feeling particularly generous. They were not.

"Ben just called. The emergency unit is on and running, so there's air . . ." Candice said, and Sam pulled the phone from her ear, letting the on-hold music play into her shoulder.

"That's great news!"

"But," Candice said with a sigh.

"Always a but."

"The damn thing is so loud he can't hear the students in the improv workshop."

"Shit, can they move the unit back?" Sam asked, still keeping an ear out for her call.

"No, he said he was going to switch to voice and movement exercises and practice projecting over the noise."

Ben was an actor who grew up taking classes at the Playhouse and now routinely came back to teach. He was a true gem and knew how to handle the challenges of being low on funds.

"Don't you just love Ben? So resourceful."

The bad music coming from the phone stopped, Sam held up her finger, signaling to Candice to hang on. The very curt credit card lady returned to tell Sam that they would give them an additional three thousand, but that was all they could do. Sam thanked her graciously, hung up, and told Candice it was approved and that she was ordering the unit. Candice sighed. For the first time that morning, she took a sip of her coffee and returned to her office.

Sam would make up the two-thousand-dollar difference. Candice never looked at the statements. She told herself when she started this job that she needed to work within the budgets, but sometimes it simply didn't work out. Sam had the money, she told herself, she was a patron too, and so she would make another anonymous donation. Candice didn't need to know. Kids needed air and Child's Play was too important. Sam ordered the unit, confirmed delivery Friday morning, and sent out an email to parents with an update that would hopefully appease them. With that fairly under control, she moved on to the next fire.

Sam pulled up the email she had been working on before the air unit fiasco. She was sure happy to see that Brad, their main housekeeper, had agreed to stay on and that he was willing to look into an organic floor cleaning product at least for the rehearsal and run of *Looking In*. Julie had managed to bring Brad to the point of resignation by yelling at him as he cleaned the stage. She was obsessing about some cleaner he was using, concerned it would pull up her masking. She also thought it was triggering her allergies. *Christ!*

Brad had humored Julie for the first couple of weeks of rehearsal, but yelling was the last straw. His resignation was stated as bold as could be, arriving in Sam's email in the morning. Sam had called Brad, first thing, and told him they could not lose him. Brad vented to her that Julie was a nutcase but agreed to stop by the supply store and return that afternoon. In turn, Sam had agreed to talk to Julie and reiterate that, while Brad was still willing to work with her, he was a grown man and would not be yelled at. Sam would stop by the theater, bring Julie some lunch, and smooth it over. Maybe a fan would work for Julie too, she thought with a smile.

Candice walked in holding doughnuts. *God bless her!*

"Do you ever wonder why we do this?" she asked, plopping herself down in a tattered yellow chair Sam had coveted and then stolen during the wrap party for their production of *Oklahoma* two years ago. It spoke to her, and she bribed the set designer with two six packs of Kilt Lifter.

"Do what . . . exactly?" Sam asked, chomping into the chocolate-covered doughnut Candice had handed her.

"This insanity. Why do I always feel like we are trudging uphill with like three hundred pounds on our backs?"

Sam laughed.

"Because we are. Today it's a two-ton air conditioning unit."

Candice rolled her eyes and leaned forward on Sam's desk.

"It's only a bad day, right? Maybe this week things will smooth out again for a few days at least."

"Sam, why do you do this? You don't need this aggravation; you could be working in Los Angeles or running a little boutique. I'm sure your daddy would buy you anything you wanted. It's days like this that I wonder what keeps you here."

Sam finished her doughnut, shamelessly licked her fingers, and took her first deep breath of the morning. She tried to ignore the "daddy" comment, she was used to it from Candice, but loved her anyway. She knew the answer to her question, this was an easy one.

"Well, I need it, aggravation and all. Everything we do from Playwright's Project to big productions, all of it. It's the soul of our city, and I want to feed that soul more than anything. And . . . I'm good at it. I like the details and maybe I like that the focus isn't all on me. It's a different kind of pressure, plus it's good to do something you love."

"And you love this, this crazy job?"

"I do. Pissed off Child's Play parents and all, I can't imagine doing anything else. Maybe it's the joy of helping an underdog or the appeal of finding a way to be in the theater without the insanity of being an actress."

"Wait, you didn't love running from one humiliating audition after another? Antacid commercials can be so exciting."

They both laughed, and Sam noticed Candice's new Jimmy Choo sandals.

"And umm, you're not stuck here either. You love it as much as I do."

"True. When it all comes together, once you sift through all the garbage . . . it's like being in charge of the glitter."

"Maybe we're just crazy?"

"Now that is probably very true."

Candice rose to head back to her office, right as Liz, their one and only assistant, came in looking a little crazed herself. Liz was still fresh-faced, right out of college. She had a short crop of brown hair, and she wore Converse.

"Um . . . I'm not sure who wants this . . . but . . ." Liz said chewing on her nail.

"Spit it out, Liz," Candice barked.

"There's a guy on line two who is very upset. He's from the Coalition for Family Something, and he's rambling about some hammer he's going to bring down on us if we proceed with staging *Bent* at the Black Box?"

Candice looked at Sam, and they both rolled their eyes. Another non-fun part of the job.

"That's not until March of next year. They're already starting?" Sam asked.

"He seems very . . . passionate about being mean. What is the Coalition . . . ?" Liz asked.

"For the Protection of Family Values!" Candice and Sam both said together.

"Is his name Gary?" Sam asked as they both laughed.

"Yes, Gary the family values guy."

She still seemed pretty flustered. Sam knew Gary, so his punch had worn off. Liz had only started a few months ago, so Sam could understand her surprise.

"Liz, Sam will handle Gary," Candice said over her shoulder as she left with her remaining doughnuts.

"Sam, tell Gary we'll give him a front row seat so when the play opens and the beautiful gay man walks out onstage in the buff, he'll get a full-frontal view."

Liz looked confused. Sam laughed and assured Candice it would be her pleasure.

"Gary, Happy Monday, to what do I owe the pleasure of your call this time?" Sam asked, picking up the phone and smiling as Liz backed out slowly and closed her door.

Gary proceeded to rant and rave about what a depraved and deviant play *Bent* was, and how they, and Sam in particular, were responsible for contributing to the moral decay of society. Gary was, and always had been, passionate about his beliefs. The problem, Sam thought, with him and other people she had spoken within his organization, was that their fire and brimstone was all based in fear. Fear of the unknown, fear or things that were different, or people and lifestyles they didn't understand.

"I'm not a big fan of that make-believe crap you put on up there anyway, but this play . . . this play is disgusting, and it makes it okay for our society to stray from what our Lord has planned for us."

How exactly did Gary know what the Lord had in store? Sam wondered but continued to listen.

Gary had probably never read *Bent*. From their conversation he clearly didn't understand the huge importance of this work, nor what could be learned and experienced through watching a performance. He must have read the notice on the Playhouse website announcing *Bent's* upcoming run at the Black Box, a sister theater. *God, did these people scour our site looking for anything to get pissed about?* The announcement mentioned it was about homosexuals during Nazi Germany and that was all he saw.

Sam actually felt sorry for people like Gary because it seemed they never saw the depth of anything. *Bent* was a disturbing play, no question, but the Black Box had always been the venue for controversial works. Patrons didn't attend that theater expecting to see *South Pacific*. They knew they were in for a play that might be upsetting or offensive yet would most likely make them think.

She tried to explain this to Gary, when he allowed her a word, but there was no point. Sam used her standard closing and decided she would increase security and put out some "tolerance" promotions closer to the run of the play. There was nothing else to really do with Gary and his band of social redeemers. She was trying to finish up, hang up if necessary.

"And . . . and, I also hear Miss Cathner that the Playhouse is putting on some new play, this *Looking In* one, which has lots of teenage angst and I'm guessing flagrant premarital sex! Again, how can you tolerate this? How can you allow young people to watch that kind of behavior? It's outrageous!"

"Gary, I'm sorry you feel that way. I respect your need to tell everyone else what to do with his or her life. Yes, yes, I hear you, and I'm sorry you'll be wasting your time upsetting our patrons. Yes, I know . . . yes, a petition. That's fine. Thank you for letting us know, and try, Gary, please try, to have a nice day."

Sam hung up before he could get another word in, took a very deep breath, and dropped her head to the desk. No wonder her family always thought she looked tired. *Peter's play was reduced to teenage angst and premarital sex? Didn't these people have jobs, hobbies? Wait, how does he even know what's in Peter's play? I barely know.* Sam tried not to let Gary get to her, but the mention of *Looking In* obviously hit closer to home than she was used to.

Opening the bottle of water sitting on her desk, Sam wondered if Peter had to deal with advocates, aka crazies, during the runs of his first play. After all, it was about his father's suicide. *Did anyone find that offensive or was violence and death all right as long as there wasn't any premarital sex?* Maybe Sam was a touch defensive because Gary was somehow privy to things so intimately personal. She didn't want someone like Gary anywhere near her memories. Sam shook it off and decided to call her mom. She usually made things better, put things into perspective. Sam probably had several more fires to put out, but they'd have to wait. She decided to spare fifteen minutes for discussions about new bed skirts, or her mother's latest finds at the open markets. Susan Cathner was the perfect antidote to Angry Gary.

Chapter Thirteen

*P*eter sat on the patio after breakfast. His mother ran into the house to get photo albums. They had started talking about Cynthia's wedding, and, per usual, his mother felt nostalgic. Of course, the buzz of the three Bloody Marys she managed before finishing her eggs was a factor too.

"I . . . you know what we should get the pictures, let's get them and we can rem . . . remin . . . reminisce. Be right back," she slurred.

Vivvie, the maid, kept her from bumping into the couch and guided her around the corner. Peter could actually feel his chest tightening. He loved his mother, but it was a challenge to like her once the vodka set in. He could write the coming scene before she even returned to the table.

They would start with his and Cynthia's births, touch on some school plays, move to the luxurious family vacations, and then she would ask Vivvie for another drink. They would skip over all pictures of his father and the little annoying fact that the pressure of keeping up with all the crap in these photos actually killed him. She would leave out the times his father stayed behind to work while she went to the spa in Ojai or to Palm Springs for weeks on end. When something became too much at Junior League or the Mothers' Guild, she would say she was stressed and needed "a little sun and shopping." His father always obliged and off she went. There would be no mention of those trips.

His mother would then jump straight to Peter's graduation from UCLA, Cynthia's engagement photos, and the picture of them at the Plaza on the night his first play opened in New York. Nice tidy story with a nice tidy bow. That's how his mother liked it. She sucked the life out of him a little more each time. It was all a lie without the details, the rough spots.

She could never handle the rough spots. After his father died, she ran to the bottle and begged it to smooth everything out. His father died the summer of his junior year in high school, and Peter escaped into himself, closed off whole sections of his childhood, in an effort to keep himself from completely crumbling apart. They never discussed his father's suicide, it was like it never happened. One minute he was there, the center of Peter's universe, and then he was gone. No discussion. Christ, it was a miracle he and Cynthia were even somewhat normal.

As she swept back to her seat with albums in hand, Peter's childhood surrounded him again. Everything he loathed and loved all in the same place, and even though he was four years older, he still couldn't sort it all out.

"Oh goodness, look at this one from when you were born."

And here we go again, Peter thought, taking another sip of his coffee as his mother flipped through the pages.

"Yes, mother, Cynthia was a beautiful baby," Peter sighed trying to feign interest in his mother's delusions.

After what seemed like an eternity of endless pictures, his mother retired to a chaise lounge in the shade for "a little nap," as she called it. Just as well, because Peter could no longer breathe. He helped Vivvie, whose hands were now shaking a little more than he remembered, clear the dishes, but she shooed him off while she cleaned up the photo albums. She was used to the routine and a faithful protector of his mother's madness. He was going to take a run, but it was raining, so he hit the gym in the basement. His father had built the gym when Peter was little. Peter learned the value of exercise when dealing with stress after his father died. After he moved to New York he found a gym and worked to exhaustion every day, finding that he needed it. A few rounds with the punching bag and he would be as good as new.

When Peter came down the stairs after his shower, his mother was on the couch. He was late meeting Grady for lunch, but still bent down to kiss her sleeping face. April's hand swept the hair from her face as her blurry eyes opened slowly.

"Why do you live in that dirty city? You should be home."

"Okay, Mom. Please rest."

Peter turned to leave.

"Marry that girl and come home. I need grandkids."

"There's no girl, mom. You really need to . . ."

"Don't be obtuse, Peter. Sam, marry her and get back home. You two will make such cute grandchildren."

She reached out to touch him. Peter let her hand fall and left. As the door closed behind him, he took his first full breath of air all day. His sister pulled up as Peter was getting into his car. She was carrying big binders.

"Need any help, Cyn?" Peter called, walking toward her.

"No, I've got it. Is mom still . . ."

"Sober?"

He tried to smile and Cynthia sighed.

"Yes, is she?"

"Well, she's taken her 'nap' so she's slept off breakfast. If you hurry in you may be able to catch her before the lunch rounds begin."

Cynthia kissed him on the cheek.

"What was that for?" he asked, walking her to the front door.

"Just for being you. Sometimes I'm not sure how I would have gotten through it all without you and that smart mouth."

Peter's face softened, and he opened the door for her.

"I've missed you. I'm glad you're home," she said, stepping into the house.

"I've missed you too."

And with that, Cynthia called to their mother, and Peter closed the door. How either of them turned out normal, he would never know, Peter thought as he pulled out of the driveway.

Grady was already at the high top table when Peter entered a dive bar that doubled as a restaurant in Grady's eyes. The guy had a thing for holes in the wall. With all his money, Grady was known for his . . . eclectic taste in hangouts. Peter didn't mind; it was refreshing, he thought, as the band went on a break, and he took the seat next to his best friend. Grady was of course flirting effortlessly with the well-endowed blonde waitress wearing what would be considered a very short skirt by any standards.

"Friend of yours?"

"Friend? Hmm . . . not sure I would call her a friend. Friendly, she's very friendly."

Grady laughed and patted him on the back.

"I'm pretty sure she has a friend. We could . . ."

"Yeah, I'm okay. Still trying to recover from the last time we 'blew off steam.'"

"Right, so when are you going making things happen?"

Peter ordered a beer from the bartender with PEACE tattooed on his fingers.

"Uh, clarification please? I thought I was making things happen. The play is going . . ."

"Not that. We all know about the play. I'm talking about the real reason you came home. When are you going to crack that mess open and start luring her back to New York with you?"

Seeing the two of them at the wedding shower, Grady was hopeful they could put the past behind them. He knew now, years later, that Peter was meant to be with Sam. When they were younger, Grady had always found their mutual attraction annoying. It upset the balance, and he'd been sure it would pass. Now, watching them dance around each other was painful. He needed to do something. Peter looked around at the collection of beer and liquor lining the bar mirrors and didn't know what to say. After his mother's drunken endorsement of Sam and marriage, he had no idea how he was going to make anything work.

"I'm here for the play, it's my hometown, and this play belongs here."

"Sure, tell that bullshit to someone else. You two are doing this little dance, and it's as fast as a glacier. While the face touching at the baby shower was promising, it doesn't seem like much is getting done. Have you said you're sorry or told her how you feel?"

Peter laughed, sipped his beer, and pretended to watch college basketball.

"You told me yourself. She was better off here. She belongs here, remember?"

"Oh Christ, man. That was a long time ago. I was stupid."

Peter looked surprised at his candor.

"Yeah, well who the hell ever listens to me? Peter, she does belong here. We all do, it's our town. I get that you needed to leave, but man, it's all over you."

"What's all over me?"

"She is. You're so in love with her. You always have been. When we were kids I thought it was lust or adoration, then you guys went to college together, and she started looking at you the same way. Even after four years apart, even now . . . it's tragic. I've seen you in New York, and you are 'the man' there. I saw you make your own life, where no one knows that you and I had a lemonade stand every summer or that your dad offed it. I understand, it suits you, but since you've been home, no, actually when you're around Sam, you're warm."

Peter raised an eyebrow at Grady's word choice.

"Fine, call it cheesy, but it's true. You did grow up here, there are parts of you here. And when you filter the shit out, when you're with Sam or even me, all that's still there. Don't you miss that history? That foundation? Because you sure as hell didn't take any of it with you to New York."

After a brief stretch of silence, Peter put his burger down.

"It doesn't matter."

"Of course it matters. You're the drama guy, love is everything, isn't it?"

Peter laughed.

"Not in this case. She doesn't want me. She's hurt and angry, and I don't blame her. She's moved on, and even if she did give me a chance, I can't give her this place. I know there's history, but it's stifling."

"When has Sam ever said she needed to live here? That's in your head. Maybe from some crap I fed you years ago, fine, but it doesn't have to be only one way. Compromise, man. I'd give up a lot of things for a woman to look at me the way Sam looks at you."

"Yeah, right."

"I'm serious. Okay fine, I'm trying to be serious. She fell apart when you left, Pete. Really fell apart."

"I know, and I don't want to talk about it."

"Well, maybe you need to. She loved you then and despite all that female temper she's throwing at you right now, she still loves you. I can see it when she's pretending to be too busy to care. She's trying to survive and protect herself. Can't blame her there. If you don't love her, then why did you come back? I travel to New York to see you. I accept our friendship on your own selfish terms."

Peter rolled his eyes.

"Selfish, I'm selfish now? That's rich."

"Why can't you love her and have a life with her?"

"Being back here isn't good for me."

"Oh, bullshit. This is where you come from and it's your home. Complicated as all hell, I'll admit, but you need to work that out. You can't run forever, man. You know what I think?" Grady asked, stuffing several fries into his mouth.

"Please, do tell."

"I think you came back to get your woman and now that you're here you're letting the past creep back in. You're chickenshit."

"Is that what you think? Well, thank you, Mr. Relationship Expert."

"Yes, I do."

Grady grinned while wiping his mouth and finishing his beer.

"I came back to put on this play and, yes, maybe I wanted to see her, be near her, but that past is still there. What happened is not going away, and I'm starting to think I should have stayed in New York. Maybe I'm hurting her more by being here. She seems like she moved on, she's fine."

"She's made a life for herself, sort of like the life you've made for yourself in New York. You two are a fine pair, a shut-off, shut-down, going through the motions pair. But she doesn't know why you ran. You left her hanging, and she doubted herself for a long time. That's not right, man."

"Christ, Grady, I know. Do you think I don't know what I did to her? I couldn't see any other way and it's not like you were super helpful, so I'm not sure where all this advice is coming from now. I would never have been enough for her back then. It was a mistake to cross that line."

"Then fix it. Talk to her, tell her what happened, tell her why you bolted. Get it out there."

Peter took a deep breath and finished off his beer.

"I've tried, but the words sound stupid. 'I left you because I couldn't cope with my own shit. You were too much for me.' Lame, it sounds absurd."

"She won't think so. She has nothing right now. For all she knows, she was a quick lay from the hometown girl before you ran off to your new and exciting life. You can't leave her with that."

"Shut the hell up. I never treated her that way."

"Really? Because it didn't seem like the two of you talked much at all after that night."

"Christ, this is perfect, Grady. You were all for me leaving her alone that night, remember? She would never be happy in New York, right?"

"Don't start, we've already been over this. I was an asshole. I didn't want the party to end, still don't, but it's time to man up. You're a different guy now, and you need to get it out, that's all I'm saying."

"Or I could work to get this play up and leave her alone. Why would anyone want to deal with all my crap anyway?"

"Beats me."

Grady bumped him with his shoulder and they both laughed. Grady wasn't going to push, but he loved them both, and this thing they were doing right now was going to hurt one, or more likely, both of them.

Chapter Fourteen

*P*eter woke up in a bad mood. Sleeping in his old house and deal-ing with his mother was not helping. He needed to find some balance, put some things back into perspective. He spent break-fast talking on the phone with his agent. Alexis would be in Los Angeles for a conference that afternoon and said she would stop by the theater. Peter was feeling a bit more like himself, maybe even a little cocky: Alexis told him his first play had been nomi-nated for a Drama Desk Award. Peter was feeling good. He needed to put this stifling town back where it belonged. He wasn't that bumbling, lovesick, insecure guy anymore, he thought, as he en-tered rehearsal.

Twenty minutes later, Sam ran through the door late and ex-hausted. She hadn't been sleeping well since Peter arrived back in town. Managing the summer programs along with *Looking In* be-came too much at times. Today seemed one of those times. Her eyes were itchy, and she had that sick, not enough sleep, feeling. Carmen asked for help with the props for the Christmas scene. *How could she say no to a pregnant woman?*

Walking in through the lobby, Sam noticed Peter was two or three rows up from the stage talking to a woman with dark hair.

He was smiling and kissed her on the cheek. She sat and crossed her very long legs. Even from a distance Sam could tell she was attractive, and the dress she wore was very urban-sophisticate, sexy.

"Peter, can we look at the scene from yesterday? I'd like you to talk us through your notes. I'm not quite understanding," Spencer finished his coffee, crumpled the cup, and tossed it in the trash backstage.

Peter hopped up on the stage with teenage Phillip and Sally. Spencer was standing on the edge of the stage. Sam quietly walked toward them.

"Sure, okay, in this scene they don't have . . . it's not quite right yet," Peter said.

"I hear you, but I'm not sure what you're saying. What's not right? They're too . . . comfortable?"

"Yeah, the audience needs to see that she shines, she's in her element, and Phillip is the background. He never has the space to grow with her there."

Peter wasn't sure what he was saying. Sometimes it felt like he was working out his actual life experiences through this damn play. He needed to focus on getting the story right.

"It's written in the dialogue, but I'm not feeling it in the scene. They're great friends, but there's tension. She's the Queen of Pasadena, and he sometimes feels like her sidekick. Get it?"

Sam stopped before anyone saw her. *She . . . Sally was what? Did he really say the Queen?*

"Peter, I'm sorry I'm not following."

"Okay, in this scene Phillip's teaching Sally. Well, he's not teaching her, but they're practicing the waltz. She has a big dance coming up, and Phillip's helping her. She, she's always so damn concerned with being correct, accepted, and well, he is helping her feel the music and be herself."

The corners of his mouth pulled up.

"Sally has an image in her mind and she's not always authentic. When she's with Phillip, she can be . . . real."

Peter was lost in his words, and everyone was silent. He found himself remembering her laugh that day and the touch of her body as they fumbled through the dance. What he wouldn't tell his actors was that she eclipsed him. Her energy and her warmth made him forget everything, even himself.

"But," he continued, pulling back to the present, "she's still Sally, popular and a little superficial. She's at home with all of this society business, and it's exactly what I said, she's the Queen of Pasadena. Everyone loves her, and she'll grow up to live this life, she'll grow into it. We need to see that. She belongs here, and Phillip, he, he knows she outshines him, and he knows he will need to make a life for himself someday. Phillip keeps everything at arm's length. Sally, Sally needs all of this."

He opened his arms to encompass the whole scene. The cast looked completely confused because they weren't sure how they were supposed to project all of that business into a dance scene. Peter stopped when he saw Sam standing a few rows from the stage.

"So the dance should show Sally as the dominant force and Phillip . . . knowing he'll need to make his own life?"

Spencer tried to make sense of it all, but Peter was clearly distracted.

"We need to show up their differences more?" Spencer asked as Peter broke away from looking at Sam.

"Exactly! They will never work. He wants the real world and can't wait to get out. She, yeah, she'll never leave, and she belongs right where she is."

Peter looked right at Sam and tried once again in vain to sort out why he left.

You bastard! She seethed. *You're going to take your shit out on poor Sally?*

"Excuse me, Peter."

Sam raised her hand, walking a little closer to the stage.

Spencer, and pretty much everyone else, turned to look at her.

"Isn't that a really generic take on Sally? I mean, with all due respect, she feels a little more complex than the . . . how did you put it? The Queen of Pasadena."

Sam was angry and Peter knew it.

"Don't you think people will see through that type of treatment for what it is: a way to make Phillip look worldly and interesting while Sally will always be remembered as a somewhat pathetic character in a sheltered little world?"

Spencer's mouth was now open and he looked back up at Peter. Peter didn't miss a beat and seemed just as pissed.

"Sam, thank you for that commentary, but I wrote Sally, the whole play for that matter, and believe me, my characterization of her is right on. Phillip and Sally are very different and at this point in the play, at this point in her life, she's in her element. Peter . . . excuse me Phillip," Peter was struggling to keep his explanation within the confines of the play, "Phillip is anything but worldly. He's eclipsed by his feelings. She's not pathetic or a victim. She is where she belongs. In Phillip's eyes, she is the Queen of . . ."

Sam cut him off and she snapped.

"That's a whole lot of bullshit. I'm about done, and I'm sure the audience will be too. What, you've been back a few weeks and every other scene seems to have a pathetic little Sam . . . Sally prancing around in a fairytale. Like the debutante luncheon scene. You didn't include the part where I threw up in the bathroom and my mother had to take me home because I was so nervous and insecure. Why wasn't that in there? I called you as soon as I got home and told you I was never doing that again. This wasn't a fairy tale for any of us, was it Peter? But I supposed it's easier to justify Phillip as a self-centered mess if you make Sally a caricature, a queen. Seriously, are you finished? Or are you looking to draw blood?"

"Come on, it's a play. You're assuming that Sally is . . ."

Julie peeked out from backstage, and the rest of the cast and crew perked up. Spencer was starting to look nervous.

"Oh, Christ! Who else would she be, Peter? Give us all a little credit here. Instead of dealing with me, you created her so you could act out your issues. Queen of Pasadena, hometown girl . . . that's easier, right? Phillip really loved Sally, but she was a little too shallow, too attached to her town, and he needed to spread his wings? Really? If the goal was to make yourself feel better through your play, make me, oh, I'm sorry Sally, feel like a superficial airhead. Justify your exit, done. We're there!"

"Sam, I . . ."

"You know what? Forget it, and leave me the hell alone. Pretend. Write it how you want, but don't try to convince those of us who were there that this is genuine. Phillip lives in the real world, give me a break. Phillip was a dreamer, and he, I thought he was so much more of a person, of a man, than what I see standing on that stage right now."

Sam's voice cracked, and she turned to leave right as tears welled in her eyes.

She would be damned if he was going to see her cry again. This was not professional at all, but she was tired, and she'd had enough. If Peter thought she was a shallow, small-town girl, if that's why he left, there was nothing she could do about that. She only wanted him to stop, but Sam's scene in front of his crew had embarrassed him. She could see it, and he hit back.

"Well, someone woke up on the wrong side of the bed," Peter said with a clear edge to his voice.

Sam recognized that tone. She'd seen Peter pissed before. Spencer, who at this point looked like he was watching a juicy soap opera, tried to smile. Sam turned halfway up the house seats and entered complete meltdown.

"I did leave. You . . . egotistical ass!" Sam raged at the top of her voice.

She was always good at projecting her voice, and, boy, this was an exceptional performance.

Peter's brow knit in confusion.

"Sam, what are you getting so upset about?"

"Pasadena, Pasadena, I did leave. Remember? The Queen set out to Hollywood. She was going to become an actress, and she fell flat on her face. Is that going to be in the play Peter? Does that make me, does that make Sally too . . . real, too human? Is it better to make her some idolized shell of a person? I mean you're the big playwright, you tell me. You're such a cliché. Poor brooding Phillip, he was the only one that had issues? Oh, let's all feel sorry for Phillip because then we will understand why he ran. No one will believe it."

By this time pretty much every actor and designer was peeking out from the wings as Sam made a complete lunatic out of herself, but she didn't care. She was fuming. Just who the hell did Peter think he was? She wasn't a child. She knew damn well what he was doing. He was rewriting history to make his point, to give his story meaning. Explain away why he ran and closed himself off from every feeling he'd ever had. Blame her, this town, put a stereotypical stamp on all of them, *his characters*.

"Sam."

Peter tried to bring things down a notch before she blew up right in front of his eyes. Part of him was glad she was at least talking, at least mad at him, but she was dissing his play and that wasn't fair.

"The play is not filled with caricatures. It's seen through the eyes of one character, Phillip, it's not necessarily an accurate depiction of what was, it's how he saw it. I'm sorry if that's painful."

"Oh please. Thank you, doctor, I'm clearly losing my mind here because it's too 'painful' for me? Anyone else you want to invite to the party, Peter? Now that your little," Sam gestured to the woman she had seen him with when she came in, "your little friend's here, who else? I mean before you show this crap to everyone who knew us growing up."

Sam walked up toward the gorgeous woman and noticed she was even more stunning up close. She certainly looked like she, unlike Sam, had time to shave her legs this morning.

"Sam," Peter called.

In retrospect she would recall that she should have simply left, but it was not to be. She swung around for her final act.

"Why did you do this? Why are you here? It wasn't enough the first time? Why did you prance back in here with your east coast entourage and . . . sorry, Julie."

"No problem. I'm okay with the entourage reference, Sam. You go right ahead and get it out," she said, peeking out onstage.

"Who the hell do you think you are? What did I ever do to you, but be your, your friend. I don't deserve this, hell none of us do, Peter. Grady wasn't some lothario with a carefree life. What about when Kara was in the hospital and Grady sat by her bedside for a month? If you're going to put us in your play, why not show the audience our color, the shades of our lives too?"

"Sam, I'm not doing anything to you or anyone else. It's only a play. It's a perspective. I'm trying. Please stop."

"Only a play, huh? Then why not make it fiction? Why put in just enough to hurt me? And when I call you on it, you hide behind your artistic license. Are you trying to tell me something, Peter? Why rehash all of this? What's wrong with you? You went to New York, stay there."

"Please, can we please have this conversation without an audience?"

"Why? You do great with an audience, right? Isn't this how you like it? Let's tell the story in front of everyone. Isn't that what this damn play is all about, Peter?"

"I'm not going to do this."

"Of course you're not."

Sam walked past his, *God, look at those cheekbones,* friend from New York.

"Sweetheart, run and run fast. He'll take you and . . ."

Sam made a bomb with her hands and made it explode in her face. She had lost her mind. She was not sure what was fueling her, but it was powerful.

"Samantha, is it?"

Ms. New York in one fluid motion uncrossed her legs and stood to try and help.

"I assure you that we're only . . ."

"Friends, right. I get it. Peter's friends with everyone. It's all so damn friendly. Good Old Peter, my buddy."

Sam walked back down toward the stage and slapped Peter on the back. He sent her a warning look. She was dialed in and pushing his buttons now. *Good!* she thought.

"Sam," Carmen said from the stage.

"Honey, you're really tired. You've been running around for me and keeping up with your own stuff. It's too much, you need to sit down."

"Carmen, thank you, but I'm sick and tired of sitting down. I *am* tired. Tired of smiling while everyone else gets to say whatever they want."

Sam looked at Peter. He had had enough.

"Spencer, can you take over here? Work a different scene for the rest of the morning?" Peter asked.

Of course he would work a different scene. It wasn't every day you got to watch a woman have a complete meltdown. Spencer nodded, they all did. Peter took Sam by the arm and tried to gently move her toward the lobby.

"Go away, go home. You don't want any of us, right? So why the hell . . ."

"All right, that's it."

Peter tightened his grip on and pulled her toward the door. He glanced back and caught Spencer's eye.

"Sorry for interrupting everyone. Sam obviously has some feelings, so we'll take this . . ."

"It's all good, Sam. Get some sleep," Spencer added as Peter pulled her out of the theater.

She was already beginning to feel incredibly foolish. She'd lost her mind, she'd let him back in. Sure enough he'd messed with her calm, ordered life. Now, worst of all, he had messed with her job. He did this. He couldn't leave well enough alone.

"Let me go, you jackass. I can see myself home. I don't need you. Everything was fine, we were all fine. Then you . . ."

"Really? Everything's fine? It sure as hell doesn't look fine. I said it right at the very beginning, when I first got here. If this was going to be too much, maybe we should . . ."

"Oh Christ, don't flatter yourself. Too much, I really don't need you right now, Peter. I have my own responsibilities, my own life. I can't play good old reliable, understanding Sam. The one who is there to help with everything Peter's going through. I don't have the room. I've got my own problems and right now . . ."

"Right now you're playing the woman scorned, is that it?"

"The woman what? Jesus, you're so self-absorbed. I'm not the woman scorned. What would that make you in this stupid play? The misunderstood hero? Please! I'm the friend, the girl who grew up with the boy. He was her very best friend in the whole world and he took everything she had to give. And then, because he's a self-centered jerk, he ran off to New York. I'm the friend who never fully understood the rejection, was left with no answers from the guy who changed everything. But you know what? I have made a life for myself and lo and behold the big ass comes back into town with his sophisticated New York set and his award-winning play tucked under his arm. Woman scorned? Hell, that's the least of my . . ."

Nothing was working, so he grabbed her, needed to kiss her. He'd managed control for weeks, but she was standing there yelling at him, and damn it he couldn't stand it anymore. He had tried talking, approaching the topic from different angles, he was trying to make amends, but she kept ignoring or avoiding or getting pissed or pissing him off, so he grabbed her. He grabbed her and kissed her. *Holy Christ!* He was starving for her. Soft lips, hair spilling through his fingers, and when a gentle moan drifted past his ear, he felt like a king, no better than a king . . . he was a god. Her hands feathered through his hair and then she pulled, she pulled his hair hard. He opened his eyes to a breathtakingly pissed woman. Peter went from a god to a gnat in three seconds.

"Ow!"

Sam pushed him away and stared. Her lips were raw, as she begged for breath. God help him, all he wanted to do was gather her back in his arms and do it all over again.

"What the hell is wrong with you? I was in the middle of a sentence and you can't . . . well, you don't . . . damn it, Peter you can't . . ."

"Kiss you?"

"No! No, you can't kiss me."

"You gave up, you quit, and I'm sorry but I've moved on and it's inappropriate. Now I know that my tirade in there was an unprofessional mess, but your play is not . . ."

"It hasn't actually won any awards."

He tried humor, humor always worked for with her before. He could usually make her laugh.

"What?"

She was confused.

"The play, you said award-winning play tucked under my arm, and it hasn't actually won any awards, but thanks for the vote of confidence."

Sam blinked.

"You're making a joke? Right now? After you? Do you think that's wise?"

He moved toward her, and she pushed him away. He tried grabbing, he tried humor, and then realized he was all out of options. Peter took her shoulders and said softly, "I'm sorry."

Sam started to cry. Just like that, her eyes spilled as if they had been brimming for weeks. Peter wanted to die for the hundredth time.

"At the time it seemed like the right thing to do. It was four years ago, and I was, I'm sorry. Please let me drive you home."

Peter felt a flood of relief, and he wanted to cry with her, but he'd given up crying a long time ago. He had finally gotten it out, told her he was sorry. Such simple words, but they needed to be said if he was ever going to reach her.

"No, I can drive myself home. I, I can't do this."

Sam wiped her eyes and walked away. She had made a complete ass out of herself, and if she still had a job, there would be plenty of apologies tomorrow, but at least she let some of the ugliness out. The damn play was the last straw, it was too much. She finally blew up, and as the wind hit her face, she somehow felt better. *How's that for keeping up appearances, Peter? Queen, my ass!* She hissed and tried desperately to ignore his apology and forget that kiss.

Chapter Fifteen

Sam had been home almost an hour. She was in her favorite boxer shorts and a tank top, sitting on the couch watching *The Bourne Ultimatum*. Action was always good for a confused heart. Her friends Ben and Jerry joined her and she was feeling better. She didn't fool herself, she could still feel his hands on her face, that kiss, but she had this strange realization that angry had felt better than sad and hiding. She hit the pause button after the knock on the door. Opening the door and getting cash from her wallet, Sam fully expected to see some high school student with her takeout Chinese. Peter walked right through the door and stood in her living room. He looked a little wound up, like he still had something to say. He took a deep breath.

"So what went wrong with the acting, why'd you move back?" he asked.

"Well, hello, Peter. Come on in, and, um, go screw yourself."

"All right, you're mad. Finally, we're getting somewhere. I'm not too happy either. That was quite a scene, and I'm not much for airing my business in front of other people."

"Weird, I thought that'd be right up your alley, Mr. Man of the World. Who cares what anyone else thinks, right? Careful Peter, caring what people think is very Pasadena."

"I said I was sorry. I'm sorry for my comments during the scene, I got carried away, but it is a perspective piece and you're personalizing it. Most importantly, I'm sorry I left. There, it's out. Thank God! I screwed up, and I'm sorry I hurt you. I'm not sorry I kissed you."

"Yeah, well you kissed your little friend in the audience too while poor Sally was getting her ass kicked up there. Someone had to come to her rescue."

"I kissed Alexis on the cheek. I missed your cheek by a mile, Sam. Alexis is my friend, and she's also my agent. When did I ever say you were Sally?"

Sam laughed.

"Alexis, of course her name is Alexis. Listen, I know us sheltered set are a little dense, but seriously? Phillip, Sally, and Greg? Hmm . . ."

"Fine, not incredibly creative, I'll admit, but they're only based on us. There are differences. The play is written to address larger themes than simply growing up. Sam, I'm not talking about the scene. Did you hear me? I'm sorry for . . ."

"Don't! I can't, I'm not ready to hear it. I'll probably never be ready."

"Sam, we need to be able to move past . . ."

"I liked my LA life. Well I lived in the house my parents bought right by campus, so what's not to like, but it was different being out of school."

Sam changed the subject, and while it caught Peter a little off guard, he was willing to go in any direction with her at this point.

"Maybe if I'd been in another part of the city. I don't know, it didn't work, and yes, I missed home. I was a mess during that time. I was searching and . . ."

Sam sat in the chair across from him and folded her legs to the side. Peter didn't push it, he knew she'd been a mess. He would wait.

"It is a great city. Remember when we were in college and we went out for a night in Hollywood on fake IDs and pretended we were foreign. Shit, life was so simple then."

Sam laughed remembering she had used the name Isabella and kept dropping her Spanish accent.

"Did you . . . ?"

"Fail miserably and come crawling home to mommy and daddy? Yeah, yeah I did."

"I'm guessing there's more to it than that. Come on, who's having the pity party now?"

"It was different from what I expected. I mean, sure I went on auditions at UCLA, but back then there wasn't the desperation to get a job. When I was out on my own I found myself trying for anything just to land a job, and eventually none of it felt like acting anymore. Fresh out of UCLA drama and ready to tackle the world. After all, I'd grown up Samantha Cathner, Queen of Pasadena, right?"

Peter started to say something, but she continued.

"Well, that's not quite how it worked out. I worked my ass off. Dance class, voice and movement, headshots, and audition after audition. I got a few things, but I missed the theater, I didn't want to hope for a sitcom or a soap opera."

Sam's arms were flailing around, she was smiling, and then her face would fall in sadness. She was a jumbled mess, letting him in, and what Peter had thought impossible happened. He loved her more.

"My parents knew something was wrong, but I kept trying to make it work. I'd convince myself I was spoiled and that I needed to work harder. It eventually got ugly. I was still reeling from you, and I spent a good two weeks on Henry's couch before he took me to lunch and introduced me to his gym. I started spinning like a mad woman, and eventually I realized I was in the wrong place."

Sam took a deep breath.

"I took a step back, worked at a flower shop for a while, finally called my parents, and spent the next six months in Europe. So, I guess you're right Peter, I am really a spoiled, sheltered . . ."

"Stop. I said I was sorry. Sam, I'm sorry things were so hard on you, I didn't know . . ."

"Yeah, well, you weren't here, you weren't here to know. You'd moved on, and there was no way I was going to lower myself . . ."

"Oh, come on. I went to New York. You still could've called."

"You're joking, right? What number should I have called? And said what? 'Hey, Peter, I realize you dumped me because I was obviously a mistake, but I'm having a hard time adjusting to the real world. Even though I was invincible in my little world, the big bad city chewed me up and spit me out.' Is that what I should've said?"

"Not exactly, but . . ."

"You never called me. I waited. I couldn't see how we were never going to talk to each other, never see each other. It wasn't just the sex. Not having the friendship actually hurt more."

"I know. I spent some time on the couch too, Sam. The professional kind, and I didn't mean to hurt you."

They sat in silence again. So many questions swirled in her head. Why was she telling him all of this now? Why hadn't he called? And, most importantly, what was wrong with her that she continued to let him into her life?

Choosing her heart over self-preservation, she let him stay for lunch. Sam looked in the kitchen for some chopsticks and tried to push away the thought that she was never going to be able to show her face in that theater again. Well, Julie should be happy. It was now clear who Sally was, no more suspense there.

"What are all of these?" Peter flicked the little Post-it notes Sam had on various things around her kitchen.

Peter looked comfortable in her home, and that was unnerving.

"Italian," she answered, while finding the chopsticks and taking two waters out of the refrigerator.

"I see that, but why are Italian words all over your kitchen?"

"They're in my bathroom too."

"Sam."

"Yeah, well, I'm teaching myself Italian."

Sam walked back into the living room.

Peter laughed.

"Of course you are," he said, following her.

"What does that mean?"

"Nothing, it's just so 'you.' Remember when you vowed to teach yourself origami? Oh and I'll never forget the summer of roller blading?"

He laughed and looked around her place like he was walking through some fascinating art exhibit.

"I'll have you know I am an origami master. I even taught it at the Y last summer, along with photography. The roller blades never really took did they?"

Sam laughed and his heart pulsed at the sound. Christ, he missed her laugh. How had he ever lived without it?

"I'm really not coordinated and I still say the toe break on those things is odd."

Sam opened one of the cartons sitting on the coffee table. Peter moved to the bookshelves. She was enjoying her Kung Pao chicken, and then she almost choked on her thought. There was no way he wouldn't notice it. Soon it would be right there in front of him, he'd know. If she jumped up now, it would look like something was wrong, like she had something to hide. Sam quickly decided it was better to stay where she was and make light of it when it came up. Peter looked at her books and joked that she still had some of her college textbooks along with a highly annotated copy of *Anna Karenina*.

"I remember this from college. I thought you hated this book."

He took it off the shelf.

"We studied for days and you barely . . ."

He looked at her.

"I keep it as a reminder of the hell I went through."

Peter smiled and put the book back and she prayed he would finally sit down.

"I've read it since. I don't like anything getting the best of me. It's not bad once you sort out all the damn names."

He smiled. Almost done, she was home free and then Peter saw it. His back was to her, but he lifted his head in the slightest way, and Sam knew he saw it. *Do something*, she begged her mind to engage. *Say something!*

"Peter, are you going to eat any of this because . . ."

"That's a great picture. Is it . . ."

"Bamboo, yeah. Thanks. Did you want an eggroll or . . ."

"When did you take this?"

"Years ago."

He picked up the small Mason jar of water next to the photograph. He turned toward her, slowly. It was all over his face. He knew what he was looking at. Sam's visual memory of that day, of him, there was no way it could be anything else. She searched her mind for something witty or an explanation, but she came up blank.

"Is this?"

He could barely get the words out.

"Water? Yeah, it's rainwater."

He looked at Sam and damn it all, she actually stammered.

"It, it's called a visual memory. I've had it forever, and I should make time to clear things off those shelves. There are things up there I didn't even know I still had."

Peter looked at the shelves and they looked pretty orderly, current, to him. Sam tried to wiggle out of the awkwardness, but there was no escape.

"Sam, that picture is the bamboo at the Huntington."

"Christ, Peter. Yes, I took it the day I finished my finals. It's not that good. Let it go."

"You took it that day."

"Yes, that day, the infamous day. Happy? The rainwater was from that night. You may recall, it poured all night, and I collected the rainwater after I got home. After we, after . . ."

"You saved the rain? The visual memory? You've kept it all this time? Even after . . . you didn't throw it out?"

"You can't throw out a visual memory."

Peter was confused.

"I read it in one of those books my mother gave me to get . . . to get past tough times. You find the pieces of the experience that were good, life affirming, and you put them on display so they become a reminder of the good. It's silly, but it helped. Can we stop now? I feel foolish, and you should eat. Sit and eat."

He sat next to her, still holding the jar.

"Sam."

He was leaning forward, elbows on his knees, and skin bunched up between the eyes. She could feel the warmth of his thigh and for an instant she thought about shutting her brain off, leaning over, and continuing the kiss from this morning. *Oh, that's a brilliant idea. It was so fun recovering from him the last time, right?* Her headache screamed.

"Sam, this is, it's incredible."

Peter set the jar on the coffee table, ran his fingers through his hair and sat back.

"Incredible, that's a lame word. I'm a writer for God's sake, and every time I try to talk to you about this I keep tripping up."

He took a deep breath.

"We should talk about . . ."

"No! Please drop it, okay? We've had enough discussion for one day, and I honestly can't take any more embarrassment. God, my head is pounding."

She got up too quickly and fell back into his lap. He held her and looked down at her face. For the second time, Sam could feel his breath on her face, warmth and Life Savers.

"You still eat them?"

"Still eat what?"

"Life Savers, your breath still smells like Life Savers."

Their eyes swam together, and Sam forced herself to sit up.

"You put it in your play. You shared that with everyone else too."

"Sam, come on, I had to put that in the play. You know most of our story is made up of great Life Savers moments. It was never bad until I took it too far."

Peter again cursed his choice of words.

"I didn't mean being with you was bad, it just made things more difficult. Shit."

"Peter, thank you for coming by. I'm not going to apologize to you for my insane rant today because you certainly had it coming, but I will make my apologies tomorrow to the cast and crew. Now, please get out. I'm falling asleep on my feet here."

Peter stood, put the jar back on her bookshelf, and then walked to face her by the door. He didn't move. He brushed the hair out of her face, tucking it behind her ear. A gesture he'd done all her life, even when they were younger, and it didn't mean what it meant now. Her heart started to cry. *Damn weak heart.*

"Peter?"

He continued to play with her hair.

"Peter, look at me."

"Oh, I am."

It was as if Sam was a fragile sculpture he desperately wanted, but was afraid to break. He barely touched her and she struggled to stay standing.

"Peter, I don't think we should . . ."

"You kept the water. Why did you keep that rainwater? I should have never gone there with you that day, made this difficult, but I did. I had to be with you, still do."

Sam shrugged to get him to drop his hands.

"Peter, what is this?"

She didn't know what to say. It certainly wasn't going to be, "I loved you, and when you left it broke my heart." That sounded pathetic. Peter was still staring as if all she needed to do was spill her heart to him and that would fix everything. Sam knew better.

"Look, I'm not sure what you want me to say, but . . ."

"The truth, I want the truth. Why did you keep the rainwater?" His voice grew tense.

"Peter, be careful," she said steady as if her life depended on it.

"Please be careful with me. I can't . . ."

He wanted to hold her, protect her from, well from himself. His hands trailed up her arms, and he was overwhelmed.

"You kept the rainwater because that day was magic. We were magic. You wanted to hold on to it. You said it yourself, that was the best part, the visual memory. That's what we need to hang on-to, right?"

"We can't."

He saw the raw pain in her eyes.

"I've moved on, and now what, you've changed your mind? I'm worth the effort now, Peter? I should simply throw myself, my life, back into your arms. No. I won't do it, and stop looking at me with those 'don't let go' eyes. You let go first, remember? The magic left."

She stepped back.

"It's only a jar, Peter. Just a picture. I don't believe in the magic anymore. I can't, it hurts too much."

"I shouldn't have left you. I should have found a way."

Peter stepped into her and she held up his jacket.

"But you didn't and it's the past, it's over. Please go, get back to your play."

Chapter Sixteen

*I*t's not that he didn't like people, they were fine. It was that he hated trying to be himself. It felt like an act to be himself in Pasadena. Actually, he wasn't even sure who he was in this town, with these people, but this was his play, and it was nothing without an audience. Peter covered up that he was a nervous, insecure mess with his best successful playwright face and walked out to meet the tour.

Sam was standing at the side door of the theater with her group when Peter walked from backstage and down the steps. She took a deep breath. She had been avoiding Peter for the past two days. She felt like she was trapped in a huge spider web. No matter how hard she tried to stay focused and keep a safe distance, things kept getting messier. She had already apologized to the cast and crew for her emotional meltdown. Even though Candice was generous with her, Sam felt stupid and ridiculous as she assured her boss nothing like that would ever happen again. She put on her best professional face.

"Ladies and gentlemen, I'd like to introduce you to the play-wright, Mr. Peter Everoad."

The small grouped clapped and a few people who remembered Peter growing up, extended their hands to greet him.

The Playhouse held this kind of event for every show as a perk to season ticket holders. They were invited to a preview, a rough performance, oftentimes with scenes still in progress, during rehearsals before opening night. The performance was the full production minus the ending. It was sort of a behind-the-scenes look or a teaser. The ticket holders would have to come back to see the ending. Meanwhile they would hopefully spread the word to as many of their friends as possible. It was not necessary for this production, because it was sold out for the entire run, but it worked well for some lesser-known works.

The group had finished a meet and greet with the cast and crew and it was now time for a brief question-and-answer session with either the playwright or the director. Peter and his play were such a draw that the Playhouse had asked, and he had agreed to do the Q&A.

"It's wonderful to meet all of you and see some familiar faces. Thank you for your continued support of the Playhouse," Peter greeted them.

For all of his initial success, he was gracious and very approachable. Sam realized that people now saw what she had known all along: Peter was confident, charming, and gorgeous in his element.

"Shall we have a seat and get started?" Sam gestured to the group and directed them to the front rows of the theater.

She moved up the aisle and sat toward the back of the house to leave Peter alone with his fans. Peter looked up at her as she backed away and then took a seat on the edge of the stage facing the group. Peter seemed softer, warmer, which made everything swimming in Sam's head worse.

"So . . ."

He took a deep breath.

"Where shall we start? Did you enjoy the performance?"

A woman in the front row perked up and said: "Mr. Everoad, it was thrilling. The scenery and the dialogue are so vivid, really wonderful. When did you write this play?"

"Thank you, and you can call me Peter."

Looking at her nametag, he continued, "Evelyn, I wrote this play about two years ago. Once the characters were developed, they wrote a lot of the dialogue themselves, in my head, of course. The scenery I owe to the director, Spencer, and lighting designer, Gordy, who came with me from New York, as well as all of the local crew. They're masters of their craft and it has been a joy to see my words come to life."

Hands went up.

"Yes, red shirt."

"Enjoyed the play, Peter," a balding man in the second row began.

"You mentioned that the characters wrote most of the dialogue once you created them. Did you base any of these characters off of actual people? People you knew as a kid? You know, is this autobiographical?"

Peter felt the question coming; Sam could see it in his face even twenty rows away. He looked up into the light, but could not see her in the darkness. Peter ran his fingers through his hair and rubbed the back of his neck. He wondered when the hometown questions would stop. *Probably when he left his damn hometown*, he thought.

"John . . . sorry, I was thinking about that for a minute. Yes, this story is very personal and many of the characters are based on people I grew up with. I think every writer draws characteristics from those around him. Or her, don't want to offend."

He smiled and the group laughed.

"I was recently told that playwrights stand on the sidelines and observe. I suppose I've been doing that my whole life."

Peter looked up again and, even safely hidden in the darkness, Sam looked away.

"Are you Phillip?" a young woman with braids and long shell earrings asked, as if she were a gossip reporter.

"Ah, well, there are pieces of me in Phillip. Yes, I see some of myself in him, but he's wiser than I was at that age. The beauty of writing is your characters can be exactly as you want them. They have the benefit of your hindsight, knowledge. Phillip's better than Peter, if that makes sense."

He smiled at the young woman.

She persisted.

"Since we didn't get to see the end of the play, can you give us a hint? Do they end up together? Does Phillip ever . . . um, does he fight for her?"

Sam's heart accelerated now, and she was uncomfortable for Peter. Knowing how private he was, she was sure this was unbearable. But he knew these types of questions would come up.

"Are you sure you're not a critic?" Peter asked, and the group laughed.

"No, seriously, Cathy is it?"

She nodded.

"Well, you'll have to come back for the full performance to see how it ends. I can't give too much away, but I can tell you that people will leave the theater satisfied. Everyone ends up where they belong, and there's a happy ending."

"So he does fight for her? I knew it."

"I didn't say that," he tried to laugh.

"Well, how could it possibly have a happy ending if he doesn't fight for her? He's madly and passionately . . ."

"Yeah, well, you'll have to wait and see. Any other questions?"

Peter was flushed and starting to fidget with his papers. A gentleman in the front row rescued him with a question about the set, which was followed by a couple of questions about his experience producing his first play in New York. Peter answered all of the questions and again shook hands. Sam collected herself in the darkness and walked toward the stage to lead the group back to the lobby.

"Well, that was a lively discussion. Thank you, Peter," Sam said as she ushered the group toward the back of the theater.

"You're very welcome. It was my pleasure. See all of you opening night."

The group walked into the darkness, and as Sam turned to follow, Peter gently touched her arm. Her heart jumped and one more time she hoped he couldn't feel it. She told herself he was playing with her and she should be upset, yet when she turned to face him, she knew she would be lucky if indifference showed on her face.

"Was that all right? I didn't seem too . . ."

Damn him. Right when I was working my way up to miffed, he goes all human on me.

"Amazing."

"What?"

"Mr. Famous Playwright nervous about a small group of theatergoers?"

"Yeah, well I was never good at talking in front of groups. I always get so . . ."

Sam could feel herself soften. Seeing underneath the facade to his nervousness, she recognized *her* Peter. For the first time since he'd been home, she reached for him. Her hand touched his face. Peter's breath caught, and this time she was certain his heart was beating as wildly as hers.

"You were great, Peter. You should have more faith in yourself. It's exactly what that woman said: a brilliant play. And people are going to . . . they are going to love you. I did notice a few changes to Sally. She's no longer so queen-like. Well done. The ending is a real cliffhanger."

"Thanks," he was having trouble breathing.

Peter always liked himself through Sam's eyes. She had a way of clearing away all the doubt and useless business in his mind. She looked at him, and he felt the most ridiculous things were possible.

"Well, things can change once rehearsals start, once actual people are up there," he smiled.

"I suppose they can."

"The ending, yeah, that is going to be. . . . Yeah, we'll see."

Sam turned to leave and halfway up the aisle he said it: "Thanks for all your help, Sally."

The group, who'd already been intrigued by their conversation, erupted in discussion. Sam whipped around, surprised he'd said it in front of other people. Peter's mouth quirked, he put his head down, and walked backstage. It was the same look he used to give her at college socials or during late nights when he would drop her off at the dorm. He'd make a comment or say something flip that had a kernel of truth to it, and then in fear, or whatever it was, he would bow his head and retreat.

She was Sally. She had known it, everyone had known it after her outburst during rehearsal, but for him to say it out loud was . . . it was a gesture. An apology maybe, definitely a gesture. Extended, yet shrouded in a tossed away remark. Every hour Sam spent with Peter made it more and more difficult to push him back into the past. They now had moments in the present, time spent together in the current day today. The pain of the past was diluted every time she added a new memory with who he was now.

After dismissing the comments and cooing from the group, Sam ushered them out of the theater and decided to walk home. Peter was right, the majority of the play was filled with wonderful memories—and Phillip's thoughts that she certainly wasn't privy to growing up. The words Phillip says to Sally, or thinks about her in the play, those beautiful, heartfelt words. Peter wrote those, felt those about her. *But words are only words,* Sam thought. As lovely as they were and as much as hearing them helped her heal the past, she couldn't build a life on sentiments. Actions build a life, and so far Peter's only action had been leaving. Sam was learning to like him again, she knew she would always love him, but she couldn't afford to trust him.

Chapter Seventeen

*I*t was late. Everyone had left after the day's rehearsal. Carmen was on her way out. Sam helped her put away the last things on the props table and finished her Coke. Carmen kissed Sam on both cheeks, thanked her for the help, and left through the green room. She locked the door, grabbed her bag, and was on her way through the house to lock up. The quiet hit her as she walked onto the stage. The house lights were down and the stage was empty except for the swing from Act II still in place.

She loved the theater when everyone was gone and the magic dimmed. Sam put her bag down and sat on the swing. The Playhouse was so beautiful and rich with history. Mocked-up pieces of her childhood sat in the wings of the stage. Sam recognized a bank of high school lockers and furniture from the Everoad house. Peter's play was very specific. Trapped in the past again, Sam tried to imagine the girl she was back then. Pretending to take the hand of a young man, she stood and danced with her imaginary friend, lover. When did everything get so . . .

"Peter," she whispered.

A light clicked on in the back of the house. A single beam illuminated a silhouette she knew all too well.

"Yes, Sam?"

She put her arms down and felt absurd.

"How long have you been . . ."

"Long enough to see you dancing around my backyard."

"Oh, well, you could have told me you were there. I thought I was alone."

"Now, that wouldn't be any fun. You'd never have danced if you knew I was here."

He hopped up on the stage, stepped stage left, and turned on a dim light overhead. It cast a warm glow as Sam sat back on the swing. Peter walked over, hands shoved firmly in his pockets, and sat next to her. The heat radiating off his body and the energy between them was again palpable. They had sat together a million times, but now it was almost painful.

Trying to ignore it, Peter looked down at his swinging feet. Breathing in the same space, he desperately needed to understand, figure things out without screwing up again. There was that need again, he needed to find a way back to her.

"Did you hear the Worthingtons are remodeling their kitchen?"

"Again? Didn't they recently," Sam caught herself, "wait a minute, are you partaking in neighborhood gossip?"

"Gotcha."

Peter bumped her with his shoulder.

"Seriously, though they are . . . remodeling. Third time in two years."

Shaking his head.

"Have these people ever heard of the term waste? How do I know this, you ask?"

"Okay, I'll play. Yes, how do you know this tidbit of information?"

"My mother. Yeah, she told me last night while I carried her up to her room. She passed out, not that that's anything new, but last night she was covered in magazines and rambling that her kitchen needed to be redone and that witch Elena Worthington, her words not mine, was trying to drive her crazy. After all these years, after everything she's been through, she still clings to kitchens and keeping up with her friends. At her age, I thought she would have figured some things out. Jesus, she's like the kid in the emergency room whose mother beats her, but she still cries for her mommy. Why does she give a crap anymore? Seriously."

"I'm sorry, Peter."

"No, don't be sorry."

He turned to face her.

"Answer the question. What is it? Why is it so damn important to have the new Viking stove or the Gucci purse? Her whole life has crumbled around her, and she still can't see it. Why, Sam?"

"Why is it important to your mother? Only she knows that, but it's how she was raised, Peter. She's the epitome of the Pasadena debutante. It's all she knows. Her parents took care of her, and then your father took care of her. It's who she is. You can't blame her for that. It's sad, yeah, but don't, I'm not telling you anything you don't already know."

"It's hard to find value in anything, in our neighborhood, when I'm around her. The way she handled my father's death . . . she closes everything off and any feelings that may creep up are drowned in a bottle. I don't want to be around it. There are better ways to live your life."

"True, but Peter, not everyone in our circle is going through what your mother has gone through. It's like what you said about your play, most of it is good. There are rough patches, and I'll give you that your mother is not easy to deal with, but that doesn't eclipse everything else."

"I know, but it's different away from here. I'm different."

Sam turned to look at him and the realization hit her.

"Peter, I don't think you are. I think you've simply pulled together the easy pieces in New York. Sort of like how your mom is with the photo albums. You don't want the ugly, the complicated, so you moved away from it, from me."

Peter stood up, appalled at the comparison.

"That's not true. I write about the ugly, I've faced my issues, Sam."

"Right, in plays, in your writing. But what about in your real life? This is my home. I, we, grew up here. The good and the bad, we have to take it all. You can't pick and choose. It's not a book or a play. This is our past, warts and all, but at least we have each other. Well, at least we had each other growing up."

Sam tried to lighten the mood, but she could hear Peter thinking.

"You honestly think I can't handle reality, that I'm hiding in my plays? I'm the only person that recognized the crap I was living in. I recognized it and thank God, I got . . ."

Peter closed his eyes. *Brilliant way to woo her back!*

"Got out? Thank God, you got out?"

"Sam, that's not what I meant. I mean, for me there was no way I was going to be able to stay here. You have to see that."

"Do I? You sure took what you wanted before you left, didn't you?"

"That's not fair."

Sam narrowed her eyes in warning. *Did he really want to discuss fair?*

"We were both there, Sam. It's not like I threw myself at you, you were there, too."

"I was, but I didn't run from everything. You never gave me, us, a chance."

"Us? Sam, there was never going to be an us back then. You are, you're you, Samantha Cathner, drama sweetheart, gorgeous in everything. My date, out of the pure kindness of your heart, to several stupid social functions I crawled through. You shine here, and I . . ."

"Ran? You ran. We spent our whole lives together. You were not some charity case, so maybe that's something you tell yourself to justify bolting. Look at me, Peter. I'm not the success story. High school and college are over. Here I am running myself ragged and living in my parents' guesthouse. I haven't seen a lot of shining lately."

"You've pulled through fine. So you're not acting, who cares? What you have is better. Only you could take something artistic and break it down into details and figures. You are so smart and different. Back then I wasn't, what is it that my shrink says? 'I wasn't equipped to handle my emotions.' If I'd stayed, I would have eventually managed to ruin that night. Once you woke up, you would have . . ."

"That's such bull, Peter. That's you running away instead of dealing with the mess of feelings you had. And that's fine, if I wasn't . . ."

"Don't! You were, you were everything. Please stop making it sound like I left because I didn't want you. Sam, that night, the night we . . ."

"Made love? In the rain? Yeah, I remember it. Seems a bit late to discuss it, but I remember every single detail. Clearly you do too, because you put it in your play. Can you say it, Peter, 'the night we made love'?"

"I'm not a child, Sam. Of course I can say it. Right, the night we made love."

He winced a little. The phrase "make love" always sounded awkward to him. The only man who ever pulled if off was Barry White, and Peter was definitely not Barry White.

"That night was, I haven't found the words, that's why you're simply a light in the play. I don't think words have been created that will do it justice. It was, it was everything I'd ever wanted to say to you."

"You didn't need words, Peter. It was passionate and tender. You were so," Sam closed her eyes.

"And then you weren't. It was like showing me everything we could be, asking me to give all of myself, and then taking it away."

"I didn't mean to hurt you. I didn't expect it to be so much. I didn't know what to do. I'd kept my feelings to myself for so long, and then we were together, and I . . . hell, I don't know. Believe me, I was not what you needed."

"Maybe you're right."

He lifted his brow at her candor.

"Maybe that night is all we were meant to be. For the longest time I tried to regret it, but it wouldn't let me go. I couldn't stop feeling, so I accepted the hurt, and moved on. And now you're back. I mean what the hell am I supposed to do with that? Why are you here?"

"I came back because. I don't know why I came back. I'm a glutton for punishment, is that the right answer?"

"I'm not looking for the right answer. I want the truth, too. Why?"

She was looking right at him and she wanted an answer. He found the simplest words, images, came to his mind.

"Because I, because I can breathe when I'm with you, Sam."

She tried not to react. She held on tightly to the swing like a child. Peter stood up and kneeled in front of her.

"There, is that a good answer? Let's see, what did my shrink say? Oh yeah, I blame this place for everything that happened to my father, and it suffocates me. You're right, I can go to New York, recreate myself, but you're here. You're mixed in with all these other parts of my life. I don't know how to make this work, but I need you, Sam, that's why I came back. I want you in my life."

She didn't know what to say, a rush of heat filled her body and she didn't like the feeling. *He needs me? Well, wasn't that just too bad.* Only a fool entertains words like that, and she was no longer a fool. She had needed him for years, and there was no way she would survive another trip around the mixed-up mind of Peter Everoad. Sam took a deep breath to quiet her heart.

"That's beautiful, Peter. Well written. I will always care about you, but what we had was rooted in this place, our past. You can't handle our past, or your past, and I won't survive when you decide to turn and run again. Thinking you need me and sticking around to have and hold me are two very different things."

Peter said nothing and Sam laughed a little to keep from crying.

"I've done a little self-help too."

"I've made something of myself outside of who I was here. I've figured some things out. I think I can do this. I mean. Shit. I want to do this. Can't we take it slow and try? Sam, I know you can still feel us, I see it when you look at me. I know I screwed up, but give me another chance. Come to New York with me for the weekend. Let's be together, spend time together."

He stood.

"You haven't dealt with any of it. You're trying to make amends with this place, with what happened between us through the right words, your play. Do you think that's going to work? Write everyone's lines and walk through all the scenes and, it's better? Peter, your father's death, that was real. I am real, not a supporting character in your story. I'm not going to run off to New York so you can hide. What happens when I bring reality with me, when I remind you of your past, and it doesn't work? Do you shut me out again? Let me help you answer: no. No, I will not allow it. I can't be the one left behind, rejected."

"I didn't reject you, damn it. I loved you. I didn't know what to do with it."

He took her shoulders and pulled her up off the swing.

"Sam, what we have is . . . give me a chance."

He kissed her and Sam felt herself spin. That familiar spin. Four years wiser and she still melted. Pulling back, she opened her eyes.

"Peter, you need to go."

"Sam."

"I'll lock up. You need to catch a flight to New York, don't you? Drama Desk Awards. I hear you're nominated. Congratulations."

"Sam, were you listening? We can do this. I'll find a way to . . ."

Sam touched his face, and he knew she wasn't going to let him in.

"Peter, I thought I'd let it go, then you came back, and I went a little nuts. But I've got my head back on straight now. I care about you. You left me alone, to love alone, and I won't risk it again. I can't. I'm sorry. Can you understand that? That I wouldn't survive?"

A tear trailed down her cheek.

Not for the first time, he felt the force of what he had done. He should have loved her when he had the chance. She trusted him and he let everything else get in the way. There was nothing he could say, there were no words to make it right. He had come home to reclaim something, yet by being here he was hurting her all over again. He could see it in her eyes. She was right. This was still all about him and his damn issues. Even after four years he still wasn't enough. He couldn't promise her the crap of his life wouldn't hurt her again. *Who am I kidding?* Peter wiped away the few tears that sat on her perfect cheeks and gently kissed her lips. As if she felt it would be the last time, Sam opened to him and returned his kiss.

"I am so, so sorry," he whispered across her lips.

"Peter, please leave."

He kissed her forehead, lingered one beat longer than was bearable, and walked toward the lobby doors. He looked back and Sam turned to walk backstage.

When she heard the doors swing closed at the back of the theater, Sam could not catch her breath. She ran her hands over her face and slid down the wall backstage. The pain was instant. He needed her, loved her, but no matter what came out of his mouth, they were only words. How could she love him so much and be so deathly afraid of him at the same time?

Chapter Eighteen

Sam pulled into her driveway. Grady was sitting in a chair on her side patio, under the glow of the outside light. She grabbed her bags, got out of the car, and walked toward him.

"Grady?"

"I'm here for a confession, damn it. I was hoping it wouldn't come to this, but since I spoke to Peter about thirty minutes ago, and he was boarding a plane without you, I think it's time I give it the old college try," he said leaning back with his legs crossed in front.

Sam really wasn't in the mood for this.

"Yeah, well I'm not taking confessions tonight, sorry. Have you been drinking again?"

She moved in closer, smelling for alcohol.

"Nope. I'm actually sober, and you're going to want to hear this confession."

"Oh, really? Well, I hope it a juicy one. Are you coming in? Coffee?"

"Sam, I said I'm not drunk. Let's not push it with the choir boy coffee on a Friday night thing. Wine?"

Sam laughed and opened the door.

"I can do that."

Grady was still in his suit, jacket off, tie loosely hanging around his neck. He looked spent and Sam knew Grady's tie always came undone when it was time for conflict or a debate. As she turned the lights on, put her things down, and grabbed the wine, Sam was caught in another memory.

Grady majored in history at Stanford, much to his father's chagrin, but he did put in a fine speech to his parents freshman year that ended with the phrase, "Mom, Dad, how can we possibly understand and guide people into the future if we don't know our past?" Grady's parents eventually let him out of majoring in political science once he explained he was not mocking his father by referencing George Orwell's *1984*. Grady slept through freshman literature, so he had no clue what his father was talking about when he'd retorted, "Riffing on a party slogan from Orwell's *1984*. Are you mocking me?" As the story goes, Grady quickly excused himself to use the bathroom and called Peter to find out who the hell George Orwell was. Peter talked him through it, and he returned to his parents with an effective response. Grady was allowed to major in history.

Many people would be surprised to know that underneath his gorgeous party boy image hid an expert on the history of the United States—and Europe. He was a complete geography nerd, too. Grady was a smart man, but not always a thinker, as Sam's father had once pointed out.

"So," Sam began, handing Grady a glass of wine and joining him in her living room.

"Okay, what do you have to confess, my son?"

She mocked him, making the sign of the cross with her wine glass.

"Well, I'm not a very good friend, and I'm starting to think I am, what's that phrase, a big fish in a little pond."

"Okay. Did something happen that brought you to this conclusion? Did you try to steal someone's girlfriend?"

Grady hesitated.

"Wife?"

148

Sam laughed, still not taking him seriously.

"Something happened years ago, and then something happened recently. And I was a jerk years ago, but I've tried to make amends lately. But maybe I'm too late. Then I got to thinking, I'm not that damn powerful, and maybe what I said years ago didn't mean as much as I thought it did. And then I thought I'd go get drunk, but then I thought it was time I was a good friend to at least one of you."

Sam felt her jaw open at some point because she had no idea what he was rambling about.

"Um, let's break this down into smaller pieces. What did you do or say years ago?"

"Ah, that's the hard part. Can't we start with the good vibes I've been putting out lately and work our way back?"

"Spill it."

"He trusted me, and I wasn't a good friend. Keep in mind that I was younger, and, at the time, I didn't understand. I honestly thought it would pass, but Christ, four years later and it's still all over him."

Sam was now getting a little anxious.

"Grady, what are you talking about? Who's he?"

"Peter. I need another glass of wine."

Sam poured, Grady slipped his tie off and leaned forward as if he were going to explain something very complex.

"Peter? He trusts you. What does this have to do with Peter?"

"Sam, please listen. I made him feel like he would never be good enough. I guess in a way I told him to go make something of himself. I mean I suppose we always knew he was going to leave, didn't we?"

Sam didn't answer, so he continued.

"I feel like maybe I had something to do with him feeling like he needed to prove himself."

"You can only make a person feel like they're not good enough if they let you. Peter . . ."

"Yeah, thank you Miss Psychologist. Listen, please. That night, the night after you two went to the gardens. The *big night*."

Grady put his fingers up to make quotes.

Sam was shocked. Grady knew she and Peter had been more than friends and that he left her, but the way he was phrasing it—"the big night"—made her think he knew about her in the gardens and the rain, with Peter. She hadn't told him, so that left one person.

"He came to my house and told me he loved you. God, he was shaking and sick over it. He told me that he'd always loved you and you were the one. I wanted to be happy for him, I wanted to help him come up with a plan, but we were finished with college and it felt like the end and . . ."

"Oh, God."

"It was so weird and I didn't know what to say, but I knew he was going to New York, and I was going to lose him. I tried, but I couldn't be happy for him. He was going to take you with him and then you would both be gone. Which I know sounds ridiculous now, but at the time you two were all I had."

He must have read something on Sam's face. Grady raked his fingers through his hair.

"See, told you. I'm a shit, right? He was so damn empowered and in love. I was a jerk, and I asked him what he had to offer you. I told him we were all friends and he should've left it that way. I told him he would never be good enough for you. I said a lot of things that a manipulative spoiled ass would say to get his way. I'm sorry, but it was a long time ago and . . ."

"What else did you say?"

Sam's heart was pounding.

"I said you, you were happy here, and he would ruin all of that if he convinced you to go with him to New York. Sam, I'm sorry. I didn't want anything to change. He said I was probably right, that he needed to make something of himself and anything else was a distraction. He left that night deflated and we never spoke about it again and then he . . ."

"Left."

She was numb, but he couldn't honestly blame himself for what happened between them.

"Okay, so you acted like a jerk, but I seriously doubt that's why things didn't work out. You're persuasive and all, but if he loved me as he said, he would have found a way to be with me and . . . well, he didn't. So, you feel horrible, I agree it was a crappy thing to do to a friend, but you're forgiven. We have all survived and moved on. I'm amazed you've been able to keep your mouth shut over the last few years. Impressive."

"Sam, it's not a joke. He loves you. Always has, but . . ."

"But? See, it always lies in the 'but' with Peter. He loves me, but . . . He wants to be with me, but . . . Grady, thank you for coming over to clear your conscience. You're absolved, and it truly doesn't change the fact that Peter can't be trusted. He wants things the way he wants them. He asked me to go to New York with him. I can't do it again, I don't want to try. My life is perfectly fine here."

"I don't think that's true. That leads me to my second story, the one where I wasn't a jerk. About a year after he left, while you were such a mess, I went to New York, we had lunch, and I apologized. Not quite in the same drawn-out way this has unfolded, but I told him that I was an ass and what I said was shitty and untrue. He forgave me too. You guys were always great friends."

Sam laughed, it was better than crying.

"He said it probably worked out for the best and that things would never work between the two of you."

She swallowed hard and continued to listen.

"I told him that was crap, and he said that when his father died, it messed him up, closed him off, so it was for the best. I told him you were already in, you know, in his heart, and how was he going to let that go? He said he'd gone through it all and his life in New York was fine. See, he used the same damn word you used . . . fine. Fine sucks, Sam. Anyway, as you know, we've kept in touch since he's been gone, and I've been to see him a couple of times. His life in New York is great, and he's a success, but he needs you Sam. I told him when he first got here that he was warm when he was around you."

"You told him he was warm?"

"Yeah, shut up. I can be sensitive."

"Clearly."

"Anyway, the point is he came back for you, he's sorted out whatever stuff he was dealing with. He knows never to listen to me, so what's the problem? You were never going to make a go of it with that . . . mountain of a man, Brian."

"That may be true, but I'm not making a go of it with Peter either. I'm fine, really. This has been good for me. I've been able to say a lot of things to him, and it feels healthier to leave it this way."

They sat in silence for a minute. Sam traced the top of her wine glass with a finger.

"Do you love him?"

She looked at Grady and told the truth.

"I do. I will always love him. It's not enough."

"Remember when we were kids, and my parents put in the diving board?"

She nodded wondering where this was going.

"Remember how all three of us were afraid to go off the board, so we came up with the thing that we only jumped in threes. Remember? So when the other kids came over we were like this cool trio and eventually we really did kick ass, doing cannonballs and flips. Remember?"

"Yes, Grady. I remember, but what's it have to do . . ."

"You're scared, Sam. Not in a weenie weak way, but in a real, terrified way. Scared that you'll let yourself love him again, and he will leave you. You're afraid to get too close, to let anyone get too close, and you can't control yourself with Peter. You love him too much. He loves you too much, too. I've known you both my whole life, and I can see it, feel it, anytime you're even in the same room."

Sam could barely form words. Grady was pleading for their love better than either of them could.

"Maybe I am scared, but you don't understand. I lost myself when he left. I will never give that kind of power over me to anyone again."

"First of all, you didn't lose yourself. You were growing up, doubting yourself anyway. You can't put that all on him. And he ran because, let's face it, great sex with you or not, who wouldn't run from Peter's childhood?"

Sam blushed and laughed. Grady was one of a kind.

"My point is: the two of you need to climb back up on the board and jump one more time. I'd join you, but I helped screw it up the last time. This time you two need to do it on your own."

Sam laughed.

"Get up there on the board with him, trust him, Sam."

Grady took her hands.

"I love you both too much to let either of you settle for fine. There are no two people more annoyingly suited for each other. Your dad's plane is gassed up and waiting for you. You already told him to kiss your ass, that probably felt good. Now go fix this thing so I can stop feeling bad."

Sam started to cry. She was scared, but right then and there she decided to climb the steps of the diving board.

"Yeah, don't do that. I can't handle the crying. You can cry on the plane."

Sam wiped her tears and kissed Grady on the cheek.

"You're a good friend, Grady. I love you."

"Okay, that's enough warm and fuzzy. Now get going."

Her mind screamed this was a dangerous idea, her heart ached with wanting. She went to her room to pack.

Chapter Nineteen

There was a line of cabs waiting outside the airport when Sam's plane arrived in New York shortly before one in the morning. She had always appreciated the benefits of coming from privilege, but nothing brought that home like using your father's private jet to fly across the country on a moment's notice. She was grateful.

The cold night air hit Sam's face with the reality of what she was doing. She had spontaneously arrived in New York uninvited and alone. For only the second time in her entire life she was fueled not by common sense or rules, but by passion and urgency. She smiled. It felt good. She was alive. While she had no idea how Peter would react, it didn't matter. Well, maybe it mattered.

Removing the piece of paper Grady had given her with Peter's address, Sam realized she hadn't been to New York since she saw Peter's play. She asked one of the cabbies to take her to 12 East Twelfth Street. Only in New York. She was sure Peter's home was warm and wonderful, but the address sounded like a cold, impersonal cellblock. If Peter lived in Pasadena, his home would probably sit on the corner of Gardenia and Whispering Pine. California was much more whimsical, but she was in the big city now, where most of the whimsy was trapped behind brick facades.

Sitting in the cab, Sam looked up at the buildings flying by and the thousands of windows. Tiny lives playing out, one on top of the other. She wondered if anyone else was on her way to declare her love. She felt certain she was not alone. Even at this hour, some of those windows held women deeply in love and about to take a chance, even a second chance. New York was magical, especially at night.

She had imagined Peter in this city dozens of times. Grady had given her some extra understanding, and she was ready to take a chance. Her heart was racing, pounding out of her chest, and there was nothing she could do to keep it quiet.

Sam paid the driver and looked up at Peter's building. There was no escaping: no sarcastic comments or dismissive glances. She had arrived. She had come all the way across the country. Bare, with her heart in her hand, standing right outside his door, she was taking the leap. Sam decided it was time to be more of a doer and not much of a thinker anymore. She needed to be brave and unlike Peter, she brought a whole foundation of love from back home with her. She knew who she was now: Peter would be a part of her life, not her everything this time.

Sam entered the lobby. It was warm, and an older man in a navy suit sat behind a rich redwood desk. He was reading and looked over his glasses as she walked further into the lobby. He then took the glasses off and came around the desk.

"Welcome, Miss?"

"Cathner, but please call me Sam."

She extended her hand.

"Sam, short for Samantha?"

She nodded.

"Very well, Sam, my name is Bobby, and I'm the doorman for the building. Is there something I can help you with? Are you here to see someone?"

"Peter, Peter Everoad," Sam blurted out, as if the words could no longer stand to be hidden away.

"Mr. Everoad, he makes sure I call him Peter too. You must be his . . . friend?"

He smiled and looked at her, trying to figure out who Sam was and how she fit in Peter's life. Sam was not sure how good a job he was doing and then it occurred to her that Bobby might not let her go up because it was so late.

"And is he expecting you, Miss . . . Sam?"

"He is not, and, well, it's a surprise. I'm his childhood friend, and you see, he left California to come home for the weekend, and I'm ready now. It's just a diving board, and everyone deserves a second chance."

Sam was lost in her own thoughts, nervous and definitely rambling.

"I see. You must be exhausted having arrived from California. I'm not sure about the diving board, but it sounds important, and I'm sure Peter will be very happy to see you."

She was glad Bobby thought so, she wasn't so sure.

"I'll call him straight away and we'll get you settled for the night."

He was going to announce her. When Sam had pictured this in her mind, there had been no doorman. Bobby was a perfectly lovely man, but she had played the scene differently. She tried to remind herself to go with the flow, that she was a doer. Bobby picked up the phone behind his desk, and Sam thought she was going to pass out.

"Good evening, Peter. Sorry to disturb, but I have a lovely young lady in the lobby that has flown some distance to see you."

He grinned at her, enjoying his little role as the messenger.

"Yes, no, Sam . . . Miss Samantha Cathner. Yes, I'm quite certain, sir. Shall I send her up? Very well, yes, you too. Goodnight."

Bobby hung up and helped Sam with her bag.

"He seemed quite shocked, but . . . thrilled to see you. Take the elevator to the top floor, and when you get off, his door is the first left."

Sam thanked Bobby and floated to the elevator. She started to sweat and was uncertain. *Just like the diving board*, she kept telling herself.

Sam stepped off the elevator and put her hand on the cool exposed stone lining the hall. She turned left, and Peter was standing in his doorway. White T-shirt, faded jeans, and socks. He looked tucked into his home, rumpled and gorgeous. Peter was always good looking, but standing in front of her, he was a man, a strong, accomplished, incredibly sexy man with a shocked look on his face. She could tell as she approached that Peter was reconciling her being in New York. She decided not to worry about that. She had something to say, a ladder to finish climbing.

"What? Sam . . . you're here. Is everything okay, did something happen?"

The whole thing felt like a dream. She remembered being a kid, and every time they went to some spectacular place like Paris, she would stand on the street and think—*Am I really here? Is that truly the Eiffel Tower?* She felt that way now looking at Peter, in a place she'd never been before. It all felt surreal. She was short of breath but managed to get out: "Yes. Yes, something happened."

"Oh, Christ, I'm sorry. Are you all right?"

Peter led her into his home, and Sam was instantly filled with warmth, brownies on a winter day, warmth. He was everywhere. It smelled like him, and everything faded. She wanted to stay there, forever wrapped in him. There was a half-eaten bowl of ice cream on the dark wood coffee table. The television was on, but muted. A scene from *The Philadelphia Story* was frozen in black and white on the flat screen hanging on a brick wall.

She loved everything about him. Now she needed to get the words out. All the conversations she'd had in her head over the past few weeks, all the doubts, everything she told herself she should be frightened of on the trip to Peter's door faded away. She slid her hands around his waist and touched her forehead to his. She felt brave and gently said, "You know that part in the play, the part where everything comes to a head, and it all changes?"

"What? Jesus, Sam, please tell me what's wrong."

"Everything's fine. What's that called? I can't remember. Hell, I can't remember anything. The part where the plot builds up and then 'boom' everything . . ."

"The climax? Are you talking about the climax? What does that . . ."

"Yes, that's it! The climax."

Sam took a deep breath.

"Peter, this, this right here, is the climax. This is where the characters have a revelation."

"Sam, you're not making any sense. Do you want to sit down?"

"No, I definitely do not want to sit down."

She pulled him close, and Peter had no idea what was going on. Her body was pressed to him, he could feel her cold hands on his back, and she was standing in his house. This was either a cruel hallucination or Samantha Cathner had just flown across the country, and she looked like she was about to kiss him.

"Sam."

He felt her breath on his face.

"Peter."

She touched the side of his face, as she had done so many times in their life.

"I'm scared. First, I felt rejected and angry, but then you came back, and now I'm scared."

"What? Sam, don't . . ."

"Do I scare you, Peter?"

Shitless, he thought, but she was so close and all he could mutter was: "yes."

"Good. Well, I'm climbing up the ladder, I'm making the gesture. I'm reaching for you this time. You are enough, Peter Everoad, you have always been enough."

He felt like he was going to die. Every system in his body raced with feelings he'd pushed away for so long. All of them knotted in this throat.

"I flew across the country to jump off the diving board with you. Remember?"

Sam sounded crazy now, but she could see in his eyes he knew. He remembered.

"I want you too. I need to be with you too. I want to be there with you at the awards ceremony tomorrow night. I want to be in your life: New York, Pasadena, wherever. I don't know what I'm doing. I'm scared you'll let go again, but I'm more afraid of missing one more memory with you."

"I won't let go, Sam. I promise."

With that Peter held her face, and Sam looked like a woman on the edge. They both looked into each other, down into the vast, unknown, dangerous water. Her breath caught for a moment as his lips touched hers and then they jumped.

Peter's mouth was urgent. He kissed her and held her so close she could barely breathe. They clung and everything they'd held in for so long simply opened. Sam was no longer Sally and Peter was definitely not Phillip. They had grown in their hurt, lived some life, and maybe it was all worth it. Peter buried his hands in Sam's hair, and trembling, they barely made it to the living room.

Chapter Twenty

"Do you have any idea how many times I've imagined you right where you are?" Peter asked, quietly stroking his fingertips along her bare shoulder.

"Of course, it was impossible for me to imagine you any more beautiful than you were the last time we were together, but you are. And I have to admit, in most of my fantasies we did at least make it to the bed."

Sam rolled over, feeling the living room rug across her skin, and gently kissed him.

"I'd like to see that bed," she smiled.

"Your wish is my command," and with that Peter slid into his boxer shorts and scooped her up in the blanket that covered them. Sam laughed as he carried her to the bedroom. Peter had learned some things since leaving Pasadena, and every part of her body was grateful.

"Oh, Peter!" Sam exclaimed, completely captivated by his bedroom.

This room was where he had brought all the best pieces of Pasadena with him. She recognized the chest his grandfather had given him when they graduated from high school. Everything was familiar. He put her on the bed, and she stood up, slipping into one of his shirts lying at the end of the bed. Sam fastened one button and walked over to the wall.

"Of course, you'd ruin my perfect chivalric moment."

She didn't respond, stunned and looking above the bed.

"Sorry, it's . . ."

"Kinda cool, right?"

She touched the canoe that was hanging on the wall over Peter's bed like a headboard. It was his father's.

"It's perfect, Peter."

"I always loved that boat, but it was insane getting it up here. Not a whole lot of canoes in Manhattan," Peter laughed.

Sam walked around the room. His bed was huge; she recognized it and the two leather chairs, one in each corner, from his dad's fishing cabin. They had gone up there a few times in high school with Grady and their dads. Peter's room was masculine and like a little outdoor oasis in this big city. He'd taken so much of what he cared about and brought it here, as if he could separate the good and take it away from what he considered the bad. His father was everywhere in his bedroom. There was a picture of the two of them fishing and a black-and-white picture of his father as a boy. That same picture had been on the mantel in his family home before his father died. Peter took Sam's arm to move her back toward the bed, and she saw it, right there, on his dresser in a black frame. She looked at him and his cheeks flushed.

"Yeah, all right, we're even. It's you, well your eyes, but it's you."

They were her eyes, only her eyes, and a few freckles on her nose.

"Oh, this is going to be so much fun. When did you take that picture, Peter?"

He rubbed the back of his neck and rolled his eyes at her as she began the same interrogation he'd given her about the bamboo photo.

"College graduation. You were smiling while your parents were taking your picture so I took my own. You looked so happy that day with them. I knew, under the circumstances, if I'd asked you for a picture I wouldn't have gotten the same smile, not after that night and . . . so, I stole it. I stole those eyes."

Sam remembered him avoiding her at graduation and thinking that he was simply keeping his distance to avoid the awkwardness of what happened. She would have never guessed he loved her that day or that he would want to steal her eyes.

"Why?"

She continued to question him, as he had her.

"Oh, here we go again."

"Turnabout is fair play, right? You wanted to know about the rainwater. You wouldn't let it go."

"I know. Fine, I love your eyes, always have. They're brown, but like a mosaic, and they change colors, I never know what I'm going to get when I look into your eyes. I wanted to take them with me."

"Only that part? Hmm, I noticed you didn't take my mouth. Too complicated, this mouth?"

"You could say that, but the mouth is great too. I love the mouth too."

He ran his thumb over her bottom lip, pulled close, kissed her gently. A warm smile crossed his entire satisfied face.

"Are you hungry?"

"Very nice. Make love to me, show me some great pictures, and then . . . food. Yes, I'm starving, but it's three o'clock in the morning, where are you going to get . . . oh, for a minute I forgot where I was, the city that never sleeps."

About forty-five minutes later the delivery guy knocked at the door. Sam made sure she was out of sight, to avoid looking like a little harlot who shows up at a man's house in the middle of the night.

Peter paid, handed the short, tired-looking, bald guy a tip and closed the door. While they opened the chicken, pitas, and tabouli, Sam asked about Bobby, the doorman. Peter told her the story of how he found this place and that Bobby had four children, all girls.

"That's why he's charming. In a house with five women, he has to be," Sam said as they sat on the living room floor and ate off the coffee table.

They fed each other, laughed, and gazed at one another without the tension that previously forced them to look away. Everything felt fresh, without all of the baggage of home. Sam was not sitting with Peter from the past; she was with and loving Peter in the present. They discussed the last four years of the Oscars and the Tony Awards. They both agreed it was a disgrace that *Shrek* made it to Broadway, and Peter said they should see *Jersey Boys* while she was in town. They talked about new music and debated the virtues of iTunes. It was like she was getting to know this gorgeous man and she happened to remember what he looked like when he got his first dog. Sam realized why Peter loved being in New York. His apartment, his life, was so rich here, and he seemed so at ease. She loved it, loved him, maybe a little too much.

Peter's home was something you see in a hip, urban magazine. Old and modern mixed together. Oak hardwood floors, exposed brick, huge windows, and a long rectangular skylight above the entry. Sam imagined that his apartment must fill with the most beautiful morning light. It then dawned on her that she would see that light, and her stomach fluttered.

After they ate, Peter showed her around the rest of the apartment with a grin on his face the whole time. He couldn't stop smiling. She was actually here, in his world, his Sam, wrapped in his shirt.

He had dreamed about her here so many times. Her laugh filled his hall, and Peter realized in that moment he had everything he had ever wanted. She opened him up, let so much light in that it was bright. Looking at her standing barefoot in his shirt, Peter hoped to God he didn't screw this up again because there was no way he would survive if he ever had to give her back again.

Sam walked through the house admiring Peter's eclectic mesh of modern and cozy. There were old pictures of his parents and newer pictures of his mother and sister together in front of the Met. They must have visited him in New York too. There was a picture of him with Grady at a Yankees game. She also noticed a group picture. It looked like a group of actors or an entire cast, with Peter in the center, holding a tattered script. He was smiling in a way she didn't often see on Peter. He looked happy, so very happy. No wonder he left, she thought, trying to tear her eyes away from the pictures. She realized there were people here she'd never met who made him, his life, happy. It was an odd feeling, and Sam wondered if there were other women. She hadn't thought about it before, and she wasn't going to start now. She was being brave, moving forward, not dwelling on the past.

They walked down the hall, past a second bedroom on the right. There were more theater pictures, a couple of artistic ones that Sam appreciated, a close-up of an old stage light and one with the edges of a torn ticket. Great shots. The walls held programs of shows Peter had seen and his own *Playbill,* under a glass frame, right by the entrance to his bedroom. Sam was so glad she had jumped on that plane; no matter what happened she would never regret seeing this side of Peter, his life away from his childhood.

They went back to the couch, talked more, nestled in each other's arms, and watched the last half of *The Philadelphia Story.* Peter was aware of Sam's warm body, his arms wrapped around her. She had let him in, her heart beat in concert with his own. As he watched, her eyes drifted closed and she sighed. He felt this strange pull and recognized what she had given him. He had a second chance, one he vowed to cherish.

Chapter Twenty-One

*S*am woke to the smell of bacon and the feel of cotton sheets. It took her a minute to figure out where she was and then she sank into a smile. It wasn't a dream. Peter had carried her from the couch in the early morning, taken her to his bed, and made love to her again. This time it was slow and achingly tender. The urgency was replaced by soft and total adoration. The warmth of the love they shared surrounded her as she reached out to touch the side Peter slept on. He had obviously gotten up to make the bacon that filled the house with its aroma along with the sound of the Police. *Good Lord, did anyone still listen to the Police?* Not even the alluring sounds of Sting, but old-school Police. Sam came around the corner wearing Peter's shirt and trying to fluff her bedhead into something appealing. Many women would go in the bathroom, brush their teeth or their hair. Some super crazy women might even put on makeup before walking out to see a lover. Sam decided she wasn't most women. She wanted to be with Peter more than she cared about her hair.

Peter turned, spatula in hand, as she walked into the kitchen, and the corner of his mouth turned up, making him look like a devilish little boy. Feeling quite sexy and fueled by that look, Sam said nothing. She kissed him slowly. Peter dropped the spatula and wrapped his arms around her. She pulled away and said: "Good morning."

Peter was in the jeans he'd worn the night before, not quite buttoned all the way, and a worn T-shirt. His hair was all over the place and he had at least two days of stubble as he stood in his bare feet with the morning light spilling into the kitchen. Sam sauntered over to the coffee machine feeling playful.

Peter's eyes hung on her as he bent to pick up the spatula.

"Good morning to you too. That is officially my favorite shirt."

Sam laughed and poured some coffee. He took the bacon off the stove and stood behind her at the counter.

"I can't get enough," he whispered into her neck.

"I know."

His hands traveled up her body.

"I keep thinking someone's going to tell me this is all some kind of mistake or a dream."

Peter spread the top part of her shirt open and kissed her neck.

"If it's a dream, it is the best dream I've ever had . . ."

He took her earlobe in his teeth and warmed it with his tongue.

"And I'd . . . be perfectly fine never waking up again."

Peter's new favorite shirt fell to the kitchen floor. His hands ran down Sam's bare back, and, with that touch, breakfast would have to wait. They had let so many things get in the way, even if they'd yet to figure out the details, they both needed each other in the most desperate way.

They eventually ate breakfast, took a shower, and dressed for their day in New York. Peter called it "Playing Tourist for a Day." They were going to take in all the tourist spots, some of which neither of them had ever seen despite Sam's having been to New York several times and Peter being a local now. They hailed cabs and gladly waited in lines. The Empire State Building line was insane, but it was a great place to people watch, and they honestly didn't care as long as they were together. Sam and Peter held hands, looked in windows, and gawked at the landmarks that made New

York such a famous city. It was fun being a tourist and time truly stood still. It was as if they were two young lovers on vacation, isolated and suspended.

They split a pastrami sandwich at Katz's Deli and walked for miles in Central Park. The weather was warm, and they sat on a bench to talk like they had done their entire lives. It was a perfect day, and even though she knew it made no sense, Sam never wanted to go home. Home was complicated. Her relationship with Peter was complicated, and there were still things that would crop up and get in their way, but in New York they were off to a brilliant start.

Later that evening, they were at the Drama Desk Awards. That afternoon Sam had found a great Elie Saab dress. It was sheer black, and she bought a pair of strappy heels to go with it. She wore her hair loosely back, exposing her neck. She felt sexy and sophisticated, inspired by the city and by being with Peter in his element. Sam met new people and was so proud of the things they were saying about Peter and his work. He was well respected and so humble. Sam was relieved to be off her feet as soon as the driver closed the door to the car. Peter pulled her legs onto his lap.

"You are breathtaking tonight. I mean I know that's overused, but there were times I looked across the room at you and actually couldn't take a breath."

"And you were brilliant. Cute too, but brilliant. You belong here and your play, well now that you know I saw it, I can honestly say it is relevant, touching work, Peter."

"Didn't win."

He started rubbing her feet.

"Oh, poor baby. What's that they say about just being nominated?"

Peter laughed.

"Did you have a good time?"

"I had a great time. I always have a great time . . ."

He leaned in to kiss her, had to taste her. Peter touched the soft skin of her neck, and Sam felt like she was falling into a deep well.

She knew he would catch her, knew he loved her, but what if he didn't, couldn't catch her? She pulled her legs off his lap and put her shoes back on.

"Sam, what's wrong?"

"Nothing. I, I needed to sit up. My head was spinning and I was . . ."

"Happy?"

She tried to smile.

"Yes, of course I'm happy. I really need to be careful. We were going to take it slow, remember?"

"Sam, be happy. We will still be happy back in Pasadena. I'm not letting go. I promised."

"I know, and it's really not bothering me, it feels, it feels like we could just live this way forever, but . . ."

"Why can't we? Haven't we wasted enough time, Sam? This, this is so right."

"It is, but it feels like a storm, too strong sometimes. I try to keep everything where I can control it. I like control these days, you know? I find myself needing you desperately and that's hard to control."

Peter took her hand.

"I need you too. It's a good storm, Sam. Whatever is up ahead, we will be fine."

Peter could feel her fear, see it when she didn't think he was looking. It killed him every time, but all he could do was keep moving forward, show her their future.

When they arrived back at the apartment, Peter closed the door as she tossed her purse on the table. They were just like any other couple coming home after a night out.

Peter turned Sam in the entry and kissed her. It became more as he pulled the few pins out of her hair that held it slightly off her neck. He touched her shoulder, caressing her with only the tips of his fingers, and then found her lips again. They backed out of the entry, still tangled in touching, and hit a wall. Sam's hands climbed into Peter's hair. Peter pulled back from the kiss, looked deep into her eyes, and began to understand what Sam meant by a storm. He saw it in her face.

"Sam."

"I . . . I need . . ." fell out of her mouth.

"I know."

He ran his hands up her back and, as her dress hit the floor, Sam stood there in nothing but La Perla and Ferragamo. Peter touched the delicate lace of her bra. Slowly.

"You are so . . . oh, Christ."

Sam knew the feeling. Peter lifted her gently, she wrapped him in her legs and the need. They simply drowned in the need.

Exhausted they collapsed down the wall. Sam laughed and Peter opened one eye.

"What? Are you seriously laughing after that? That was a world-rocking, heart racing, up against the wall explosion and you, you're giggling?"

She covered her mouth.

"Sorry. I was just wondering if this tops the black dress I wore the night you rescued me from Harrison?"

His head fell back, still hoping for a full breath, and he tried to imagine seventeen-year-old Peter.

"Thank God you saved this for our adult life. I would have gone up in flames back then."

Sam kissed him, still laughing, and then untangled herself.

"Are those shoes, by any chance, comfortable? Because it would be all right if you never took them off. You know like jeans and those shoes, sweatpants and the shoes, or hell, only those pieces of lace and the shoes, forever."

"I think that would get old."

She smiled and made sure to bend slowly when she reached for and slipped into his jacket.

"I don't think it would get old. Ever."

Peter zipped his pants, ran his hands over his face, and looked at Sam standing in his tuxedo jacket.

"That's a great look too."

"For that, I'm going to cook for you in the shoes. Follow me."

She pulled on his pant loop having the very best time being the sexy siren. Sam felt powerful and so comfortable.

She made omelets that they ate in bed. Sam fell asleep curled into Peter as the sun began to peek over the skyline. As Peter watched her slide into sleep, he kissed her forehead and knew he would never see anything more beautiful for the rest of his life. She was it for him, and his heart felt as if it rolled in his chest.

Chapter Twenty-Two

*P*eter came out of the shower the next morning, and Sam was awake, but still in bed. She was looking around his room and smiling.

"Tell me something I don't know," she said.

"Oh God, I remember this game. Okay, give me a minute."

Peter dropped his towel and climbed back into bed next to her warm body.

"Oh, here's one, I eat the same breakfast now, every morning. Well, this morning and yesterday morning were a pleasant surprise, but every morning that I don't begin making love to you . . . I eat the same breakfast."

Sam turned to face him.

"Give it up, what's the breakfast?"

"Raisin Bran, bananas, and strawberries."

"Every morning?"

"Every morning."

"What if you run out of bananas, or you forget to pick up Raisin Bran?"

"I don't."

She laughed right as Peter continued, "Tell me something I don't know."

"Hmm . . . I, I count in Italian during my spin class."

"Excuse me?"

"Seriously, it takes my mind off the pain, and I can count to a hundred now. It's like the ultimate multitask."

Peter laughed and imagined her in spin class. She had never done that when he knew her. Then he started picturing her all hot and sweaty and counting in Italian, and he had to stop thinking or they would never get through the game.

"Tell me something I don't know," she said.

"I stole your sweatshirt when I left for New York. A little deranged, I'll admit, but something you don't know."

"Which one?"

"You had so many I knew you wouldn't miss it. It's the UCLA one with the bear on the front, has a hood, royal blue."

"I loved that one."

"You didn't even know it was gone."

"Did too. I assumed I lost it."

Sam sat up, holding the sheets to her chest.

"You left it in my car and I took it with me. Now I'll get super creepy."

Peter folded his arms behind his head and looked at her sitting in his bed all rumpled and was sure he was smiling like an idiot.

"It smelled like you for a while, and when I missed you, which was often, at least I had the sweatshirt."

"Peter."

Her heart swelled.

"Yeah, well it doesn't smell like you anymore."

"We can remedy that. Where is it?"

"Top shelf in the closet, left side."

Sam got out of bed completely naked and walked to the closet. Found the sweatshirt and put it on.

"It's much better with you in it, especially like that. Please get back over here."

She crawled back on the bed and kissed him, her lover, the slow lazy kiss of two people connected. Peter rolled over until she was beneath him and wrapped in his arms.

"Tell me something I don't know."

"You could've had me in the sweatshirt all along. After that night, after we were together, I would have gone to the end of the earth with you."

"You say that now, but at the time, we were young and you had . . ."

"That's why the game is Tell Me Something I Don't Know. You didn't see it, or you didn't look, but I'm telling you now that no matter what you thought, no matter where you needed to go, I would have. Not easy for me to admit, considering how it played out, but I was so in love with you."

"Sam."

"You don't need to say anything. I'm only playing the game."

"But I do, I'm sorry. I couldn't find a way to be with you. I needed to be more, I needed out, so I could find myself. I took a piece of you with me first, and that wasn't fair. But you are rooted in home, you would have missed your family. And even though I put us both through hell, look what we have now."

"Maybe it's easier for you now. You've enjoyed being home, admit it."

"I have. It's been great working in the Playhouse, but mostly it's been great being with you. Even when we were fighting, it was better than nothing."

"Have you dated a lot of women?"

"Whoa, left field."

They both laughed.

"Should we be naked when we have this conversation?"

She wasn't letting him out of it, so he answered truthfully.

"Yes, I've dated and had women in my life."

Sam said nothing, so he added, "And you clearly have had men. A firefighter no less. I will say that Brian was a surprise and not the kind of guy I expected you to date."

"See how you did that? Moved right off my questions about the women you've dated and on to Brian."

She said pointing a finger at him.

"Well, Brian is pretty hard to forget. What do you think that guy benches?"

She laughed.

"He's lovely, and not only because of his body, although that's lovely too."

"Really? I'm naked here."

Sam crawled on top of him.

"Aww, is someone feeling threatened, do you need me tell you how much I love your body, Peter?"

Peter's breath caught as her hands moved down his chest.

"I, well, if something comes to mind. I have all afternoon. I mean I should finish this damn play, and we do have a flight to catch at some point, but maybe . . . you do what you need to do."

"Should I start at your feet or the top of your head? I was thinking I would do a running narrative?"

She kissed his neck, and Peter no longer cared where she started, as long as she kept going. She stopped right above his navel, covers draping her head, looking so damn adorable, he almost burst.

"Hey, Peter."

"Yeah, Sam," he managed as her hands grabbed the sheets.

"Probably best that we don't talk about those other women. I don't need to know."

Peter laughed as her head went back under the covers.

"What other women? I can't remember a single one of them."

And just like that she undid him once again.

They arrived back in Pasadena late that night, and they both needed to be at the theater the next morning. Peter dropped Sam off at her house. After spending three nights in Peter's bed, Sam felt odd sleeping alone, and it bothered her. She was already attached. She told herself to stop whining as her body begged for some much-needed sleep. Sam closed her eyes and allowed herself to be happy. What's that saying that used to hang in her grandmother's house? *With Love, All Things Are Possible.* Sam sure hoped so.

Peter floated back to his mother's house and deflated once he walked through the door. The weight was immediate and all he wanted to do was get back on that plane with Sam. Go back to his apartment, back into her arms, but it was time to start figuring this out, meshing the two worlds. There was no going back now. He loved her to desperation and he would make it work. Peter checked to make sure his mother had made it to her room and went to bed.

Chapter Twenty-Three

Sam had spent only a couple of days at the theater since getting back from New York. The rest of the week she had been in the office working on promotional materials and press releases for *Looking In*. The graphic designer they were working with really understood Peter's play and Sam was hoping the proof would be in before they left for Cynthia's wedding. She and Peter had gone to dinner with Sam's parents. They held hands, and her mother and father moved past cautiously optimistic to thrilled that Sam and Peter had finally figured it out.

Peter told his mother they were dating, but he wasn't sure how much actually registered through her drunken fog. He spent most nights at Sam's house, and they had gone on a couple of actual dates. They drove into the city over the weekend and saw a play they had both wanted to see at a small local house. Peter was amazed that even in Pasadena they were the same couple they'd been in New York, but their lifetime of friendship and memories made it even better. It was and felt wonderful. Sam told herself the lingering feeling that all of this was temporary was only negative thinking. They even went out for drinks with Grady and one of his Barbie Dolls the night before. They had fun together. The three of them, all grown up: life seemed to be finally moving forward.

It was Saturday morning. At this point in rehearsals, Sam was there to help with just about anything. Yesterday, Gordon had asked her to stand on certain marks for about an hour while he adjusted angles and made some last-minute changes to his lighting design. This morning, Carmen gave Sam a few pages of dialogue and asked her to sit in the balcony and follow along. They needed to make sure that all props were created and onstage during the scene. If anything was missing, Sam would circle it, and they would figure it out later. She walked through the house seats. It was early. The smell of coffee and sounds of low grumbling voices were soothing. Peter and Spencer were seated in their usual spots discussing something about the color of a door. Sam walked past them and Peter smiled mid-sentence. It was as if they coursed through one another, like a beautiful, much-needed storm. Sam climbed the stairs and sat at the edge of the balcony. She was alone. There were no house lights, only the glow of lighting directed at the stage. Sam loved the theater, this theater. She looked at the pages Carmen had given her as the actors came on the stage.

"Good morning, all," Spencer said, throwing his glasses on the table and walking toward the stage.

"Thank you for being on time this morning. We're in for a long day, so I need a lot of energy. We're going to circle back to Act I, Scene 4 for about an hour. We need to rework some of the blocking. Please see my additional notes from last night's rehearsal."

With that, he handed pages to each of the actors.

"This is a huge scene. Yeah, I know I say that about all of them, but this is where the audience sees Phillip break. We need to show the tenderness and still keep the humor that runs throughout the play. We don't want this to be too depressing, but we are talking about a young man who lost his father to suicide."

Hearing Peter's life discussed in such literal terms was bizarre. Step here, look this way, and cry because your father killed himself. It was strange listening to his life, or a piece of it, discussed in terms of lighting and stage presence. It had to be weird for him, or maybe it wasn't. Maybe he liked it this way, removed and distant. From the balcony Sam couldn't see Peter—probably just as well. Spencer jumped off the stage, the actors took their places, and she read along.

(Sally enters SL. She is a seventeen-year-old girl, hair in a ponytail, wearing shorts and a sweatshirt. She looks around and sits in the first row of the balcony seats of the quiet theater. It's Monday, the theater is dark. Sally crosses her legs, breathes deeply and closes her eyes. Phillip enters from the audience. He is a seventeen-year-old boy. He's wearing jeans and a sweatshirt. Phillip runs up the house stairs, SR of the actual stage. Stops center stage, which would put him in the house seats of the theater depicted onstage. He does not see Sally. He hunches over halfway down the center aisle, hands on knees, and begins to cry.

Sally hears something, sits up, looks over the balcony railing, and sees Phillip lit by the dim house lights. Phillip falls to the ground in a ball. He is sobbing. Sally leaves the balcony and runs to him.)

Sally: Phillip? *(Sally calls to him as she approaches from behind. Phillip is startled, jumps to his feet, and quickly wipes his eyes. Tears still stream down his face.)*

Phillip: Sally, Jesus . . . you scared me. I was . . . I needed to . . . why are you here?

Sally: *(Sally crosses SL to Phillip.)* Are you all right? I mean I know you're not all right, but . . . did something happen? Is your mom . . .

Phillip: *(looking uncomfortable)* She's fine. I really needed to get out of there. My aunt is over and they're going through my dad's things and I . . . *(Phillip begins to sob again. Sally puts her arms around him.)*

Sally: It's all right. Phillip, you need to be sad. It's okay. *(Phillip holds her tight and cries.)* You know, I was worried when you didn't cry at the funeral last week. I guess this is it. I'm so sorry. I know how close you were and . . .

(Phillip continues to hug her and then pulls back to see Sally's face. She wipes the tears from his eyes, he brushes her bangs off her face, and they linger, looking at each other for several beats.)

Phillip: You didn't tell me why you're here.

Sally: Oh, well it sounds stupid compared to what you're going through, but I needed to get away too. Mrs. Mason is over for lunch, and we are playing the "Let's Dress Sally for Cotillion" game. I mean with everything that's gone on with your family? We need to be discussing ruffles, really? This dance is still going on? It's so weird. When they brought out the one that looks like a pink cake, I bolted. I needed some fresh air.*(Phillip laughs, and they both sit in the theater seats on-stage, heads back, looking up at the ceiling.)* But who cares about that? You, your dad . . . do you miss him? Is that why you were crying?

Phillip: I, well, of course I miss him, but I couldn't sit there and watch them comb through his things. I don't know, I just feel like she killed him sometimes. You know with all her cars and clothes. I know he liked to prance around and brag too, but I think it all killed him and . . . it makes me sick sometimes. I know I'm part of it, but the man hasn't even been dead a week. He shot himself for Christ's sake, and you're already checking out his desk drawers? What's left of him? As if she didn't suck the life out of him while he was alive, now let's rummage through his shit. I'm sorry, sometimes I . . .

Sally: Don't be sorry. I'm sure your mom's probably trying. She's . . .

Phillip: Putting her affairs in order so she can get ready to snag another rich husband?

Again in the dark familiar theater, Sam looked away, tears welling in her eyes. Damn, these actors were good. Peter had walked to the front row and was sitting next to Spencer. This had to be a difficult scene not only to write, but also to watch. The pain Peter had to deal with their junior year in high school was really unimaginable, but for him and for Sam and Grady, it was all too real.

His father, Robert "Bob" Everoad, had been a huge, charismatic man with a booming voice. Sam loved going to Peter's house while his dad was alive. He had crazy stories about safaris and trips to the Galapagos Islands. He was like their very own Indiana Jones. Peter's mother, on the other hand, was a classic debutante, proper and social. She was friends with Sam's and Grady's mothers, but when they were kids Peter's mom always seemed like the leader of the group. Even though Bindi Malendar was married to a senator, April Everoad was known to throw the best parties, to wear the most perfect dresses. She always erred on the side of propriety and in so doing she came across as cold and controlling. Grady used to say, "We could keep a six-pack cold on Mrs. Everoad's ass," and he was right. She was about five years younger than her husband and while he was alive, she was the social scene. She was a good mother to Peter and Cynthia, but Sam always got the feeling they were treated more as extensions of the family name rather than as individual people.

Mr. Everoad had married later in life and was quite successful in banking and investments. He was a self-made man and people could tell. Unlike most of the trust-fund parents in Pasadena, he was so normal and likable. He too hung out with Senator Malendar and Sam's dad. They went on fishing trips and barbecued. Peter loved and idolized his father. When his dad wasn't working they did everything together. Yet by his junior year it seemed as if all his father did was work. Peter became angry, convinced his father was struggling to keep his mother in diamonds and BMWs. He resented her and then he came home from school after rehearsals for a school play to the paramedics at his house. Mr. Everoad had killed himself in his study. No note, just all of their financial papers on his desk. He'd lost millions in investments, but it didn't make any sense, they were still quite wealthy. Sam had heard her father talking to friends about Bob's depression, saying something about how maybe his medication was off. There were rumors that he was devastated about a bad land deal. Whatever the reason, something took over his spirit, their neighborhood lost a great man, and Peter lost his dad.

His father's body, zipped up in a body bag, was being wheeled into the ambulance by the time Peter arrived. That was the day Peter's world shattered, yet from that day until the day now being played out on the stage, Peter had never cried. He went through the entire funeral and the days that followed without one tear. Even after he finally cried with Sam in the theater, he was still shut off for months, and there was nothing Sam or Grady could do for a while. Peter eventually emerged as they approached high school graduation, but he was never the same. He was always a unique and funny guy, but he became uncomfortable and agitated, he wrote volumes and he . . . changed.

Once they went to UCLA, Peter blossomed out of the confines and beyond the eyes of Pasadena. He still had Sam, but the rest of the school knew him for his writing, and no one knew enough about his life to feel pity. There were plenty of holidays Sam had to drag Peter home, but he came. She was the bridge between his new world and their past. Sam always told him he had to take care of his roots, even if he didn't like where he was planted.

"Roots help the plant grow. You can't make it without them," she would say.

He'd laugh at her and say, "Mine are a pain in the ass. What's wrong with wanting a different pot?"

Thinking about it now, Sam looked over at Peter. He sensed her stare and met her eyes. Peter smiled at her and she was filled with pride and love. He had survived, had grown in New York, and returned to her. She looked at her notes and felt the pain and doubt fall away. Peter was hers and she was his. It was time to stop questioning.

Chapter Twenty-Four

Catalina Island had always been a special place. Sam's father had practically grown up on the island; it's where he had proposed to her mother. It was nothing short of romantic folklore that her grandparents fell madly in love on Catalina. The island had been an important place for her family, immediate and extended, for as long as Sam could remember.

Until their children went to college, the Cathners had vacationed there with the Malendars and the Everoads at least once every summer and always over the long Labor Day weekend. Even after Peter's father had died, Mrs. Everoad brought Peter and Cynthia. For years she just stayed up in their house overlooking Avalon, but after some time she joined Sam's mother and Bindi for walks on the pier and lunch at the country club. Catalina was a healing place, and when Sam was on the island, even as a grown woman, she felt as if anything were possible.

Cynthia Leigh Everoad was going to marry Alan Christian Ferrimore the week Peter and Sam arrived on Catalina. Alan was the sort of man that women never really swooned over, but nevertheless wanted to marry. He was educated, successful, trilingual, and very wealthy. Raised in Connecticut, Alan came to the West

Coast for college and, as the story goes, was in love with Cynthia at first sight. Alan annoyed Sam; to be honest he annoyed everyone and that may have even included Cynthia. He was a slightly less anal version of the Daniel Day Lewis character in the Merchant and Ivory adaptation of *A Room with a View*. He was tight and awkward, but he worshipped Cynthia, and she deserved to be worshipped.

Cynthia was a stunning woman. On the boat ride over to Catalina, Sam tried to imagine how beautiful she would look in her wedding dress. She had a version of Peter's green eyes, but her mother's pale complexion and blonde hair. Unlike Peter, she was frail, a dancer, and Sam always felt the urge to feed her. She was tiny and like her mother, always impeccably dressed.

When they were growing up, Sam had always felt a little envious of Cynthia because everything was mapped out for her, and she didn't seem to mind. Whatever was put in front of her, she went along with it. Her mother had her in cotillion and cooking classes; she even made aprons one year as Christmas gifts. She was pretty damn perfect, never complained, and never wanted more. For as long as Sam could remember Cynthia had been set to get married, have a home, and raise a family. As Sam got older she realized what she envied was the simplicity. There's something to be said for simple. Sam's mind never worked that way.

Sam's parents were a little looser with the reins growing up. She liked to play basketball with her brother, her two best friends were guys, and while she dressed up well and smiled through all her cotillion classes, Sam had always preferred jeans and the theater. All she ever really thought about growing up was being an actress. She never entertained the idea of marriage until after college. Making a decent omelet was the extent of her cooking expertise. Sam liked her life, but it was full of choices, and choices often turned into mistakes.

Sam and Peter came over on the ferry together. Their families had arrived a day early by plane. There were some last-minute program changes at the Playhouse before everything was sent to the printer, so Sam and Peter needed an extra day. Their relationship was handling the stress of the production and even though Peter seemed distracted and had flown back to New York because they had lost a principal actor from the cast of his first play, things were good.

Candice had given Sam the week off. Their Friday meeting had been productive. She and Candice discussed the upcoming season following the already sold-out run of *Looking In*. She was optimistic that the Playhouse would be stronger than ever. But now, taking in a deep breath of sea air, Sam was ready for a week away with her family and Peter. On Catalina the past and present seemed to blend together nicely like in a rich painting.

Peter waved off the driver sent to meet them. They wheeled their bags toward the house. They did it each time they came to Catalina together, yet Peter's mother continued to send Terry in his stretch golf cart to pick them up. It had become a game. Terry always joked that someday they would be too old and would accept the ride from him.

Peter had felt a weight lift as soon as they stepped onto the island. The wind blew through Sam's dark hair, and he knew her nose would freckle by tomorrow morning. Everything about her was like the island, warmth and fun, mixed with history and stunning beauty.

"What's behind that smile, Peter Everoad?"

"I'm realizing there are so many things to smile about, but right this minute, this smile? This is a 'you're all windswept-flushed, and how long before I can kiss you senseless?' smile."

"Well, that's a very good smile."

She kissed him, lingering.

"If you want more of that, as is tradition, you'll have to race me home."

"Oh, come on. Are you kidding me? Aren't we too old for this?"

"Tradition is tradition. It's bad luck to start a Catalina trip any other way. Think about your sister's happiness."

"What does that . . . oh, forget it."

They took off running, bags wheeling behind them. Sam had to stop midway and take off her shoes. She was so full of life and as her feet felt the sand that had escaped the beach, she knew it was possible for the past to resolve itself. Even the deepest wounds healed. They ran out of breath and bent over laughing halfway up the hill to Peter's family home. They were happy and that was more than enough.

Chapter Twenty-Five

Two days later, following a rehearsal dinner at the country club and a combination bachelorette and bachelor's party, Sam took her seat at the wedding. Guests quietly visited and found their seats among the white chairs set up on Descanso Beach right as the sun began to dip into the ocean. The string quartet glided through Bach's Cello Suite in G major even as their sheet music tried to escape in the ocean breeze. The aisle was lined with bright coral roses and delicate pale orchids. Alan stood by his best man and groomsmen next to a huge arch that framed the ocean view with a burst of more of the same blooms. Grady walked down the aisle and took his seat in front of Sam, next to his parents.

He turned around, saying, "Peter looks good. Doesn't seem nearly as nervous as poor Alan does."

Sam was taken in by the setting, and she was already starting to tear up. Even though she'd never imagined herself the bride, she enjoyed weddings. They were the ultimate beginning, and she always loved the beginning.

"Oh Christ, are you starting with the tears already?"

She opened her eyes wide, trying to contain the tears, and smacked Grady's arm.

"Just turn around. You're making me cry."

"I'm making you cry. Okay, that makes no sense, but I'll do as I'm told."

He laughed and turned around as her father joined her and her mother approached from the front of the aisle after kissing April Everoad. The sun was now setting and huge candles filled the darkness with the most romantic glow. The quartet began playing Pachelbel's Canon in D and everyone stood for the bride.

Cynthia looked iridescent in a soft, white, strapless gown that had the slightest shimmer and hugged her body right to her tiny waist. It then blew out into a full skirt with a small train. Her hair was swept to one side. Even beneath her veil, she was radiant, a perfect bride. Peter's mother stood surrounded by her two sisters and other relatives who had flown in for the wedding.

The guests were looking at the bride and taking in the gorgeous setting, but Sam's eyes were on Peter. The wind messed his hair as he confidently walked his sister down the aisle toward a married adult life with a man who clearly adored her. It struck Sam what a rare opportunity it was to know a person his entire life. She had been there when Peter lost his father and she was here now, watching him assume that responsibility and give his sister away. Most people meet the man they love in college or at their job, but Sam had known all the phases of Peter.

Walking Cynthia toward her fiancé, Peter felt calm. He held her arm and noticed she was shaking just under the surface. He was proud to be there for her. Somewhere deeper he knew he was there for his father. He would have expected Peter to be a man and give his sister away, honor the family. As the ocean breeze caressed Cynthia's veil, Peter knew it all still mattered. His home, his family, his father, it was a deep-rooted part of him, and it always would be. Maybe it was being with Sam, maybe it was the island, but Peter welcomed the peace.

They approached the flower arch, and Peter saw his mother squeeze her sister's hand. She looked vulnerable. As often happened, Peter wondered what she was thinking, if she was proud or sad. Had she found some shred of happiness? He would never know.

Cynthia looked up at him with such hope, just as she had when she still wore pigtails. Peter gently passed her hand to Alan's and turned to take his seat. Cynthia stopped him, gave him a real hug, and whispered, "I love you and thank you."

Peter kissed her cheek and took the seat next to his mother. He had no idea where it came from, but Peter held his mother's hand and kissed it. She looked at him, smiled through her tears. He allowed himself to feel, and in that moment, he wished things had been different.

Peter watched his sister get married and realized his heart broke for the pain they had gone through. Not the pain everyone witnessed, but the pain only they knew, experienced together. The quiet pain of lying in their rooms as already confused teenagers and wondering what happened to their world, how their family was ever going to be whole again. But here they were on this moonlit evening at a very happy time in Cynthia's life and they were fine. Even though the absence of their father loomed over her walk down the aisle, Cynthia seemed happy, and Peter was alive and feeling again. It was painful, but his sense of calm made it bearable. He glanced back at Sam, took in the evening, the importance of what he had just done, and realized that these times were well worth the messy parts in life.

Sam remembered her father saying Peter's father "got twisted up." Looking at Peter's face now as he lovingly watched his sister, Sam felt sorry for his father, sorry that he could not make it through and be here for his daughter. Could not sit next to his wife and relish in the strong and wonderful man his son had become. The guests stood as Cynthia and Alan sealed their marriage with a kiss. Pretty passionate too, who knew Alan had it in him?

The reception was in the ballroom of the casino. The entire wedding party carried candles and followed the bride and groom along the walk from Descanso to their grand party. It reminded Sam of an old English wedding where the party walks in procession throughout the town. The air became crisp and Peter draped his jacket over Sam's shoulders. Her parents walked up next to them and Jack put his arm around Peter.

"Great wedding."

"Yes, it was, exactly what she wanted, and she looks so happy," Peter said, taking a deep breath.

"Were you nervous up there?"

"I was before the wedding started, but once she took my arm, it was weird, but it was only the two of us."

"I thought you did a terrific job," Sam's mother said, as she tried to keep her candle from blowing out.

"Peter, I'm proud of you and . . ." Jack said as he stopped Peter, pulled him aside, "and your dad would have been too. You're a fine, fine young man. We may not be able to see him, but he's here. Looking down on you and your sister, your mom, and he's so proud. I can feel it."

Peter hugged him, and right as Sam's eyes filled with tears again, Grady arrived with the comic relief.

"Can you believe that sexy mermaid above the entrance is your grandmother? Kinda weird, right?"

Sam laughed and Grady put his arm around her.

"Jesus, is this a wedding or a wake? Wipe those tears, gorgeous, and let's see if we can get Alan drunk."

Peter came up next to Grady.

"Couldn't have done it better myself, man. Great ceremony. I mean it," Grady said, patting Peter on the back.

"Thanks."

Grady put his other arm around Peter.

"Now, enough with the warm and fuzzies. I need a drink and a lonely bridesmaid."

They all laughed and walked into the casino, the three of them, together again.

There really were not words to describe the reception. The ballroom looked like a wonderland. April had hired some hotshot wedding planner for Cynthia, and no expense had been spared.

Blush linens draped each table to the floor. Candles, circled with delicate orchids, sat on each table. The candles each guest brought from the wedding were placed in a huge centerpiece at the wedding party's table. The glow of all of those candles seemed to warm the bride and groom. It was a great touch. The lights in the ballroom were dim and it looked like the entire room was lit by candlelight. All of the floor-to-ceiling doors were open to the circular balcony and the cool night air. There were sheer panels of darker blush framing each door, tied at the sides with more flowers. The balcony that circled the entire ballroom and looked out to the ocean was also lined with candles and bouquets.

The ballroom began to fill with laughter and so many people from the couple's life: Cynthia's friends from college, Alan's colleagues, and a fairly large, older set that Sam was certain were friends of parents on both sides. Sam greeted some guests from Pasadena and recognized several of Cynthia's friends from the shower. Peter walked over to his mother, who was sitting at the table with the Malendars and drinking sparkling water. She was off to a good start. Peter had spoken with her earlier and she had agreed to not drink at the reception. She'd had a couple of Bloody Marys with breakfast but had fully agreed that she wanted to be present, alive, for her daughter's wedding and would not drink herself otherwise. She looked lovely in aqua blue. She was laughing at some story Grady's mother was telling. Peter had faint memories of his mother this way, sober and genuine. He would miss her when the wedding was over and she chose to climb back into the bottle.

Sam ordered drinks with Grady, and they joined Peter at the table next to all of their parents. Peter pulled open his bow tie and Grady did the same. They were different in so many ways, but they shared a familiarity that only boys who grew up together possessed.

"Okay, the maid of honor is off limits," Grady said.

"Married?" Sam asked, as Peter pulled out a chair for her.

"No, but I'm waiting for our drinks, and we start talking. She seems normal and has incredible legs; I'm off to a good start. She then proceeds to tell me that she loves the bride's dress and her own wedding dress is quite similar."

Peter and Sam both look puzzled.

"She's engaged?"

"Nope, that's where it turns. Not only is her wedding dress bought and paid for, but the shoes too, and she's on the mailing list for all the most popular honeymoon spots, that's what she says. Just waiting for the right guy, she says batting her eyelashes at me. Christ, I started to sweat."

Peter and Sam laughed.

The wedding party was seated. A woman in a great Armani suit, who Sam assumed was the wedding planner, asked everyone else to take a seat for the speeches. The best man, a tall redhead with glasses, made a brief and funny speech. After the applause, Peter sensed he was on, took a deep breath, stood, clinked his glass and said: "Thank you all for coming tonight. It certainly is a happy time for our families and close friends to join Cynthia and Alan as they begin their lives together."

Peter cleared his throat and willed his nerves away.

"Cyn, being here on Catalina brings back so many great memories. I can hardly believe, looking at you now, that you were that little blonde tagalong I rowed around this harbor. You've grown into such a beautiful and loving woman. You make our family proud every day. We love you."

Cynthia blew him a kiss. Peter didn't realize at first that he did it, but his hand went to his heart as he looked back at his sister. Their father used to do that. He would say his "heart ached with love." Peter let the chill hit his spine and continued.

"Alan, first of all, who knew you had that passionate kiss in you? Wow, man, nicely done!"

Everyone laughed, and Alan blushed.

"But seriously, you are a good, honest man, and those are harder and harder to come by. You respect and love my sister and for that I thank you. To quote one of my favorite American poets, Nikki Giovanni, 'We love because it's the only true adventure.' May you both cherish what makes the other unique and share a life built on love, trust, and that kiss."

Laughs again and with that Peter raised his glass, and they all toasted the bride and groom. Cynthia dried her tears.

Following dinner, they ate cake and Mr. and Mrs. Ferrimore danced their first dance to "Awake" by Josh Groban. The sounds of the orchestra spilled out of the ballroom as Cynthia and Alan twirled around the dance floor. It was such a winsome image that Sam felt for a second like she was in a dream. They both looked so in sync and delighted with each other. If this evening represented marriage, everyone should be clamoring for the altar. The realist in her knew love was complicated and didn't always work out, but for tonight she enjoyed the magic of two people finding each other and having the courage to start the adventure. It was a phenomenal wedding.

Peter led Sam onto the dance floor, placed his hand on her lower back to pull her close. Peter nestled into her neck and gently led her through a dance.

"I feel like I've barely seen you all night. Have I told you you're stunning, yet?"

"You've been busy with the wedding and the guests. Speaking of the wedding, my God, did you see the sunset right as the ceremony started?" Sam sighed.

"I love weddings, beginnings, but sunsets are my favorite time of day. Doesn't make any sense, does it?"

"It makes perfect sense. You love it all, Sam."

Her cheeks flushed in the night air and Peter tried to remember how to dance as his throat knotted. She was so free, open, and in spite of it all, in love with him. For an instant he wondered what he had done right in his life to deserve her again.

"Oh, and to answer your question, yes, you did tell me I looked stunning, right before the wedding started. You never fail to make me feel cherished these days."

Peter took a deep breath.

"Making up for lost time."

He squeezed her in closer.

"Let me know if I start slipping."

"Oh, believe me, I will."

They both laughed as he swept her past the orchestra. Peter looked into her eyes. They were still dancing as he cradled her face. He looked into her, hoping he was giving her whatever she needed to calm her heart and allow him to stay.

"I love you. I love you so much," he said, hovering near her mouth.

He kissed her. A tender, pulling kiss that had most of the people at the wedding turning from the bride and groom for just a moment. Many of these people had watched them grow up together. Many now saw them in a different light. It was such a long time coming for Sam that she simply kissed him back. In that one dance, that one kiss, the past slipped farther away.

"I love you too," she whispered.

Chapter Twenty-Six

Wrapped in a blanket and still in their wedding wear, Peter and Sam played Scrabble on his patio after the wedding. She played a word worth eighty-nine points, and then Peter stood, swept her into his arms, and took her to bed. Normally Sam would argue he was being a sore loser, but curled into his neck, she couldn't care less.

Peter slowly took off Sam's shoes and moved his way up her body. It wasn't urgent or restless, but the slow, relaxed touch, caress, and ecstasy of two people letting each other into places no one had ever been. Peter took his time exploring every inch of her in the glow of moonlight. He held her face, stroked her hair, and kissed her slowly, deeply. Her entire body let go. Right when she thought she had given him everything, she gave him more. Their bodies melted together in perfect unison and then slipped over the edge.

Sam lay on top of Peter, her head resting on his warm chest. She could barely hear his breath. His heart thumped quietly in concert.

"Sam."

"Hmm . . ."

"Remember when I asked you if you'd ever thought about marriage?"

He could feel her body tense. When she didn't respond, Peter gently rolled her next to him and pushed the hair off her face.

"What?"

"It's so all of sudden, you know. I mean, a couple of months ago, I was trying to figure out how I was going to see you again without passing out and now . . . now we're here. I'm with you, I love you, but I can't help feeling like somewhere a shoe is going to drop and I'm going to be left picking up the pieces."

Peter sighed and rolled on his back.

"I can't help it. I mean, you still live in New York. I live and work in Pasadena. I heard you on the phone last week talking about finishing up your next play."

Peter touched her and she sat up clutching the blanket to her chest.

"How is this going to work, Peter? Don't feed me flowery words or questions about my thoughts on marriage. Tell me how we are going to move this forward, in real tangible ways. How am I not eventually going to be standing in some doorway or at some airport saying goodbye?"

"Sam, we just got back from a wedding. We're naked. What do you want me to do, break out the yellow pad and start planning?"

She didn't laugh, so he pulled her back down, and hovered over her. Sam closed her eyes.

"Hey," he said, kissing her.

He could see a tear pooling.

"Hey, look at me."

Sam opened her eyes.

"I don't have a plan right now. I'm working and you're working. We will figure it out. I'm here right now. *Looking In* hasn't even opened yet. We will make a plan. I'm flying back and forth. We can continue to do that for a while."

Sam went to turn over and Peter held her.

"What do you want me to say? It's working, we are working. Why can't that be enough for now?"

Sam got out of bed and wrapped herself in a robe. She didn't know why. She was happy, but when he asked her again if she'd ever thought about marriage, something snapped. What was she doing? Was this going to end in happily ever after? Did she even believe in that anymore? Sam was a ball of confusion. Rather than open her mouth just to sound pathetic and needy, she got dressed.

"What? Where are you going?" Peter asked, getting up, and putting his jeans on.

"I'm going to head back to my parents' house. I'm sure I'll see you at breakfast in the morning. I've got some things to do."

"Sam."

She kept dressing, so he held her still.

"What's going on, why are you doing this? Please talk to me."

She didn't know what to say.

"I need to take a break for a minute, okay."

"Was it the marriage thing? I was only talking."

"I know. We do a lot of that . . . talking."

"What's that supposed to mean?"

Sam slipped into Peter's sweatshirt and her flip-flops, grabbed her dress, and walked toward the door.

"It doesn't mean anything, Peter. I just need some space tonight. Lots of emotions and we've been busy with the wedding."

She kissed him and left before he could offer to drive her home. Peter sat on the bed. He knew she was pulling away, but he had no idea why. *Terrific*, he thought. *A bunch of emotions and no explanation.* This must be what if felt like for her when he left. He didn't like it, but he would give her some space. He had no choice.

The next morning the wedding guests were on their own. Some of them rented boats or bikes. Others, including the bride and groom, slept in. Sam had barely closed her eyes. She finally gave up trying around seven o'clock. She pulled on her running shorts and laced up her shoes. She needed to sweat. Her mother and Henry were sitting at the dining room table with a laptop in front of them, when she came down the stairs. Henry was showing their mother something on YouTube. Probably a clip of a project he was working on, or some new filmmaker Henry was discovering. They both looked up, surprised to see Sam.

"Hey, didn't know you were here," Henry said, looking suspicious and concerned.

"Yeah, sorry. I got back late last night."

Sam tried for carefree, relaxed.

"Late? Sam, you haven't slept here since we got to the island. Why would you? What's going on?"

"Sam, honey, come sit. Is everything all right?"

She didn't know what to say, she didn't know what was wrong, other than this uneasy feeling that she was losing herself, that she was being swallowed up again. Her eyes burned from last night's tears, and Sam searched her mind for a way to explain as she stood next to her mother.

"I . . . I can't sit right now. I need to go for a run. Too much wedding cake."

She joked, but her mother and Henry still looked like they were waiting for an explanation.

"What? I felt like coming home last night. Is that no longer an option? Why are the two of you looking at me like that?"

Her mother stood up.

"Of course it's an option, don't be silly."

She hugged Sam.

"Good morning. We were just surprised to see you."

Her mother looked to Henry, unsure what to say.

"So, what gives? You and Peter have a fight?"

Henry cut right to the chase, and Sam began to move toward the door.

"No, not at all. I needed a little space, my own bed. You know? No . . . we're fine."

"Fine, huh?"

Henry took a sip of his coffee.

"Henry, stop. We're good. I need to run, I'll be back."

She kissed them both on the cheek and left before she'd have to continue talking about something she couldn't explain. Henry and her mother looked at each other. After a beat, he said: "Okay, well, that was weird."

"She's figuring things out. Leave her be, Henry."

With that they both returned to the laptop.

Sam ran down the three front steps of the house. It was a foggy morning. As the sea air hit her lungs, she woke up and took off running. By the time she reached Pebbly Beach Road, her lungs were burning. She stopped by the boat terminal to breathe. The sun was barely peeking through the marine layer, and Sam heard the horn of a boat leaving for the mainland. Sam remembered being a little girl and coming over on the same boat. She used to be afraid any time there were rough seas. Henry would tease her that it felt like the boat was in trouble. He would lean over and whisper: "If I were you, I'd start locating your life vest." Sam's eyes would get huge, she'd hold on to his arm, and then he would laugh and tickle her. Preparing to head up Claressa Avenue, toward the Wrigley Memorial, Sam realized she had never taken the boat to Catalina by herself. She was always with family, never had to worry about rough seas on her own. What did that say about her? She wasn't sure and she continued running.

Sam reached the entrance to the Wrigley Memorial and Botanic Garden. Her shirt was drenched and her breathing was steady. She felt energized and stronger. The thin gravel crunched beneath her feet, and the smell of blooms from the garden whispered in the morning air. A memorial to William Wrigley Jr., the chewing gum magnate and father of Catalina Island, loomed ahead. It was a massive structure created out of all of the materials that made up the island. Michael Cathner, Sam's grandfather, helped Mrs. Wrigley plan the memorial and Sam thought of her grandparents every time she saw it. They'd had a great romance, but it was not without bumps in the road and trouble. Sam's grandmother, Gwendolyn Ross, grew up during a time when women were only expected to be wives. She was spunky, graduated from Mount Holyoke, and seriously thought of becoming a doctor. Instead she modernized and expanded the island hospital. Sam remembered her grandmother always smelled like lavender, remembered she had an unbelievable laugh that took over her whole face. Sam's grandfather had big hands and always hated wearing his reading glasses, so she would read to him. They must have been scared as well, when they fell into the desperation and need of love, she thought. Or maybe not, maybe it was easy for them. Was it supposed to be easy?

God, Sam wished she was still naive. She longed for the girl who willingly wrapped her arms around Peter and simply gave in. She would never have her back. She'd been hurt and that scar would stay. Sam knew it made her stronger and she knew she loved Peter, could trust him even, but she felt as if she had climbed back onto the diving board. She was scared again.

At the top of the memorial, Sam looked through the arch out to Avalon.

"Incredible what one person can accomplish," Peter said from behind.

Sam spun around and saw him standing, hands in the pockets of his tan pants. He was wearing a jean button-up shirt, left out. He hadn't shaved and he looked tired.

"What?"

She held her hand to her chest to ease the surprise.

"How did you know I was here?"

"I went by your house. Your mother said you went for a run. I knew you'd come here. I took the golf cart. Rough night, so I didn't feel like running."

His mouth curved just a little as he walked toward her.

"Yeah," Sam took a deep breath.

"Sorry about the rough night."

"You don't need to be sorry."

He stood behind her and gently ran his hands up her arms.

"I'm sweaty."

"I can see that."

He kissed the back of her neck.

"Do you want to talk about anything?"

"Sure, what's your next play about?"

"Whoa, not what I expected."

Sam smiled, and they both kept looking through the arch out to sea.

"I'm tired of talking about the past, our past, people in the past. I want to look ahead. What's coming up, instead of what's already happened."

"Okay. It's a comedy."

"Thank God!"

They both laughed.

"Yeah, I thought so too. I'm getting a little tired of myself. Too much introspection is not always a good thing."

"I'm getting a little tired of you too."

"Are you now?" he joked, turning her around for a kiss.

"Not completely, but you're pushing it."

Sam took his hand, and they started back toward the gardens.

"Tell me about it, where does it take place?"

"It's about four men. They play chess at the Chinese Culture Center of San Francisco. Four different nationalities, four different backgrounds, and chess."

"Doesn't sound like a comedy."

"Oh, it is. It's funny, but of course there's a message."

"Of course. You wouldn't be you, if there weren't some sort of message or lesson."

They walked through the vast collection of indigenous and imported trees and plants, then stopped for a while to marvel at the hundreds of different cacti that formed only a small part of the entire garden. Peter noticed he was again standing in a garden with Sam. They'd both always liked gardens, were both interested in collections and different regions. Maybe that came from growing up in California or maybe it was simply something else they shared. Sam seemed less agitated, more at ease, and Peter let their conversation from last night lie. He was sure she still had doubts or fears, but she was still with him, moving forward. She didn't want to talk about it, and he didn't push.

Peter gave Sam a ride back into town, and they talked about *Looking In* and the upcoming premiere. They would be flying back to Pasadena in the morning, and Peter would again fly back to New York later that week for meetings and to check in on the play there, as it had been picked up for six more weeks on Broadway. Sam decided to head back to her house. At the wedding reception, Henry had mentioned wanting to take her sailing before they left the island. She felt like taking him up on that offer. Peter was going to meet Grady at the country club before he left to head back to Los Angeles.

Peter kissed her outside the Cathner house.

"Movie tonight?"

"What's playing?"

"Does it even matter? You only go there for the theater and snacks."

"True. Sure, we'll have Movie Dinner, so don't eat before you pick me up."

"Ugh, I'm always sick after Movie Dinner."

"Your point? It's . . ."

"Tradition, I know. I'll pick you up at seven, and we'll walk over. I'll even spring for the M&M'S."

"You are a prince."

Sam kissed him again and turned toward the door. Peter started to walk away when she turned.

"Hey, I love you," she said softly.

He knew he would never tire of hearing those words slip off her perfect lips.

"I've loved you longer."

She bit her bottom lip as if figuring out a tough math problem.

"We'll have to argue about that later. See you tonight."

Chapter Twenty-Seven

*H*enry was already out with a potential rebound girlfriend he'd met at the wedding, when Peter arrived at the Cathners, so he was spared the third degree regarding his intentions toward Sam. Henry wouldn't have dared bring it up at Cynthia's wedding, but in the privacy of their own home? Most definitely. Henry loved to watch Peter sweat, always had. They all secretly got along, but the Cathner men loved to jibe. After Peter had tasted Mrs. Cathner's zucchini muffins and talked baseball with Sam's father, they were free to go.

"You dressed up," Sam said as he closed the door behind them.

It felt like a date. The day they had spent apart created a newness in Sam, and it slowed things down. They were dating, that was the plan. Peter's hair, still wet from a shower, was brushed back off his face, and he had on dark jeans and a navy linen shirt. It was open at the neck, and Sam noticed he'd gotten sun while they were on the island. Every time Peter tanned, the green in his eyes seemed to lighten. Standing in front of her, he was the very best-looking date she had ever seen.

"You too."

Peter was carrying her sweater. As they hit the night air, he stopped to put it over the green cotton dress she had put on for their movie date. He paused to lay a kiss on her bare shoulder and then covered it with her sweater. She smelled like the sun and Chanel. Her smell had become part of his life again. It was everywhere, on his clothes, in his bed. It was becoming as much a part of his life as she was. Peter had switched from convincing Sam that everything was fine to . . . wooing her. He'd decided when she left the night of the wedding that maybe he needed to earn her back, put in some effort.

"The dress is new. I just felt like I wanted to . . ."

"Yeah, me too."

Peter pulled her to him under a dimly lit street lamp and kissed her. The moon was huge and Sam could hear the ocean crashing on the beach below.

"I have a surprise," Peter said, easing back, and brushing Sam's hair out of her freckled flush face.

"Extra M&M'S?"

He laughed.

"I do have extra M&M'S, but that's not the surprise."

Peter put his arm around her. As they walked toward the movie theater, she tried to wrangle the surprise out of him, but Peter did not budge. He was good at secrets. The Avalon Theatre sat beneath the casino where they'd held Cynthia's wedding reception. It was never a real casino in the modern-day sense, but the word *casino* actually meant "large room used for entertainment and dancing." There was only one casino on Catalina and beneath its grand ballroom was the most spectacular movie theater either of them had ever seen.

Sam loved movies, especially classic romance. The acting was not always realistic, but there was an innocence or simplicity to the stories and a sense of class Sam felt was lacking in modern movies. She and Peter didn't always appreciate the same types of movies. Peter leaned toward art films or '80s movies. He was a sucker for anything John Hughes. His personal collection was a little bit eclectic because he had also seen just about every movie Katharine Hepburn had ever made. Even the bad ones. Sam and

Peter both agreed, however, that movies were best when seen in a theater, sticky floor and all.

The Avalon Theatre was the palace of movie theaters. It was like being in a real theater, complete with beautifully upholstered chairs, murals on the walls, and a heavy velvet curtain. Watching any movie in this theater took Sam back to a time she felt strongly needed to be preserved because it would never come again.

Movie Dinner was Sam's favorite. She had come up with it when they were teenagers in high school. Every Friday was movie night and most of the time she, Peter, Grady and any other assortment of girlfriends or friends would skip out on dinner and fill up on popcorn and candy: Movie Dinner. Peter was never a huge fan of sweets. Sam never understood that part of him. So, he was the guy buying nachos or one of those nasty hot dogs spinning under the case. Grady and Sam usually shared a bucket of popcorn, layered with butter, as well as two big bags of peanut M&M'S. All of that was washed down with two large cherry Slurpees. By the time the movie was over, they were sick, but it was all in the name of tradition. Peter crossed over to the dark side with popcorn in his later years, but he still drank a bottle of water instead of the Slurpee. "Progress, not perfection," was Grady's remark.

They arrived at the theater and Peter walked up to the ticket booth. There were no posters outside and the sign above the ticket booth did not have the name of the movie playing. Sam was confused as Peter gestured her through the glass door. There was no one else around. Sam thought it was strange because they seemed to be the only two people at the eight o'clock showing. Catalina had one showing a night, so something was up. Sam tilted her head in question as they walked into the warm burgundy lobby. There were two women, both fairly tall, both in uniform, one with graying hair, standing by the entrance to the theater. One of them had a jumbo tub of popcorn and two big bags of M&M'S. The other woman was holding a tray of fried shrimp and clams from the little green shack right across from Antonio's. Sam recognized the red and white paper. She looked at Peter and he smiled right up to his exquisite green eyes.

"Peter, what?"

"*Movie Dinner*, right?"

"Yes, but where's everyone else and . . ."

"I never said anything about other people joining us."

"Peter."

"Okay, I pulled some strings. I know some people. The whole place is ours for the night."

"The night! Well, we have enough food. Of course you brought regular food," Sam said, snatching a fried clam out of the basket.

"Cheater."

"A man cannot live on M&M'S and grease alone. If you're nice to me, I might share."

"What's playing?"

"Well, I sort of took the liberty. We're watching *An Affair to Remember* for you and *Some Kind of Wonderful* for me."

Sam was pretty sure Peter knew all the lines to that movie. He'd watched it at least a hundred times.

"That's quite a pairing. *An Affair to Remember*," Sam sighed, "I love . . ."

"I know, when Cary Grant looks at her while she's singing at the grandmother's house. I know."

He laughed and then kissed her. Sam was a sucker for a great romance and believed nothing was more romantic than Cary Grant and Deborah Kerr.

"*Some Kind of Wonderful*, again?"

"It's a classic, never gets old. The teenage angst, not to mention the Psychedelic Furs."

Sam laughed.

"And for you, there's the kissing scene where they cut in to his hands clenching into her jeans. Very romantic in a hormonal sort of way."

"That really is a great scene. Almost makes up for the Psychedelic Furs."

Peter shook his head as he led the way to their seats. Waiting on a tray were two large cherry Slurpees.

Sam raised an eyebrow.

"You're going to drink a Slurpee?"

He nodded and said, "I am. So, if I slip into some kind of sugar coma you'll have to get me home."

They both laughed and sat. Sam was so excited. Peter had thought of everything and there they sat, as they had throughout their life, in a theater. Sam loved that it was empty and they were alone. The house lights dimmed and the minute the screen filled with falling snow in New York City and Vic Damone began crooning Sam was in heaven. She leaned over and kissed Peter.

"Thank you."

"You're welcome. Now, watch the movie. No one likes a talker during the movie."

Their eyes held and just like that one more warm memory was added to their present, their future. Peter put his arm around Sam and handed her the popcorn. She threw a piece of popcorn at him, and without missing a beat, he threw a french fry at her and smirked. That was Peter. Silly and serious mixed together with intelligence and those sexy eyes.

A little after midnight, they walked home from the theater feeling the crash of the sugar rush they had enjoyed earlier in the evening.

"I do like it when she says, 'What makes life so difficult?' and Grant deadpans it and says, 'People'—that's the best line in the movie. Almost makes up for all the damn singing. What's with all the kids singing?"

Sam pushed his shoulder and laughed.

"No, I'm serious, there are like two full songs in that movie and . . . bad songs."

"It shows the innocence of the children she was working with. Without the songs . . . yeah, okay, maybe one too many songs."

"More like two songs too many."

Sam laughed.

"Okay, I noticed a similar image in both movies this time," she said, pulling her sweater closed.

"Hmm . . . okay, this should be good."

"The big kiss in both of them. You know the scene on the boat stairs when Grant and Kerr kiss for the first time, and you can't see their faces? It builds the intensity, it's so good. The same thing happens in *Some Kind of Wonderful*. When he kisses Watts, and they cut to his hands clenching her jeans. No faces, same intensity."

Peter got that little wrinkle between his eyebrows and had to admit she was right.

"Only you could find a similarity between those two films. You always notice the details, the framework. That must be what makes you so good at your job. You take in the whole thing and then tend to the details within the context."

Sam thought about it as they walked.

"You might be right, I've never thought about it that way, but I do notice things. Hmm . . . I suppose you know me after all."

Peter pulled her in as they approached the end of the arch on the casino walkway. He gently backed her up against the arch and kissed her in the moonlight. Her hands wrapped around his neck, and the kiss deepened. Sam pulled back first and tucked her bottom lip between her teeth.

"Do you ever notice," she said, her voice still husky from the kiss, "how they stop the movie before you see the complications of the romance? You don't see Grant schlepping that wheelchair around New York City or what Keith in *Some Kind of Wonderful* is going to do now that he has blown all of his college money on those damn earrings. You never see that."

Peter knew what she was saying, he knew he was the reason she was no longer a wide-eyed optimist, but there was nothing he could do about that. Besides, he liked her this way, a little darker, a little warier. She certainly made him work harder.

"Are you suggesting they put all that messy business in a movie? Who would want to see that? People only want to see the happy stuff, or indulge in their morbid fascination with tragedy. It's like the masks, you know? Comedy and Tragedy, which is ironic because most of life is somewhere in the middle. Don't you think?"

"I suppose you're right. Life is not like the movies."

"Oh stop, you are such a diehard romantic. I'm not buying this deep brooding cynicism. Just because some ass left you after college without a word doesn't mean you're suddenly Greta Garbo. You're not fooling me."

Peter put the back of his hand to his head in the classic drama queen pose. Sam couldn't help but laugh.

"Maybe I am a cynic: you bring this out in me. Maybe I'm under the spell of all those romantic words in your play. I'm out of control with you."

He kissed her again, and she was again swirling in the storm.

"Good. I'm glad I bring out your romantic. You're not out of control, Sam. You're . . . how did you say it? You're in the storm with me. We're tossing and turning together. We need to hold on."

He held her hand and walked her toward her house.

"See, there you go again with the metaphors," she sighed.

"Well, we're home, so I'll give you a break tonight."

Peter held her close and bowed his head to rest against hers.

"We leave tomorrow," she said.

"I know."

"Back to . . ."

"Work, back to work, we have a play to premiere."

"Yes we do. Do you have an ending yet?"

"I do. Finishing it up."

"The movie's almost over. Things are going to get complicated again."

"You can take it. I hear you're pretty tough."

Peter kissed her.

"See you tomorrow?" he whispered over her lips.

Sam opened her eyes.

"You will. Goodnight, Peter. Thanks for the . . . the great date."

She touched her lips to his one last time.

"You're welcome. Sleep tight."

Sam walked toward the door, her fingers brushed out of his hand, and she looked over her shoulder. Peter was watching her with a look that told her this life was possible, even after the movie ended, but she still didn't have the details. Her mind couldn't figure it all out, and she knew, despite Peter's lovely words, that nothing was simple.

Chapter Twenty-Eight

The week following the wedding was hectic, as everyone started to focus on the final details of the production. The Playhouse was less than a month away from opening night and there was still a lot to be done. The scrim for Phillip's dream scene had torn, yet Sam was being told with she wouldn't be able to have a new one until three days before opening. That was cutting it too close, so she was working with the costume and scenery department to see if the tear could be repaired.

Carmen had the baby three days prior to Sam's return, so Sam was filling in as Carmen tried to juggle working from home. Candice was busy with casting and rehearsals for *Bent* at the Black Box. *Bent* was still six months out, but the protests had already started. *Clearly people didn't have enough to do*, Sam thought. It was all normal stress. Sam was back to going to her spin class in the morning. There was nothing she couldn't handle.

Peter had stayed at her house a couple of nights. They'd tried a new Vietnamese place two nights ago, but for the most part they were well into a routine of up late, fall asleep, wake up, and do it all over again. Peter was tired from flying back and forth to New York to deal with a new principal actor there who was not adjusting well.

When Peter was in Pasadena, he was distracted and constantly on the phone with his director back East. The pressure was mounting for his play in Pasadena, and even though Spencer and Julie were handling almost every decision, Sam could tell Peter was being pulled.

On top of everything else, they were asked to attend a fundraiser for Grady's father's campaign. Sam didn't mind these events; it would give her a chance to promote the theater and dress up. She actually looked forward to a little break. Peter on the other hand would rather as he put it, "Gouge my eyes out before standing in a monkey suit and talking about absolutely nothing." He had work to do and didn't have time for this "society crap." Sam left the theater at five, right after Spencer called the rehearsal. She had to get home and change. She had asked; Peter mumbled that he wasn't sure if he would be there or not. She gave him his space. They decided they would meet there, if he attended at all.

"Hello, gorgeous."

Grady kissed Sam's cheek and took her hand to help her down the last two steps as she entered the ballroom. The place was packed and Grady was on. He was in his Armani and playing the dutiful senator's son.

Returning the kiss to Grady's smooth cheek, Sam straightened his tie for the society-page photographers snapping away. Sam had played this game her whole life and watched her parents play it with aplomb. She hadn't been to a fundraiser since the one at the Norton Simon, but it was like riding a bike. She pretended that her shoes didn't hurt and rolled her shoulders back.

"You're pretty gorgeous yourself there, mister."

"Our table's over there. I'll walk you over, but then I need to go say hello to Senator Grafton. He wants me to look at pictures of his new parrot."

Grady rolled his eyes.

"The sacrifices I make."

He smiled his movie star smile, took Sam's arm, and began to lead her toward the table. He leaned in as they walked, talking through his sparkling teeth.

"You see the enchanting woman sitting next to my father?"

Sam nodded.

"That's my new babysitter, at least for the campaign. Can you imagine? For some reason my father thinks I'm threatening his chances of re-election."

"Hmm, do you think it was when you did karaoke at that biker bar? Or when you and Peter were photographed playing flip cup at the club bar?" Sam asked, still smiling.

"Yeah, I don't know, but he's hired a damn firm to babysit me, and she, yeah, she's a piece of work. Told me to lay low and keep my zipper up. I'm staying home nights, Sam. Can you imagine?"

"Hmm . . . she is lovely, maybe you'll learn something."

"I doubt it. She's like an iceberg."

Sam laughed as they approached the table and the men stood. Grady left her to go talk about the parrot. She looked toward the gentlemen, standing to make her greetings and niceties. To her left, hands stuck in his tuxedo pants, jacket over the back of his chair, looking rumpled with a fairly decent chip on his shoulder, was Peter. She was surprised to see him.

The whole event was painful for him. Anyone could see it in his eyes, but he was there for Grady, and to show his support for Senator Malendar. Another obligation bestowed on the head of the Everoad house while he was in Pasadena. But it was just one night. While Sam didn't know what it was like to manage one production and bring up another, she felt as if Peter could spare one night.

Sam kissed her father on the cheek and then made her way around the table to the seat next to Peter. She kissed him gently and he took her hand. She looked into his eyes, and in the middle of this formal event, she pictured him laying next to her. He stared straight at her, not through her, into her eyes. With a gentle tug he pulled Sam closer and gracefully, it was downright graceful, drew her hand to his lips. Sam could feel his warm breath on her hand, and he paused, lingered. Once again, everyone else in the room faded away, and there she was with Peter. The kiss to her hand was soft, but strong, as if he was trying to hold her.

"Hi," he said, still standing.

"Hi. How did things . . . ?"

"How long are you going to keep these poor men standing, Sam?"

Grady had returned to the table carrying a glass of champagne for Sam and noticed everyone was still standing.

"I know they're a cute couple, but we can all sit," he said, pulling out her chair.

Sam was beginning to wonder how many cocktails Grady had already had. The table laughed, except Peter who was not in a laughing mood. Grady threw his arm around Peter and handed him a glass of champagne.

"She can't take her eyes off you, man. What have you done to this girl?"

Peter shifted his eyes to the table and gave Grady his usual sarcastic grin.

"You know, maybe if this thing works out at the Playhouse, we can lure you back here."

Yup, Grady was one too many drinks into the evening, Sam thought.

Peter laughed mid-champagne sip and said: "Thing? You mean my play? No, I belong in New York. I don't think I could be lured . . ."

"Oh, come on, what's New York have that we don't?"

"Um, Broadway and . . . my life. Once I'm done here, that is."

"Oh, yeah, there is that."

Grady looked to the table, and as if on cue, they erupted with laughter. Peter realized a little too late what had flown out of his mouth. He could feel Sam's reaction, but he was too tired to care. *This was a bad idea, I should not have come tonight.* He couldn't take one more minute of useless small talk and watching the Sam and Grady show. They were always more comfortable with this crap. He needed to catch the red-eye to New York. They were having an emergency casting call in the morning in the hopes of replacing the lead before the next six-week run started. Promotional materials would need to be reprinted. It was becoming a small nightmare, and he was sitting here once again drinking champagne. *Christ, was that all these people did?*

Sam got the message loud and clear. She told herself to cut him some slack, but the sentiment, the need to return to his "life" as he called it, had been strong since they had returned from Catalina. There was pressure now, and Peter lost some of his flowery luster under pressure. His words became clipped and he could bite back if necessary. Grady's comments were ridiculous, but Peter's reaction truthful, unfiltered. Sam could feel her throat tighten.

Grady headed back to the bar, but his PR "babysitter" as he called her, very subtly cut him off by trying to start a conversation. He smiled at her but Sam could tell he was annoyed. Attempting to defuse the situation, Sam grabbed Grady and they hit the dance floor. They laughed and had a great time, in spite of Peter and "the babysitter." Grady was always up for a good time. Dinner was the standard rubber chicken, and even though the speeches were slow, it reaffirmed for Sam that Senator Malendar was one of the good guys in Washington. His campaign was important. Sam would be supportive financially and give of her time, as she had in elections past.

Peter chewed the ice from his water glass and watched Sam dancing with Grady. She was avoiding him, and quite frankly, he didn't have the energy to deal with it right now. He received confirmation from Alexis that she'd booked his flight. He needed to get to the airport. He looked up to find his mother asking Mr. Cathner to take her for a "spin around the dance floor." *Christ,* Peter thought his jaw would shatter under the pressure. He was leaving. He couldn't find Sam. She was probably off somewhere with Grady. *And wasn't that just the cherry on the cake of his day?*

Jack, of course, danced with his mother, and Peter then quickly grabbed her wrap, as he'd done at hundreds of events since his father died, and ushered her out the door. He would escort her home and get to the airport. Sam was walking back from the bathroom when she saw Peter tip the valet and drive away. She pushed through the glass doors to try and catch him, but she was too late.

Chapter Twenty-Nine

Grady agreed to take Sam home. Right as Norah Jones started singing "Turn Me On," the other car's headlights flashed in her face. She felt nothing but a heavy push. She heard metal crunch and something screeching, followed by spinning like she was on a fair ride. She felt her head slam into the side window. Pain pulsed down her cheek, and her chest was in a vise that she thought may have been the seatbelt holding on for dear life. As the car continued to spin, Sam heard Grady's voice, but she couldn't understand what he was saying. She tried to turn and face him, but the force wouldn't allow her to move her head. It felt like a slow motion movie scene, but was painfully real. The car jerked to a stop, Sam felt her head hit the side window again, and then everything went black.

Sam woke up in a hospital bed as the sun peeked through the blinds of the window. It was morning, but which morning? She tried to focus. Grady was asleep in the chair next to the bed. He was still in his tux, so she couldn't have been out that long. *What*

the hell happened? She reached for the plastic pitcher of water, knocked over the cup, and Grady sat upright, startled, eyes heavy. He had a bandage on his head and moved stiffly out of the chair to stand next to her.

"I'm in big trouble now," he said, carefully taking her hand.

"Why's that?" she managed to croak out.

"I made a deal with God that I'd never do anything stupid again if he pulled you through this with minimal damage."

Sam started to laugh, but it hurt. She was sore.

"Easy there. See, so I'm screwed because I'll never be able to leave the house again, or I'll break the deal."

He poured her a glass of water and eased the back of the bed up.

"Before I tell you why you're in the hospital, I want to say, in case I've never said it before, I love you."

His eyes watered, and then he started to laugh.

"I'm fine."

"I know . . . but when I saw you in my car it was so . . . Christ . . ."

He wiped away a tear.

"What happened?"

"Some jackass ran a red light, that's what happened, and he completely ruined our evening. You took most of the impact and some very strapping firefighters came to your rescue. You were knocked out. You have a minor concussion and a broken arm."

Henry and her parents entered the room with coffee from the cafeteria. Henry handed Grady a coffee and something in a bag, then leaned over, and gently kissed Sam's cheek.

"Scared me to death, sis. How're you feeling?"

"I think I remember waking up for the cast, but I missed the firefighters. Damn!"

Sam's voice was back with the help of the water. She felt like someone beat her up, but she would be fine. She had never broken anything before.

"Thank God, you're okay, honey," her mother said, taking her hand, and sitting in the chair Grady offered.

"Brian was on the scene. Poor guy had no idea who he was rescuing. Had to cut you out of the car, Button," her father added gently, brushing her cheek, and then he too sat down.

"Brian? Was there? Oh, I need to thank him."

Sam tried to sit up too quickly, and her body sent a reminder she had been in a car accident. She lay back down.

"He's already checked on you. He's back at the station. I'm sure you can thank him later," Grady added, carefully biting into a bagel.

Sam noticed his lip was cut. She moved her legs and did a mental inventory of her body. She was sore, but everything appeared to be in the right place.

"Do I even want to look at my face?" Sam asked her mother.

"It's fine, honey. You were wearing your seatbelt, so there are some scratches, but nothing major."

Her mom dug a mirror out of her purse and handed it to Sam. She looked through the small, round mirror and noticed she had a black and blue knot on her forehead and a cut on her cheek. Other than that, she was lucky. Really lucky. Sam rested her head back on the pillow and then she realized what was missing.

"Peter," she said, looking at Grady.

"Did . . . please tell me someone called Peter."

With that everyone except Grady stood, kissed Sam again, and said they were going to let her rest and they would be in the waiting area. It was a mass exodus because no one wanted to have this conversation. Grady stood alone. Thank God he'd had some coffee because he was going to need it.

"Where the hell is everyone going? Is he here?"

Grady took a deep breath, as deep as his aching ribs would allow.

"Henry called him, Sam. He knows, and he's on his way back."

"On his way back from where?"

Sam scooted up a little in the bed.

"New York. He was on a plane when Henry called, but he called me back when he landed."

"What? Why the hell was he on a plane? I didn't even know he was flying last night. When did he leave?"

"I guess his agent booked the flight. He left right after the fundraiser. Something about the principal actor. It doesn't matter, Sam. He's on his way back. I think his flight gets in at two. He's worried sick and called again right before he got on the plane," Grady added as Sam's face continued to look confused and then deflated.

"So he was in New York, off to New York again."

Sam stared straight ahead, as if she were in a trance.

"Sam, he had no way of knowing we were going to be in an accident. It was just weird timing."

"Did you know he was flying to New York last night?"

Grady hesitated. He knew where this was going.

"No. When I talked to him he said he couldn't find us before he left the fundraiser. He said he tried to find you, but he needed to . . ."

"Run," Sam interrupted, looking right at Grady.

"Is that what he needed to do, he needed to run? Back to New York, something super urgent in the great big city? Didn't have five damn minutes to wait for me to return from the bathroom, or hell, even tell the woman he's, once again sleeping with, that he needed to catch a flight across the damn country."

Sam was wincing from raising her voice, her ribs hurt, and Grady had no idea what to say. He opted to stand up for Peter.

"He didn't run, Sam. He had to deal with some things. There are big issues with his show in New York, you know this. Come on, it was a shitty coincidence."

Sam let out a small pained laugh.

"Am I the only one who sees the irony here? I am in a hospital bed, a car accident that could have taken both of our lives, put me here. I'm surrounded by my family. Christ, I was even cut out of a car by my ex-boyfriend. Even he was there. I woke up to you, even though you're hurt too and in pain. What's missing, once again, Grady? Who's not here when I need him? Who's off to New York, Grady?"

Sam didn't wait for him to answer, she knew he wouldn't. Sam was stunned and angry. Things had been building up over the past week, and sure, she knew Peter had responsibilities, but they all did. How were they ever going to make a life if she's lying in a hospital bed and he's not there? If he flew off to New York without even mentioning it to her? Was this how it was always going to be? She'd be left hanging while Peter did what Peter needed to do? *Sam, you stupid fool. That's why there's never a plan. He has no intentions of making a life with you.* Her head fell back to the pillow, and she closed her eyes.

"Sam, I don't know what to say. It was one of those things. He's on his way. He turned right around. It's not like he doesn't care. He loves you."

"I don't care. Did he even ask how you were? If you were okay?"

"He was out of his mind with worry and trying to catch another flight. Come on, Sam. Cut the guy some slack. He was on the phone with me. He knew I was fine."

Sam said nothing. Grady rose to get more coffee.

"Sam, please relax and rest."

Chapter Thirty

The Cathners brought Sam home from the hospital later that afternoon. The doctor gave her pain medication, but she was tired of feeling whacked out, so she was sticking with Tylenol. Her body was sore, but with the exception of her right arm, everything worked. Sam's mom pleaded with her to stay in the main house, but she wanted to be alone. She was fine. Her mother said she would send dinner over and to call if she needed anything. Sam walked her parents to the door, assuring them she was going to lie on the couch and rest. When they left, she curled up on the couch, resting her cast across her chest.

Peter knocked on the door as the sun was going down. Sam was sleeping, propped up with pillows. She opened her eyes and knew immediately who was at the door. She took her time getting up, partly because her body would only move so fast, but mostly because she was angry, and didn't want to have the conversation.

She opened the door. Peter was standing in front of her, bathed in the setting sun, and her heart began to fall apart. He looked worse than she felt. He took in her scraped-up face and then stared at her arm. He wasn't sure how to reach out to her without hurting her, but before he had a chance, Sam shook her head in disgust, and walked back to the couch, leaving him in the doorway. Peter closed the door.

"Sam."

"You know what, save it. I'm not sure why you're even here."

"Sam, I'm sorry . . . I . . ."

"Sorry? You're sorry for what exactly Peter? Sulking at the fundraiser because you didn't want to be there? Flying off to your precious New York without so much as a goodbye?"

Peter was well into twenty-four hours without sleep, so he interrupted before this got out of hand.

"I was going to call you from the airport, I couldn't find you, and I really needed to . . ."

"Just don't!"

She held up the hand that worked and winced at the pain in her shoulder. Peter moved to sit next to her.

"Please stop. You're in pain. Can't we talk about this later? I'm here. I'm sorry I didn't tell you I had to leave, but I turned right back around as soon as I spoke to Grady. I wanted to make sure you were okay."

Sam said nothing.

"Grady told me what happened on the phone. Jesus, Sam, you guys were so lucky."

He touched her knee and then went to brush her bangs off her face, and Sam moved away. Peter had a bad feeling, a very bad feeling, as she slowly stood.

"I can't do this. I can't love like this. I don't want to."

Peter closed his eyes and rubbed the bridge of his nose.

"Aw, Christ, Sam, what does that mean?"

"It means I'm done. I don't want this relationship. I don't want to compete with New York and your precious life. I don't want it, I don't want any of it."

Peter stood. She was hurting, and he needed to find a way to calm her down. She was talking crazy. She moved away again.

"Don't. You shut down, think of yourself, and I'm left hanging. That's not a relationship, that's not going anywhere. I'm tired of hanging on for you. I have a life, I need things, and I need you to be . . ."

"Where the hell is this coming from? Because I had one bad day, I got on a plane, and so now you can't do this?"

He tried to be gentle; she had a cast and the bruise on her head looked awful, but damn it, he was tired of apologizing.

"How long is this going to hang over us, Sam? How long am I going to have to pay for leaving you?"

She turned and her eyes bore right through him.

"What?"

"I'm serious, I mean: what's it going to take? I'm in love with you, we're together, and you still can't let it go."

"I can't let it go? I can't . . . are you kidding me? I've let it go, Peter, I let you back in. The problem is you're the same selfish son-of-a-bitch who left me the first time. You just have better excuses now. You're still running, hiding behind New York or your job. You still cringe at some stupid fundraiser. You're always first in your mind, Peter, and hell, I don't know, maybe that's because of your past."

She sat back down on the couch, her face was warm and her head was starting to throb. Peter took a deep breath and kneeled in front of her, resting his hands on her knees.

"That's not true. I put you first, you are first, but I have responsibilities. I'm not hiding, I mean, sure I have issues being home, but we'll work those out. Once the play opens, we'll figure it out. This is crazy, Sam. I love you."

He looked up at her, and her eyes were cold. She was gone.

"Sure, we'll figure it out. It will all work out."

She was mocking him.

"Once the play is up, I'll know what the hell we're doing. Who's going to make those decisions, Peter? You? Will you dole out the next scene when it's written? Will you tell me what's coming up when you're good and ready?"

He stood up and so did Sam. They were face to face, and he could feel her anger, years of it that she'd never let out.

"No! You won't do that to me. I'm done waiting for you, done figuring you out, done trying to understand your next move. I know it sounds crazy, but you were on a plane when I needed you. You never even told me you were leaving. You said nothing. My heart was resting in your hands, and you left. Sound familiar?"

"I'm sorry," was all he could say.

"I'm sure you are. I'm done. Please leave."

Peter began to shake, physically shake.

"You can't be done. Sam, we love each other, we need . . ."

"No. I don't need, I can't. It hurts too much. I'm not made like you. There is no plan, there never will be, because you can't find a way to me without dealing with everything else. You dodge and avoid, that's you, Peter. The only one who loses in that deal is me. You're skimming the surface, you always have. You risk nothing."

"Bullshit. I don't live my life that way anymore. I came back for you. I'm trying, damn it. I know you think I'm self-centered, and you're probably right, but I never pretended to be anything more than completely screwed up. Your father blows his brains out and your mother basically abandons you for a bottle of whatever she can get her hands on, yeah, it leaves a mark, and I know I've hurt you. I've hurt myself, but this is going to work, Sam. I can't live without you anymore. I need you too much."

Tears burned Sam's eyes. There was no fixing this.

"You, you, you. What else do you need, Peter?"

"That's not what I meant. Stop it. We love each other. Why are you doing this? There isn't a choice here?"

"There is. You can leave. I choose to not let it in anymore. It's a matter of survival, Peter, and if it means hurting you, I'm sorry, but I tried."

Peter drew his hand over his mouth and watched Sam give up.

"What are you saying?"

"I'll take your play to the premiere, do my part, and then you need to go back to New York where you belong. *I* need to get back to my life, and *I* can't do that with you here."

Peter wasn't going to win. He could see it in her face. He stepped closer, careful not to hurt her, and said: "Look who's running now, Sam. You are. Closing the door. You can't let yourself love me because you're afraid I'll take too much, or I'll hurt you. Those are the messy parts you're always preaching about Sam. You're not jumping off the board with me. You're still at the bottom of the ladder because I don't have a plan, and you forgot how to trust me."

His breath was warm on her face, and Sam felt like she was going to pass out.

"I'll leave, fine, but you'll never escape this; you'll never be able to fully get this out of your system, no matter how much you close down. I'll always be here."

He gently touched her heart, and Sam recoiled in pain that had nothing to do with the accident. The tears spilled down her cheeks.

He touched her face gently as she started to turn away.

"Samantha Cathner, I've loved you my whole life, and I know you love me. Losing you, watching you walk away this time, that doesn't change anything. I'm letting go of what happened to my father, I'm moving through my childhood on my way to a plan, but maybe you're the one reliving the past, maybe you're the one that's letting it paralyze you."

Sam looked away.

"I can't promise you something won't happen to me or you won't get hurt. I can't tell you that you won't be left behind, but . . ."

Peter took her face again.

"I can tell you that I love you more than I ever thought was possible, and I will never willingly leave you. I'll probably disappoint you from time to time, but I'm here. I may not be standing on the stage yet like you want me to, but you're not the only one who is scared. There's no other path for us, Sam, is there?"

As her tears touched Peter's hands, she pulled away, walked to the door and opened it. Peter hung his head and walked out without another word. He had given it everything he had and she was gone. Sam closed the door and collapsed to the floor. She no longer cared that her body ached from the accident. Her heart was broken again, but this time the optimism of youth was not there to soften the blow. This was a very adult heartbreak, and she had done it to herself.

Chapter Thirty-One

Sam's physical bruises had healed, and she was no longer working on Peter's production. She used the accident as an excuse, and Candice took over for the final rehearsals. The play would premiere in a week.

After the senator's fundraiser and a nasty fall down the stairs, Peter's mother had asked him to put her into an alcohol treatment facility. She was out now. According to Grady, she looked ten years younger and actually seemed happy. Sam was glad that she was finding her way back, but she was surprised when Mrs. Everoad called and asked her to come over for tea. Sam still received the rehearsal schedule, so she made sure Peter would be in rehearsals when she agreed to meet her later in the day.

Sam had not been to the Everoad house since Peter had left for New York over four years ago. Even now, standing in front of the large wooden door with the brass pineapple knocker, she felt small, young all over again. Peter's house was huge, even by Pasadena standards, but it was welcoming. There was always a wreath on the door and beautiful planters filled with flowers of the season.

Their house was yellow when Peter's father was alive, but once Mr. Everoad was gone, Peter's mother had redone the entire house from top to bottom and painted the outside white. Peter had never understood why his mother made all of the changes, none of them did. At the time it had been whispered she was a cold, heartless woman.

Now, as a woman herself, it occurred to Sam that maybe his mother couldn't live in the same house. Age has a way of introducing experiences and all sorts of shades of grey. Nothing appeared black and white to Sam anymore, not even Peter's mother. Why she'd invited her for tea, Sam wasn't sure, but she felt privileged that she wanted to talk to her alone.

As Sam rang the bell, she realized that she had never even hugged Peter's mother when his father died. To her knowledge, no one had. Sam's mother had taken April's hand. Her father had offered to help with the arrangements. But, had anyone hugged her? Wrapped their arms around her and allowed her to collapse? Sam did not remember that happening, and as Vivvie, their housekeeper, answered the door, Sam felt deep sadness for Peter's mother. She had spent so much time feeling bad for Peter, and it had never occurred to her that his mother was in pain. *Oh, she must have been so alone.*

"Miss Cathner, I haven't seen you in years."

Vivvie, short for Vivian, hugged Sam and ran her hands down her hair, just as she had done when Sam was a child.

"Your hair has grown. Well, you've grown. Into such a beautiful woman."

Her eyes were filled with the years she'd spent in this house and the things she had seen from the sidelines. Vivvie was now a little shorter than Sam, but Sam would always see her as taller. She had tiny little feet and long, slender fingers. *It's funny the things you notice as a child,* Sam thought. As an adult, Sam noticed the grey in her hair and her incredible, almost golden, eyes. Sam had probably not spent much time looking into her eyes as a child, but she sure noticed them now.

"Vivvie, so good to see you. You look exactly the same."

"Oh, sweetheart, you need to come around more often. My aging ego loves you."

Sam laughed.

"I'm here to see . . ."

"Mrs. Everoad. Yes, I know dear. I set up tea on the patio. She's putzing in her garden. Been a little obsessed of late, if you ask me, but . . ."

Her voice lowered to a whisper.

"She hasn't touched a drop for almost a month now, so I say, 'Garden away!' Right?"

"Absolutely, that's wonderful."

"Ever since Mr. Peter brought her home from that treatment place. She spent two days in bed after that and woke up a different woman."

"Really?"

Vivvie looked out toward the patio to make sure they were still alone.

"Well, not exactly a new person, she's not been her old self, since before the mister died. She's got something behind those eyes again. She's, well, let's say it warms my heart."

Vivvie changed the subject before Sam could even comment, careful not to be disrespectful or say too much.

"It's lovely out today, you'll have tea on the patio. Still drinking black tea? Mr. Peter's into the green tea now."

At the mention of Peter's name Sam's pulse tripped. She smiled and recovered.

"I'm a traditionalist, Vivvie. Tea is black."

She patted Sam on the shoulder with a laugh and gestured her out to the patio.

"You'll see her out there, elbow-deep in dirt. Make yourself comfortable, and let me know if you need anything."

Vivvie pulled the French doors toward her and left Sam on the patio. She turned and saw a big, bright green hat shading matching gloves digging in the planters along the stairs off the patio.

"Mrs. Everoad," Sam called out, not wanting to startle her.

April Everoad looked up. One soiled garden glove raised to shade her eyes as she looked toward the patio. Even from a distance she looked different. Mrs. Everoad was the epitome of class and elegance; at least she had been before her husband passed away. Even on her off days, and there had been many over the years, she was stunning. Honey-blonde hair, always in a bob right below her ears, and green-blue hazel eyes. She was a "head turner" as Peter's father would always brag when they were kids and the parents were going out for the evening. "I'll have to fight them off," he'd say with a thundering laugh, and he was right. April Everoad was a beautiful woman, but as she approached in her hot pink gardening clogs and rolled chambray pants Sam had never seen her lovelier.

Sam met her at the top of the stairs. April reached out to pat her on the shoulder. Sam looked at her slightly older face, void of all makeup, and she grabbed her. Consumed with emotion, Sam did what she thought she should have done, what they all should have done, years ago. She hugged her. It was sudden and pretty tight. April began to laugh.

"My goodness, dear. It hasn't been that long."

She held Sam's shoulders and gently pushed her back. Sam smiled.

"Samantha, now cut that out. What the Dickens has gotten in to you? Just because I'm sober, don't start thinking we're friends."

After a minute where Sam was stunned by her candor, they both laughed.

"I'm sure my busybody housekeeper told you that I've stopped drinking."

Sam nodded and let her continue.

"Well, it's true. Peter checked me into a great place. I became incredibly tired of feeling sorry for myself, so . . ."

"Mrs. Everoad, you don't . . ."

"No, dear. I do. I wanted to apologize for, well for everything that's happened since, since my husband decided to leave us. It's part of my steps, you see. I need to own my mistakes. I sort of like that idea, so I've been moving down my list. So, Samantha dear, I've made more than a few parties uncomfortable for you and Peter's friends. I'm sure there were plenty of times I wasn't nice to you. I can't promise I'll always be nice going forward, but at least you'll know it's me and not the booze."

They both laughed.

"Really, you don't need to apologize to me."

April Everoad's face grew serious.

"Oh, but I do. I'm sorry Samantha, I truly am. I'm afraid I haven't been much use to anyone for the past few years, and I'm afraid my son . . ."

"Mom? Vivvie, where is she?"

Sam froze as the French doors rattled and Peter's voice got louder. Then like a child playing a game, Sam ducked down.

"Mrs. Everoad, please, I'm so glad you are well, but I do not want to be here if Peter . . ."

Sam looked toward the doors and back at April.

"Sam, it's only Peter . . ."

"No!"

She couldn't be polite about this. Her heart was pounding; she could not be there. April must have seen it all over Sam's face because she took her arm and walked her toward the doors as Peter came out to the patio. He froze at the sight of Sam. He hadn't seen her in weeks, and she hadn't called. He threw himself into work, told himself he was doing fine, and then he looked at her, and the air crackled. Peter tried to steady himself, be casual, anything other than pathetically heartbroken, but nothing worked. He wanted her more than his next breath.

"Peter, I didn't expect you, thought you were at rehearsals. I'm showing Sam out. There's tea if you want some. I'll only be a minute."

Peter said nothing as April rushed past with Sam. Sam's eyes betrayed her and she glanced at him. She looked away quickly and headed straight for the front door.

"Poor thing, looked struck dumb," April said with a little chuckle.

Sam tried to smile politely, but found nothing funny about the look on Peter's face. April kissed her on her cheek and took her hands.

"I'm not sure what happened, the two of you seemed like things were finally working out. A touch stupid that you broke his heart right when he was getting his act together, but I know that boy can be a handful," she said on a sigh.

Again, Sam was struck by the new and improved Mrs. Everoad. She liked the direct, cold water on the situation. Maybe she was right. Seeing Peter now, Sam felt pretty stupid, but what was done was done.

"I'll let you go, dear. Thank you so much for coming by, and I'm sorry our visit was cut short."

"That's fine. I'm sorry, I can't stay," Sam replied, fighting back the lump in her throat.

This was so ridiculous, she thought, running from Peter. How sad things had become. Sam turned to leave, but April held her arm.

"I'm sorry too, Sam."

With those words, April gave her one last squeeze and turned into the house. The apology was layered with years of regret. Sam felt nothing but pain as she walked out and closed the door.

April walked out to the patio, found her son sitting at the round teak table. She sat next to him and watched as he tried to pretend away all of his feelings for Sam.

"Mom, what the hell is . . . wow, you look great," he said, finally making eye contact.

He laughed.

"Nice hat."

"Don't make fun of your mother. I was on a gardening roll before you showed up. I've fertilized the rose bushes and the lilies are trimmed. I'm thinking of putting in a succulent garden, what are your thoughts on succulents?"

She took her hat off, set it on the table, and fluffed her hair.

"I can't say that I have any thoughts on succulents, Mom," Peter said looking out over the grounds.

"Don't you have gardeners for this?"

"I do, Mr. Smarty Pants, but I want to get my hands dirty. I want to, I want to do this myself," she said, taking the tea Peter finished pouring.

"I'm having fun. I haven't had fun in an eternity. You're supposed to be at the theater. Why are you here?"

"I was in town for lunch and I ran into two of the little hens you used to hang out with, Sissy and Mrs. Fleming. They said you all played bridge yesterday and you looked, and I quote, 'super fantabulous.'"

His mimicking and sarcasm were thick. There were reasons Peter was in the theater.

"Okay, so you came home to tell me . . ."

"Is it true? Were you honestly in the hen house with . . ."

"My friends? Are you asking me if I played bridge with my old friends? Yes, the answer is yes, and we had the most . . ."

"Mom, don't you think it's a little soon to be back in the swing of things? Don't they drink mimosas when you play bridge? Why would you, Christ, Mom, you've only been home a week. You're starting to feel better and you . . ."

"I'll ask you not to use that tone of voice with me, young man. Please remember who you are talking to."

April threw her small yellow napkin on the table. Peter was well aware that gesture meant his mother was pissed. He braced himself as his five-foot-two mother in pink garden clogs rose from the table.

"Mom, you can't possibly blame me for worrying about this, you need to start fresh and get . . ."

"Is that what I need, Peter?"

She put her hands on her hips.

"Oh honey, you don't even know what you need. You're going to tell me what I need too? I will have you know that my friends no longer drink mimosas when we play bridge, at least not for now. They care about me, so we drink tea."

Peter raked his hands through his hair.

"I only want you to be careful. It's a long road and some of these people are the problem, Mom."

April leaned toward her son and prepared for battle. *When did my son become such an elitist,* she thought.

"Some of these people? All of these people are my friends. They made me casseroles and checked in on us when your father, your wonderful, fabulous, could-do-no-wrong father upped and killed himself."

Her face was red now.

"These people made sure your sister got to ballet when I was too drunk to take her. All of these people will be filling that theater this weekend to support your play."

Peter sat back in the cushioned chair and shook his head.

"Mom, please, you know what I mean. Remember what the counselor said, it's easy to fall into old habits, you're a product of your . . ."

"Peter Alexander, for a smart boy, you are so, so oblivious. Was I really too drunk to see how self-righteous you've become? They teach you that in New York?"

She had never been this honest with him.

"All these people, Mr. Perfect, they love you. When are you going to stop this? It's my fault that I've been drunk for the last . . . Christ, eight years!"

Her voice was raised and Peter started to play with his spoon.

"It's not their fault. For God's sake, now that I can see things through clearer eyes, Peter, stop running."

At that, Peter looked up at her, and she took his hand. The jolt of warmth hit something inside of him, it felt like a craving he'd had for years. His mother's affection, acknowledgement, anything, that's what he needed when his father died, and she never delivered. Looking at her now, he felt certain that she simply hadn't known how.

"You know Pete, your father loved you so much, and I adored him, but he left us. He made that choice. This neighborhood, our circle, is not responsible. I'm not to blame and neither are you. He loved it here and wanted to make a life for us. We lost him somewhere along the way but stop trying to undo everything we've built here."

"Mom," he took her hands, and she sat down, "I'm not trying to undo anything. I live in New York now. I was asked to come home and put on this play. I'm helping, I just have a hard time being here. I don't understand why he left, so maybe in the past I've blamed you or this place."

"I'm not perfect, and I've stumbled more times than I can count, but I lost the only man I've ever loved. The sunlight is a little dimmer now, and nothing will ever be the same. Cut me a break. I'm trying to piece myself back together. I know I've hurt you, embarrassed you, but there's no handbook on this stuff. Things turned ugly, but I," she touched his face and continued, "I love you and your sister so much. There are no words. Love's that way. A person can get sick with love. Your father, oh, I was so weak for that man, and then he was gone. Maybe I pulled back from you and your sister because my heart couldn't take it, but, I'm here, I'm repairing myself, and we'll be fine."

Peter pushed away from the table, stood, and looked out over the yard. April could see the pain in his eyes and she knew so much of it was hers to heal. She had struck a chord, but Peter was not about reality since his father left. He needed someone to be the bad guy. He needed a villain. If there was no evildoer, well, that simply meant things were unfair or his father gave up. So Peter dealt in the abstract, kept it loose. That way he never had to really put himself out there.

"You need to stop judging everyone and assuming they're judging you. This is your home, these are your roots."

Peter stared straight ahead, cursing himself for stopping by. He saw this going differently in his mind when he had stormed in to talk with his mother.

"So how are you going to get her back?"

Peter's head snapped to look at her. *Shit,* he thought, *things just got worse.*

"I mean I hope you've got a plan because she seems pretty content to leave your ass in the dirt. I can't say that I blame her, you're a slippery one. You really need to work on that."

Peter laughed, he couldn't help it. His mother was giving him advice, putting him in his place. *Well, this was rich.*

"Mom, I'm not slippery. I was working on a plan. Christ, I came back for her, and things were fine, but then she can't get over what happened. She thinks I'm self-centered, that I'll leave."

"And what exactly have you done to show her she's wrong?"

Peter fumbled, it was a simple question, but he didn't have one answer. What had he done to prove her wrong? Well, he flew to New York without talking to her first. That was a brilliant move.

"I'm not sure."

"You're not sure. That's a ridiculous answer. You know what your father would say, don't you?"

Peter was pretty sure this was the first time his mother had ever casually mentioned his father since he died. He was really going to have to get used to this new April Everoad.

"He'd tell you exactly what he used to tell you before all those talent shows you put on. He'd sit you down and say, 'Sure, this is going to be a challenge, but everything can be accomplished with a plan. You need to know your end game, son.'"

April laughed, "Oh, remember that. He was like some coach in a movie, and you would sit on that couch and look at him like he had all the answers."

She was lost in her memory, and when she turned to Peter he was silent, looking out over the garden, and tears were streaming down his face.

She turned and wrapped her arms around him. It was like a dam broke somewhere. His mother held such sadness and love for him at the same time. Peter sobbed, and they both stood holding on to each other. The ache in Peter's heart was soothed by her honesty and the memory of his father. He hugged her tightly and felt like he was giving her something back too. How long had she gone without feeling, without really noticing, her children's hugs?

Peter sighed and quickly wiped his tears. He still had one arm around her as they walked into the house.

"It's good to have you back, Mom."

"Yeah, well you better fix this thing with Samantha and give me grandchildren. All this drama may drive me back to the bottle."

Peter laughed and heard his father's voice, "What's your end game, son?"

Chapter Thirty-Two

Sam got out of the shower and dried off. She felt beaten up. She had decided last week after leaving the Everoad house that even if it was too late for her and Peter, a lot of things still worked out. Peter's mom was sober, his sister was happily married, and somehow Sam knew he would be all right. He would go back to New York and find some lesser-than version of happiness, and she would find the same. She was resolved, but she was still crying.

Last night had been difficult because Sam and Henry had been dining at the Raymond when Peter walked in with Spencer and Julie. He'd acknowledged them and shaken Henry's hand. Julie and Spencer even made small talk with Sam. They asked how she was feeling since the accident, told her they were excited and ready for the premiere, and that they both missed her. They finally took a table, Peter looked up at her a couple of times while they were eating, and when she couldn't take it anymore, Sam pleaded with Henry to take her home. It was all perfectly civil, perfectly distant, and completely awful. Sam fell asleep on the couch watching *Some Kind of Wonderful*. It was in her Netflix queue; she couldn't resist torturing herself a bit further.

Sam had spent the last four years feeling rejected and— there were no pretty words for it—angry. Angry that her love was not returned, angry that she was not only rejected personally, but on some level professionally as well. When she was little, her father used to tell her to take her anger outside and that when she had kicked its butt, she could come back inside. Last night, some time before the movie started, Sam had kicked her anger's ass. She let it go, and she realized that she loved Peter enough to wish him genuine peace and happiness.

Sam's eyes were burning, and she was sure, as she cleared a spot with her hand on the fogged mirror, that she looked like Quasimodo. Sam's face came into focus in the mirror, and she was thankful she felt worse than she actually looked. Some cucumbers, a little ice, and she would be fine by tonight. *In time to cry at the premiere*, she thought. As the benefits of crawling back under the covers rolled through Sam's groggy mind, there was a knock at her door. Before she could get to the knob, a key turned and Piper, her old roommate from LA, was pushing her way through the door with bags and boxes.

"Good morning, sun . . ."

She dropped everything and looked at Sam.

"Okay, maybe not sunshine just yet."

She touched her cheeks.

"We can work with this. Oh, Lord, we'll have to start right away."

"Good morning to you too. That key was for emergencies," Sam mentioned as she grabbed a bagel from the bag Piper was holding.

"What the hell are you doing here, and God, why are you so chipper?"

Piper set everything down and smoothed her bright yellow sundress.

"Well, your luscious brother called me last night, and unfortunately, it wasn't because he wanted to climb into my bed. He told me you needed me, but were too stubborn to ask," she said, reaching toward her bags.

"So . . . I decided, that's right, I made the decision, because you're, well, you're a mess. So, I decided that your little collection of black dresses would not work for tonight's festivities."

"Oh, Christ."

Sam threw herself on the couch and picked the soft part out of the bagel. She closed her burning Quasimodo eyes and tried to will her friend mute. *Why had Henry unleashed the fashion dragon?*

"Don't 'Christ' me. Henry called me last night."

Mistake, clearly a lapse in judgment, Sam thought.

"And he told me you're being very adult about all of this. I get that you wish Peter the best, and you're moving on, but honey, I've seen Peter, and, Lord, if there wasn't the 'never date your oldest friend's ex' rule, I'd be all over him."

"Thank you, Piper," Sam moaned from under the pillow she now had over her face.

"This is such a great help. Can we talk more about how sexy Peter is too? Maybe we can also talk about how brilliant he is and how talented. I'm so glad you're here to help reinforce that I made the right decision."

"Yeah, well I'll never understand that one, but it's your life, sweetheart. Do you have any coffee in this tiny little place?"

"Ahhhh! Try the little counter in the tiny kitchen. It's on a little timer, so it should be all ready. Will it shut you up?"

Thick with sarcasm, Sam threw the pillow to the end of the couch.

"Nope," she said, still talking as she went for coffee.

"Anyway, you may have accepted you don't want Peter ... oh, too harsh, that Peter's incapable giving you what you need? Yes, that's prettier, that sounds better."

"Yes, much better," Sam nodded, chewing on her bagel.

"Right, anyway, you need to knock him to his knees one more time, so he remembers forever what he messed up. Wait, are we sure he messed up, or was that you?"

"Oh, shut up please. I'm a little concerned about what's in those bags."

Looking again at the tight-as-sin yellow sundress Piper was prancing around in, Sam knew she had good taste, but Piper also had no problem sharing her body with, well, lots of people.

Piper made a face at the coffee and ran over to her packages.

"You need to wear . . . this."

She pulled the zipper on the garment bag and pulled out the most indescribable dress Sam had ever seen, and she had been in some pretty great dresses. It was dark, but it shimmered; it was floor length, but sexy and understated. It was not black and Sam loved it instantly. Piper swept the dress back and forth in front of her as if she were waving a flag.

"Where, where did you get it?" Sam asked.

"Interested now, aren't you? Well, the seamstress that does all of my dresses in LA, you know the one who works for Dolce?"

Sam nodded.

"She made this for a client, and at the last minute she started losing her hair, the client did, and I guess couldn't go or checked into a detox place or maybe it was a . . ."

"What?"

Sam was sitting up now.

"Yeah, I don't know, and I didn't care, because when Silvia, that's my lady, showed me the dress, all I could think of was you. I took it and then brought every shoe I could think of to go with it. This dress, this dress, Sam, is your goodbye. You can't say goodbye to the love of your life in another damn black dress."

She'd exhausted herself, it was a common occurrence for Piper, and she dropped into the chair across from Sam.

"Piper."

"What? I'm not taking no for an answer on this one. There's no way I'm going to let you. Sam, this is tragic and you need to look absolutely . . ."

"Piper."

"What?"

"Thank you."

Sam would have cried if she had tears left, but instead she plopped herself right in Piper's lap and hugged her.

"Oh, honey. You're welcome. You're going to look so gorgeous. I really want you enjoy tonight. He'll drool. I know you dumped his ass, and I can't say I agreed with that decision, but he'll definitely drool."

They both laughed.

"Well, drool is good, right? We'll settle for drooling, but we need a proper breakfast."

"I couldn't agree more. Let's get you up and out. We have spa appointments this afternoon, and we need a few Bellinis before we get you all purified and beautiful."

Sam felt better, she truly did. Tonight would be fine. She would say goodbye, make her peace, survive. The idea of Peter drooling one last time did have merit.

Before they left for the spa, Sam called Candice to make sure she didn't need anything. Even though she had been away from the production, Sam was back to working in the office, and she'd received and reviewed the final programs. They were perfect. When they arrived last week, Sam had remembered when she and Peter proofed them before leaving for Catalina. *That was a much better time,* she thought. *Why did it always seem like her life with Peter was in memories?* Candice said everything was great and all Sam needed to do was show up.

After her day with Piper, Sam was shiny and manicured. Piper dropped her off at the house, but then had to leave for a date with her "man of the month" as she called him. He was probably way too old for her. Piper was great at giving advice, but she was clueless when it came to herself. "When a man's children are older than you are, it's a clear indicator that something is wrong," Sam had said. Piper had laughed her off. Sam thanked her again and waved goodbye.

Maybe Sam's parents were right, maybe she was always tired, because walking into her house she felt relaxed and pampered. She looked at herself in the mirror as she put away the yummy bath stuff from the spa. Leaning into the mirror Sam noticed the whites of her eyes seemed whiter. The spa agreed with her.

Sam didn't really know how to relax. Maybe Peter wasn't the only one running—except she was running in place, running herself ragged. Since she started working at the Playhouse, Sam had been going nonstop to prove, mainly to herself, that she wasn't a trust-fund girl, that she had value and could be good at something. Looking at her exfoliated and glowing face in the mirror, Sam decided it might be time to give herself a break and to learn to relax.

She put on the kettle for hot water. Piper had instructed her to only drink hot green tea for the next three hours until she left for the theater. Sam put on John Mayer and followed directions. After about a half hour of sitting on her couch, John Mayer proved too sad, too introspective, so she changed playlists. By the time she was finishing her makeup it was Lady Gaga. Even if she understood what the hell she was singing, there was no way she was crying to Lady Gaga. Gaga was safe. "Absolutely no crying" was another Piper Rule.

The dress was strapless with a heart-shaped neckline. The base of the dress was dark purple and then a sheer, silvery blue tulle flowed from a crystal-encrusted bodice that fit Sam perfectly. The same crystals then dripped down into the skirt of the dress as it fell to the floor. It looked weightless, but was actually quite heavy. Her shoes were barely-there sandals made of the same crystals. Piper was good. She was very good.

Sam's dark hair had dried into her natural wave, and she swept it up loosely into a side knot. Diamond earrings her father had given her when she graduated from high school and a gorgeous clamshell purse Piper had found in Santa Barbara completed the look. Sam did her own makeup because she didn't wear a lot, and every time she had it professionally done she walked out looking like a clown. Standing in front of the mirror, Sam took a deep breath.

No more green tea. Another Piper Rule: "Once the dress goes on, no more tea, no food, nothing." She was kind of a scary control freak, and what was really sick was even though she was gone, Sam still followed all the rules. Good friends seem to have that power.

Sam stood up straight, looked in the mirror, and smiled. She did look beautiful. She could count on one hand how many times she had said that about herself, but tonight was one of them. She felt good, alone in a gorgeous dress, but good.

Her mom and dad had offered to go with her in the same car, but Sam had arranged her own driver on the off chance that she needed to make an escape. She put two Altoids in her mouth. *That doesn't count as food, does it?* The driver knocked at the door. She grabbed her purse and was off like Cinderella, but it was different, very different.

Chapter Thirty-Three

The Pasadena Playhouse was completed in 1924. The pamphlets the Playhouse distributed during tours and the blurbs in all of the programs explained that the playhouse was Spanish Colonial, designed by Pasadena artist and architect Elmer Grey. The theater company was actually started years earlier, in 1917, by Gilmor Brown. He produced plays out of an old burlesque house called the Savoy. Brown's company rose to such prominence that the citizens of Pasadena raised the funds to build what was now the Pasadena Playhouse. The theater was built by, and has always been loyally supported by, the community of Pasadena.

The Playhouse has housed productions by some very famous writers, everyone from Fitzgerald to O'Neill. It has a proud history, and even though the theater sat dormant for almost seventeen years when Sam was very young, it would always be a legend and an important part of the community. As with all theaters, the Playhouse had some very difficult years. Financial nightmares, internal struggles, temperamental actors, and times when all hope seemed to be lost, but the Playhouse always managed to pull through and be there for its audience. It was a place where Pasadena's community and people from other areas came together to escape their own drama and slip into a world of make-believe.

Sam loved what she considered *her* theater for so many reasons. New York and Los Angeles, San Francisco and London all had wonderful theaters, but the Playhouse was special. The first time she ever heard Shakespeare's words spoken, Sam had been in very itchy tights, sitting in her theater. When she came home from her Hollywood dream, lost and confused, the Playhouse had inspired her to make her own way, to create a job that now perfectly suited her. She had worked tirelessly to ensure the theater was run efficiently and maintained with loving care. She helped Candice and the rest of the staff fill its seats with laughing school groups and aging arts patrons. They were a team, she and the theater.

Standing in the lobby, Sam felt grateful and so sad at the same time. Six months ago, this theater had brought Peter back to her, and tonight Sam would watch his play, laugh, cry, and then she would let him go. Things didn't work out, but the Playhouse was still here with its glittering lights and warm wood to give her and Peter one more night of magic before the curtain fell and life went on.

"Wow, that's fantastic, now that's a dress!" Jack Cathner said, looking incredibly debonair himself, standing next to Sam's mother. She wore a black pants suit and red heels. Her mother could pull of anything, Sam thought.

"You two look pretty fantastic yourselves."

Sam kissed both of them.

"How you doing, Button?"

Sam took a deep breath.

"Good, everything's good."

Her parents knew things with Peter hadn't worked out. They sensed there was trouble brewing when he wasn't at the hospital, and she told them when she had made the decision to end it.

"Sam, you look magnificent," her mother said.

"Thanks, Mom. Piper found the dress. She's a one-woman fashion advisor."

They all laughed.

"We saw Peter, met the director," her father said not so subtly, and her mother lightly smacked his shoulder.

"Okay. That's great. Listen, I need to check with Candice before I take my seat. I'll see you guys in there. Our seats are marked, so you shouldn't have any trouble."

"Sure. Sam," he said, looking at her with a strange expression.

It was kind of the look he used to get when she was in high school, and he'd sneak into the garage to smoke his cigar.

"Enjoy the play, be sure to enjoy all of it."

Jack kissed her forehead with that look still on his face. Sam walked away. *What was that all about? Enjoy the play. Okay?*

Sam checked with the box office manager to make sure there were no last-minute ticket issues and everything was running smoothly. She saw Grady and met his "babysitter" as he called her. She was in a long, navy blue silk dress. It hugged every curve; Sam thought she was the sexiest public relations person she'd ever seen. Grady seemed quite captivated by whatever she was telling him. Sam could not help but wonder where that was headed. What would be more scandalous than Grady seducing the woman his father hired to keep him out of trouble during the campaign? Sam laughed to herself as she ushered them to their seats. She turned to walk back to the lobby as Peter and Spencer were walking in to take their seats. Her chest hurt and the smile dropped from her face. Peter looked at her and the dress. No drooling that she could see, but his eyes softened. Visible confirmations of its effects were all over Peter's face. *Thank you, Piper.*

If only life were as simple as a good-looking guy and a great dress. Peter paused for a minute, tilted his head, and rubbed the back of his neck. Sam thought she saw him grinning, but then it was gone. He looked away and took his seat. Spencer walked over to Sam and thanked her. He wore a bow tie with his suit and Converse. He was relaxed now. The show was in the hands of his very capable stage manager, Julie.

Sam took the seat next to her mother as the house lights dimmed for the last time. This was it. She wanted to congratulate

Peter, tell him that she was so proud of him, but that was not going to happen. She glanced over her shoulder, and he was looking right at her. *Breathe, Sam.* She tried to smile. The house went dark and the curtain opened on the day Phillip's parents brought his little sister home from the hospital.

The audience laughed at all the right spots, mostly at Greg's antics. Greg encompassed all the nuances of Grady when he was young. The dialogue was witty, but intelligent. The audience was belly laughing when Sally tried to teach Phillip and Greg the Macarena at their junior high school dance. Sam remembered that day like it was yesterday, although Peter took artistic license because she had never flirted with Peter at that dance. The theater was appropriately silent during the more difficult scenes. Sam was happy to see that Gordy nailed the lighting on the theater scene where Phillip cries for the first time. It was a much softer spot and the backlighting accentuated the immensity of the dark theater. It was brilliant work. When Sally, Peter, and Greg graduated from college, the montage of scenes from their childhood that filled the stage brought the audience to its feet in applause at the end of Act II. By the time Sam stood for intermission, Peter had left his seat. She told herself it was for the best as they filed out into the lobby. Her father brought champagne over for Sam and her mother.

"Sam," Grady said approaching from the theater.

"Will you please tell Kate that Peter based Greg, the incredibly handsome and charismatic character in the play, on me? Tell her. I'm Greg, right?"

They all laughed.

"I'm sorry. I don't see it," Kate said, pursing her lips. *Oh, I like her,* Sam thought.

Sam tried to keep a serious face.

"Grady, all I can tell you is that the characters are loosely based on people from the playwright's life."

She smiled at Kate.

"Loosely, what? Sam, come on. Phillip, Sally, and Greg. Who the hell else would Greg be?"

"Well, maybe it's a compilation of several people in his life," Kate teased.

"Greg seems far too harmless to be, yeah, you."

They laughed again. Grady shook his head in defeat and drank his champagne, as Kate walked outside for some fresh air.

"I like her, Grady," Susan Cathner said.

"Of course you do. She's my babysitter. Here for the sole purpose of keeping me in line. To make sure my puppet strings don't get tangled and, this just in, to mock me."

Laughter again. It was fun to see Grady frustrated and not his usually suave self.

"Traitors, all of you. Enjoy."

Grady walked toward the men's room.

After a few words with Peter's mother, who was still sober and looking more radiant every day, Sam's parents stepped over to look at the actors' headshots and bios. Sam was left standing by Mrs. Pennyfred, who awkwardly tried to set Sam up with her nephew. She was rescued when the house lights dimmed, signaling the end of intermission. She excused herself from the clutches of matchmaking and took her seat for the second half. Peter was not in his seat. Sam reminded herself that it was no longer her business where Peter was.

Chapter Thirty-Four

*H*e was crazy. He had lost his damn mind, Peter told himself as his breathing went into overdrive backstage. Surely there was an easier way to do this. There were all kinds of gestures, and this one was totally nuts, unprofessional even. He had an obligation to the audience and to his supporters. His agent, his backers from New York, they were all out there and he was most definitely out of this mind.

He peeked out into the house. The audience was once again taking their seats. Peter felt the entire place twirl on its axis while he cursed love, and then he saw her. He was able to draw a breath, his head quieted, and the edges of his mouth curved into a stupid, completely irrational smile. She was pointing at something along the stage, in that dress that had nearly killed him on the spot. It looked like her mother was asking her a question, and Sam was probably explaining some historical tidbit about the theater they both knew so well. He had no choice; he had never had a choice when it came to Sam. She was his person, his woman. He adored her up close, working in the theater, or all the way across the country. He couldn't shake her, and now she had tried to push him away, he knew she needed the gesture, she wanted a plan. As the house lights dimmed, and the stage was filled with the blue-green flush of Act III, Peter saw her face again and knew there was no gesture too grand.

The second half was much more emotional for Sam. Her father looked over at her during the Huntington scene, and she looked straight ahead. Sam was certain he knew she was a grown woman who had intimate relationships with men, but she still felt ten years old and in big trouble. Her mother cried during the flashback, when the audience saw the actual day Phillip's father died. Peter's mother cried during Phillip's seventeenth birthday party, most likely at the cruelty of the intoxicated mother she hoped she had left behind. Come to think of it, Peter's mother cried through most of the second half.

Sam felt a pull at her heart as Phillip got on the plane for New York. There were things said, feelings Phillip had, that Sam never knew existed. It was like having access to Peter's mind, and while she already knew he loved her, it was incredibly written, and the words held her suspended. The lights dimmed onstage, the audience clapped, and after the scene change almost all of the characters were back on stage, frozen in place. This must be the final scene; Sam had not yet seen the ending. Her eyes grew cloudy. Not because the scene was particularly upsetting, it hadn't even started yet, but because she was going to miss Peter. Her heart was going to break all over again, and she was sad. The stage flooded with light for the last scene. Peter stepped out onstage.

"Ladies and Gentlemen, thank you so much for coming tonight, and I hope you've enjoyed the story so far. My name is Peter Everoad, and I am the playwright."

The audience clapped and Sam was stunned that Peter was onstage. *Why? Had something happened?* Her first thought was to get up and check backstage, but she stayed seated, not wanting to look like a fool if this was something he had worked into the play. Maybe the theater had wanted him to introduce himself for the premiere? She had no idea because she had stepped away weeks ago, but surely Candice would have said something.

Sam turned to her mother with a puzzled look, but Susan only patted her hand as Peter continued.

"Many of you came to the rehearsal, as well as the question and answer session, a couple of months ago. There was a young woman in the group who asked me how the story ended. She asked if Phillip fought for Sally. At the time I told her everything ends well. Our cast and crew have worked tirelessly and brought my story to life with such brilliance, I couldn't have asked for more, but I have to tell you that unfortunately . . ."

Sam got up, something was wrong. Unfortunately is a word no one wants to hear on opening night. *Crap. Maybe if he'd solidified the damn ending instead of waiting until the last minute this wouldn't be happening.* Putting her bag in her mother's lap, Sam's mind began to spin, thinking about all of the things that could possibly be wrong. She discreetly stepped into the aisle. This was such an important night for the Playhouse, and if Peter was onstage, something was definitely not right. He hated the attention, especially with this group of people. What could be so wrong that he would need to do this himself? She thought as she glanced over to where Spencer had been sitting. *Where in God's name was Spencer?*

Peter's voice quickened, and his words began fumbling out when he saw Sam get up. *Where the hell was she going?* Maybe he had not thought this through. He needed to finish before she hit that door, or he would look like a, well he would look like the complete nutcase he was.

"Unfortunately, the ending took me some time. I had a few hurdles, and over the past few months I've written three or four endings, but none of them felt right. I've decided I may need some audience participation."

The crowd laughed nervously and began to shift in their seats.

"Because to tell you the truth, I have no idea how this thing is going to end."

The audience mumbled a bit more, and Sam started to sweat. Her fantastic shoes, it turns out, were not the best for making fast and frantic exits. She'd made it to the door, ready to push through to the lobby, when she heard Peter say,

"I once had someone tell me all I ever do is write lines for other people to say. That I sit on the sidelines."

She froze, hands on the cool, gold plate of the door. Sam stared at the door and couldn't physically move. Peter took a deep breath.

"She was right. It's pretty damn terrifying up here."

The audience laughed, and Sam could feel the whispers.

"So, here I am on the stage at the end of my play. If you'll bear with me, I'll take over for the incredibly talented Jacob Pratt, who has been playing Phillip. I need to read these lines myself, and if I could get Samantha Cathner to turn around and come to the stage, maybe together we can give the audience an ending. Sam?"

The house lights warmed enough for everyone in the entire audience to turn and see Sam with her face in the door. She slowly turned toward the stage. The cast was frozen in their places. Young Phillip and Sally and Greg were on the stage sitting in an imaginary back yard, just as Peter, Grady, and Sam had done so many times in their childhood. The parents were gathered around a dining room table poised over plastic food behind a sheer scrim that separated them from the children. Everything hit slow motion for Sam and she still couldn't process what was going on.

Jacob, the actor playing older Phillip, broke character when he heard his name, shook Peter's hand, and exited stage left. Minka, the actress playing older Sally, broke also at the mention of Sam's name, kissed Peter on the cheek, and exited the stage. The entire theater was quiet, not one rustling of a program or a candy wrapper, no one moving in their seats, nothing. Sam swallowed hard and looked at Peter. He smiled. She could tell he was nervous even from the back of the house, but his face was absolutely magnificent. He stood there, all eyes on him, with his hand confidently outstretched to her. His energy, his warmth, radiated all the way up to her, and he said, "Sam, I have a plan. If you could get to the stage before the audience gets restless, that would be great."

Laughter filled the theater again as Peter raised his eyebrows and gestured again. *He had a plan.* All on their own Sam's legs began to move.

Never taking her eyes off him, she approached the stage as the whispering in the audience grew louder. Her heart was thundering, but all she saw was Peter. He met her at the stage stairs with a yellow pad in his hand. She held her dress with one hand and took his hand with the other as he guided her center stage.

"You look unbelievable, as if it's not obvious."

She tried to respond, but nothing came out.

The lights were warm and bright. The audience clapped and, still looking at Peter, Sam bowed her head in acknowledgement of the applause. This was crazy, but somehow it didn't matter. His face, that smile, whatever he was going to do was worth it, if only to see that look. The theater was packed with everyone Sam knew in all of Pasadena and some bigwigs from New York. She was standing center stage on the opening night of Peter's new play, and he was clearly having some sort of a breakdown, but she didn't care. Sure, her face was five shades of scarlet. Sam stood facing Peter and like the rest of the audience, she was looking to him for what was coming next.

Peter held her hand, and for an instant, it was exactly like the movies, he thought. The room became a gauzy fuzz, and Sam was the only thing in focus. It was so clear now, and even as he felt a bead of sweat trickle down the back of his shirt, Peter was certain.

"Thank you, Samantha, Sam. Now," with one hand shading his face, Peter looked up to the lighting booth, "if I could please have my lighting cue, Gordy."

The house lights went dark, and the stage flooded with the most fantastic blues, oranges, and pinks. Marvelous lighting, as if they were standing right in the middle of a sunset. Peter whispered: "If I'm going to do this I thought we might as well create your favorite time of day. Sunset for you, Sam. Gotta love the theater."

He kissed her hand. Sam was bathing in that beautiful light when Peter turned toward the audience.

"Ladies and gentlemen, thank you for your patience, I give you the final scene of *Looking In.*"

What? "Peter, I don't have any lines. What are you . . ."

"All you have to do is respond to what I say. This is *our* ending, you don't need lines. We're going to finish this up with messy, real life. Kinda like reality television, but hopefully better."

He laughed, and Sam tried to swallow past the swell in her throat. *Maybe he was actually losing it,* she thought and squeezed his hand harder.

"Listen and say what you want to say. Don't worry, I have most of the lines. Oh, and pay no attention to the hundreds of people staring at us, just look at me."

He laughed nervously this time, his hands were sweating.

Sam started to shake. They were quite a pair. She did exactly what Peter said, mostly out of complete terror. He held both her hands and faced her.

"Samantha Cathner, I ... I've loved you my whole life. I've written pages about you and to you. My first thoughts of friendship, laughter, love, comfort, passion, all have you swirling around in them. I wasn't ready for you the first time. I blew it. But I came back, and even though you say you don't want me, I don't believe you. You wanted a plan. I have one."

He flipped through the pages on the yellow pad. They were filled with writing and arrows. Sam saw the words "live in New York and summer in Pasadena." She took the pad and turned the pages. It was a plan. He'd written it all out with little notes in the margin that said: "Ask Sam."

Sam held the pad to her chest and for the hundredth time, tears welled in her eyes. The audience clapped and Peter continued.

"You drive me absolutely crazy."

Sam laughed.

"And I know I scare the hell out of you when I climb into my head, but it doesn't matter. A light turned on in our world that day under the bamboo, Sam, and our lives have never been the same. You are my shelter from the storms in my mind, and in your eyes, I am everything I've ever hoped to be. We will always be scared of losing each other, that's part of needing, and I need you desperately. I love you, Sam."

He squeezed her hand, and the audience was silent, like they didn't want to disturb.

"This is our path. We are part of the same beginning and the same sunset, the same Sunday morning breakfast and Saturday farmer's market. So, I'm here onstage with you and I've got my game plan. I've followed your need for tradition and already spoken to your father."

Sam didn't think it possible, but Peter suddenly looked even more nervous. His hand was shaking as it left hers and reached into his pocket.

She stopped crying and looked at her parents in the audience who were now both crying for her. She was squeezing the one hand of his she had left as Peter dropped to one knee right there on the stage in front of everyone. If the audience knew Peter the way Sam knew him, they would see that this was the most spectacular gesture of love and courage.

"Samantha Cathner, I love you with everything I am, you are my very best friend. This play is about our past. I promise to make plans and cherish you every moment, for the rest of my life. This is the only ending that works. Will you, will you marry me?"

Peter looked up into Sam's eyes, the eyes he knew so well, and saw that he was loved. He knew her answer. He knew after that day at the Huntington. He knew when they were on Catalina. Even when she pushed him away, he still knew. He gave her space and made a plan. Now Sam knew she needed to stop blubbering and find her ability to speak. The theater was silent. Sam wasn't sure anyone was even breathing. Peter was still kneeling, holding an exquisite antique diamond ring in a quilted box. She pulled him to his feet and looked deep into those eyes. She knew she would spend the rest of her life with Peter Everoad and that she would look back on this day thousands of times. She wanted to remember it. Remember Peter, those eyes, his plan, and their very own beginning. Through her tears and a radiant smile Sam said: "Yes."

The theater, onstage, backstage, and in the audience erupted, clapping, and hooting. Well, Grady was the only one hooting. Peter shook as he put the ring on her finger and then held her face and kissed her as if no one was watching. He gently wiped the tears from Sam's eyes and whispered across her lips: "You were right. Reading your own lines is much better."

They both laughed, Sam smelled Life Savers, and he kissed her again. Everyone in the theater was on their feet as Sam and Peter turned toward the actors onstage to acknowledge their performances, as the clapping continued. They then turned toward the audience for their own curtain call.

Holding Peter's hand and looking out over the people who supported them and challenged them, Sam and Peter knew this was only the beginning, the premiere, of their life together.

Thank you for reading *Premiere – A Love Story*! I hope you enjoyed Sam and Peter's story. If you liked the book, please consider leaving a review at the book retailer of your choice, as well as Goodreads, to help other readers find this story.

Please make sure you're on my newsletter mailing list at: tracyewens.com to keep up with the latest news about my books.

Thank you, wonderful readers, for making this amazing journey possible. I appreciate each and every one of you! Keep reading for a look at *Candidate – A Love Story*, which is Kate and Grady's story.

All the best,
Tracy

Chapter One

Kate Galloway didn't remember buying apple Toaster Strudel. She could have sworn all the boxes were cherry, but biting into the fresh out-of-the-toaster goodness, she definitely tasted apple.

It didn't matter though, because she was going to be late if she didn't find her other black pump in the sea of partially unpacked boxes that littered her apartment.

It was to the point now that she was using the boxes as furniture and storage, moving them around to create spaces. So, her shoe was probably thrown back into a "closet" box, somewhere. She was trying to get her earring clipped, while wobbling on one heel, when she noticed the time. If she left within five minutes, there would still be time for coffee. Her boss had called at 5:30 this morning, something important, could she be in by seven? So yeah, coffee was essential.

Finding the errant shoe behind her bedroom door, Kate took another bite of her strudel and walked to the bathroom to tackle her hair. Grateful that messy buns were still in, she wrapped an elastic around the mass of damp curls, grabbed a yogurt from the kitchen, and her keys, phone, purse, and a folder off her bed. By the time she finished shoving the folder into her briefcase, she was at the front door. Twirling around one last time, she surveyed the chaos of her apartment and told herself, as she had almost every morning for the past two years, that she would start unpacking when she got home. Kate licked a last bit of frosting from the corner of her mouth and left for her morning pilgrimage.

"Kate, we've retained a new client as of last night, and I'm assigning a large part of the project to you. While I'm sure your colleagues here would love this one, you're the best person for the job—we all agreed, right guys?" Her boss Mark turned to the rest of their staff at Bracknell and Stevens, his fear well masked behind a smile, and they all nodded in turn.

Kate had a feeling she wasn't going to like what Mark was about to say next.

He continued, "So just let me finish before you judge or say anything. I really need you to not judge, okay?" he pleaded as he sipped his coffee.

Kate took a seat, looking puzzled, and waited for him to go on.

"Senator Malendar's—"

"I voted for him. He's great, why—" The caffeine had kicked in and she interrupted anyway.

"Kate, please." Mark took a breath and gave her a pointed look, as if he needed her to focus. "Senator Malendar is running for re-election, as you know. He has hired us to bring a fresh perspective to his campaign. Truth be told, his opponent Jeff Driggs is giving him a run for his money. This guy's a Republican, mid-thirties, and from what I was told last night, he's drawing a lot of votes from the younger demographic. The senator's office would like us to help him with his PR and outreach to these same young voters."

Kate was still listening, but still not sure where he was going. Mark took another deep breath. Javier and Max both reached for another doughnut across the conference table, and when Kate looked to them for a clue, they just smiled. Big Cheshire smiles. This was not going to be good.

"There are several components to this, the most challenging being revamping the senator's son's image."

"Mark—" Kate's eyes narrowed.

"Grady Malendar is a direct link to the demographic the campaign is looking for, but he needs reining in. There have been a few situations lately, but he seems to appeal to—"

Kate couldn't hold back any longer. "Situations? Are you joking, that man's a walking situation. Which underage debutante did they find him with now?" she said, setting her pencil down as warmth crept up her face. *This was a joke, right? Was it April first?*

"Kate, this isn't funny. From what I hear he's an asset, has a good relationship with the community, but needs—"

"To grow up?" Kate said, leaning back in her chair and biting her thumb. It was a nervous habit. She caught herself and put her hand in her lap.

"Probably, but he's willing to campaign. We just need to work on his image, play up . . . "

Kate raised an eyebrow.

"Play up whatever we can, and help turn that into something for the campaign." Mark said, and then looked to the rest of the table, hoping someone would chime in, throw him a lifeline, as Kate grew more and more disillusioned.

"I . . . I will be working on the social media components, younger voters, you . . . we'll get to work together," Javier added, chomping into his second doughnut.

Kate tried to meet his eyes, but they averted, and she looked to Max, who cleared his throat.

"Right, this is a really exciting project. I mean, a United States senator's campaign and the youth vote." Max looked back at Javier for words. "That's, um, cool and Grady Malendar is important."

Christ, this was ridiculous. What is going on, and who turned their staff into puppets? Kate thought.

"And let me guess, the son, Grady. That's my all-important, call me at zero-dark-hundred this morning part of the job? Why me?" Kate tried to remain calm.

"Because you can do this and you'll do it well. Grady Malendar is extremely popular and charismatic. You can channel this into a winning re-election bid for his father, I know you can. Remember Randy Nelson, coach at UCLA who was caught selling pot to his players?"

Everyone nodded at the table and Kate could feel Mark winding up for his You Can Do It speech. "You got him a medical marijuana license, convinced the entire university board that he was helping them, for medicinal purposes. Remember that, Kate."

Kate nodded. It was a great save.

"He agreed to cut it out, close up his shop once the dust settled. The man retired last year with full benefits. That was brilliant work. Tough assignment, but those are your specialty. Listen, I know this is going to be a challenge. I'll admit that from the media coverage, Grady is tough, but you're good at this. You know you are. So, that's that." Mark picked up his notes and Kate could see him trying to finish strong, and hand down the order. "Kate, you will head up the Grady Malendar part of the campaign. You will work with Javier and Max, be with Mr. Malendar for the next six months. The senator has specifically asked for someone dedicated to Grady's relationship with the community and voters. You will help him prepare speeches, manage his media exposure, clean up any messes, and accompany him to campaign events to ensure the public sees him in the best light. Congratulations, Kate. This is a big assignment."

The other people sitting at the conference room, her colleagues, as Mark put it, snickered and clapped.

"This is just great. Thank you so much for your confidence in me." Kate stood up and bowed as the clapping now evolved into cheers and whistling. "All of you, I can't wait to work on this very important project. Where is the spoiled little—"

"Kate!"

The room grew quiet and all gazes were now fixed on the door behind her. Javier and Max stood. Without turning around she sensed something, someone was there.

Mark looked panicked. "Kate, I believe you already know Senator Malendar."

She put on her very best PR smile and turned around. Standing just outside the conference room and taking up most of the doorway was a good-looking man in a perfectly cut navy-blue suit. He wore a red tie that complemented his salt and pepper hair. Kate recognized him immediately as Senator Patrick Malendar of California. Through the glass encasing of the door, she could see a group of other suits, not as expensive, standing behind the senator with various electronic devices.

"Yes, of course. So good to see you, sir, and a pleasure to be working with you," Kate said, extending her hand.

The senator, who had either not heard the beginnings of her jabs at his son, or chose to ignore them, smiled, stepped further into the room, and took Kate's hand in a warm and firm handshake.

"Great to see you too, Kate. You guys seemed like you were having fun. Did I interrupt? Are we early?" The senator asked, and Kate turned to Mark hoping he had an answer.

"Not at all, senator. We will be going just down the hall to the larger conference room. It should be all set for our meeting. Your staff can head in there, and we'll meet you in a moment," Mark explained.

"Sounds good." The senator hesitated and turned to the … what was the right word? Dashing, yes, that was it, the dashing younger man standing just outside the doorway. Kate had seen photographs of Grady Malendar, often of him doing something completely asinine, but they didn't do him justice. He was tall, broad shoulders, short honey-brown hair, and he had—hands down—the most stunning, ice-blue eyes she'd ever seen. Kate had sworn off men for the rest of her life, but this man was at least fun to look at. His father gestured, and Grady walked into the conference room. Grady nodded to Mark, whom he'd obviously already met, shook Javier's hand, and then turned to Kate.

"Kate, I'd like you to meet Grady Malendar," Mark introduced, and Mr. Blue Eyes smiled a sort of runway model smoldering, but professional smile.

You've got to be kidding? Does that work? Of course it does. Kate, look at the smile for crying out loud. She started to roll her own blue eyes, but Mark gave her a pleading look for best behavior, and she obeyed.

"Mr. Malendar, it is a pleasure. I'm—"

"You're Katherine Galloway." He shook her hand. Firm handshake, and it served its purpose. Kate was thrown off for a beat. He came out of the gate collected, almost mature. The strength in his voice, his whole demeanor was unexpected and the public relations part of her was thrilled that there appeared to be something to work with. It was as if there might be something of substance behind the lady-killer smile. She saw it for just a moment.

"Kate, please call me Kate." She took her hand back.

"Kate it is. Thank you for meeting with us. Shall we?" He gestured, and everyone began filing toward the large conference room. Kate stayed behind to collect her notes.

Grady popped his head back into the smaller conference room. "Hey, Kate. You coming?"

"I . . . I just need to get my things. I'll be right there."

"Okay, because you surely don't want to miss a moment of how we're going to contain the spoiled-son strategy." Sarcasm? No, maybe that was anger mixed with his smooth silky voice. Either way, he was still standing there. *Say something clever, Kate.*

"I'm sure our strategy encompasses much more than just following you around, Mr. Malendar."

"Grady, please call me Grady, and from what I hear you've been assigned to keep me in line. Am I mistaken? Kind of like a babysitter?"

So much for clever, it was time to break out the credentials. "Mr. Mal . . . Grady, I graduated top of my class at Columbia. I've been with Bracknell and Stevens for over five years. Now clearly someone thinks you need an image makeover, but I can assure you that I am not a babysitter."

He stood there with his hands in the pockets of his light tan suit, leaning against the door and smiling.

She had just met him five minutes ago and already she was unnerved and a little pissed. *Babysitter? Just who the hell does this guy think he is?* Grady moved off the door jamb to let Kate pass, and to spite him she gestured that he should go first. She could tell it upset his prep school sense of propriety, and she saw first-hand what she already suspected, that Grady knew all about maneuvering. His father clearly liked being in control, but Grady was like an ice skater. He glided, smiled, and moved with efficiency. As he walked past Mandy and Sabrina, normally very astute office assistants, both women strained for one last glimpse. Kate rolled her eyes at both of them, shaking her head. Christ, she should have gone for the double latte.

Grady seemed to have a way of walking that assumed people were following him. He did glance over his shoulder to check on her, so that was something at least. He walked with purpose, made quick and fleeting eye contact with those he passed, and carried an air of importance. His laid-back demeanor was not present in his walk, and Kate found that interesting. She wasn't sure if this was his "being made to do something" walk, or if he always carried himself this way. They both entered the conference room, and Kate moved toward the empty leather chair on the far side of the dark-lacquered conference table. Everyone had taken their seats as the senator stood by the window with Mark. He looked as if he was telling a story that required a bird's-eye view of the city. Kate stepped over wires and found Grady, pulling out a chair for her.

"Let's start over, Kate. After all, I didn't realize you graduated from Columbia." Grady spoke close to her ear. "Impressive, indeed. Allow me."

Kate eyed him suspiciously and tried for a smile. She failed. "That's not necessary, but thank you," she said as she sat.

Grady smiled a full dazzling smile for the audience of onlookers around the table, and then Kate fell a bit forward as he pushed her chair harder than was necessary.

She couldn't see his face, but she was sure the smile was now a smirk.

Acknowledgements

I would like to thank:

The Pasadena Playhouse and the community that keeps her going.

The Catalina Island Conservancy for protecting and preserving one of my favorite places.

Maya Rock for editing me into fewer words, more meaning.

Mr. Kenyon, at Barry Goldwater High School, for putting me on my very first stage.

Tracy Ewens is a recovered theatre major who writes smart con-
temporary romance from a beautiful piece of Arizona desert.
When not working on her next book, she drinks copious amounts
of tea, prefers an exit row seat, and reads well past her bedtime.

www.tracyewens.com